EXILES
ON THE SAINT JOHNS

ISBN: 978-0-9821223-3-4
Library of Congress Control Number: 2008944195
Published by Global Authors Publications

Filling the GAP in publishing

Edited by Barbara Sachs Sloan
Interior Design by Kathleen Walls
Cover Design by Kathleen Walls
Front Cover Photo credit: The drawing of "Confederate cavalry crossing the St. Johns River to the eastern shore" is from Dickison and His Men, by Mary Elisabeth Dickison. The map is an 1865 Union Army map of St. Johns County, Florida.

Printed in USA for Global Authors Publications

Exiles on the Saint Johns

Lydia Hawke

Dedication:

To My Confederate ancestors, James Lewis Colee, Francis P. Andreu, Frederick Newton Varn, Zachariah Groom Seward and John Hardy Bolton. Also their brothers, George A. Colee, William Charles Colee, Charles Henry Colee, William Baker Varn, and Josiah Varn. All of them except the Georgian, John Hardy Bolton, resided in Florida and served in Florida regiments.

Foreword

Thanks to the Florida Memory online project, I discovered the Confederate pension records for my great, great grandfather, James Lewis Colee. He served in Baya's Artillery, which was organized into the 8th Florida and sent to Virginia. He was discharged "on account of disability" in October of 1862. He returned home, near Picolata, and hired a substitute to serve in his place.

One can understand why he would not want to reenlist due to personal responsibilities; he and his wife had four children and would produce another during the war. However, despite his exemption, he did not stay out of the service after the restoration of his health. He assisted Confederate Captain J. J. Dickison with his forays into St. Johns County, and apparently served in Company H of the 2nd Florida Cavalry for the last few months of the war.

Knowing what was going on in St. Johns County during that period, I believed I can reconstruct his motivations for kicking in with Dickison's command despite his legal exemption. St. Augustine was under Federal control from May 1862 through the end of the war. It was off limits to anyone who refused to take the Oath of Allegiance, which James Colee, a Confederate veteran, forswore. In the meantime, Union soldiers terrorized the countryside east of the St. Johns River, trying to drive out anyone with Confederate sympathies.

The Confederate cavalry under Dickison strove to protect the citizens wherever and whenever possible. With Yankee depredations making a normal living impossible, the veteran apparently rejoined the Confederates to fight his tormentors and try to protect his home and family.

James Colee had three brothers, all of whom served in the Confederate Army. The youngest brother, teenaged Charles Henry Colee, enlisted in Dickison's cavalry in 1863. In Captain Dickison's writings, he mentioned a "young soldier" in his command whose father lived within the Union picket lines at Picolata after a garrison was established there. The trooper infiltrated the lines and brought out his father. The older man's information prevented a suicidal attack on the fort and led to a much more enjoyable raid resulting in the capture of partying Union soldiers and musicians. I have conjectured that the unnamed young trooper may have been Charles. George and Tryphenia Riz Colee, who founded the St. Augustine Colee clan, resided near the river landing at Picolata.

James' son, my great grandfather, Raymond J. Colee, married a Minorcan lady, Florence Constancia Andreu, who was the daughter of Francis P. Andreu, a Confederate veteran from St. Augustine. My grandfather, Raymond Francis Colee, Sr., represented a blend of some of the longest-standing northeast Florida pioneer families.

Of course the main characters in *Exiles on the St. Johns* are fictional people, who, I hope, bear little resemblance to the people who inspired this story. However, I wished to honor my ancestors by giving them minor roles. For instance, the Catholic Church established a mission at Picolata. I found out George Colee, Sr. hosted the St. Augustine based priest, who held Mass at the Colee home whenever he visited that remote area.

Coincidences happen during the writing of historical fiction, which can give one those Twilight Zone moments. I placed Jack Farrell in the St. Johns Grays, which was organized into the 2nd Florida Infantry. That unit, along with the St. Augustine Rifles, served in the Army of Northern Virginia. Later I found two John Farrells on the roster of the St. Johns Grays. Again, I trust Jack Farrell bears no resemblance to his namesakes. I decided to leave his name intact to honor those individuals who performed their duty as they saw it.

Also, a Google Earth search located Jack Farrell's fictional home as just about where Kathleen Walls, the publisher of this book, lives, on the south end of Colee Cove.

The main historical events in this novel are accurate. However, I took a few liberties. Some of the skirmishes in the story are purely fictional, though they are based on actual incidents and depict the style of fighting Dickison and his men employed.

Early in the war, which is the scope of this story, Dickison's company was not as heavily engaged as during the last year and a half of the conflict. As hostilities dragged on, the United States government took greater notice of Florida. Although a sparsely populated frontier, the state provided the Confederacy with much of its provisions. Eventually the Union military invested more effort in trying to occupy territory and disrupt the flow of beef, citrus, salt and other necessities northward to the Confederate armies. Many historians give Captain Dickison and his command major credit for keeping the interior of the state under Confederate control.

I am working on a sequel, *Raiders on the St. Johns,* which will endeavor to bring to life Dickison's exploits during the last half of the war, which rivaled those of his Virginia counterpart, Colonel John S. Mosby.

CHAPTER ONE

Near Sharpsburg, Maryland
September 1862

Over time, Jack Farrell had schooled himself to think of his targets as objects rather than men. He was no murderer, just a skilled marksman.

Fellow skirmishers ran past as he claimed a likely spot. He dropped his haversack and blanket at the bottom of the tree trunk, leaving his canteen and cartridge box on his waist belt. He propped himself against the rough bark and tightened the leg straps anchoring the climber gaffs to his shoes. The nearby crackle of rifle fire, the boom of artillery, and the screech of shells overhead made deadly music.

He swept his gaze upward, regarding the big oak tree, searching for the best way to scale it. He studied the curve of the branches, gauging the climb to the crotch of the tree, one well sheltered by leaves, still thick in early autumn. The screen could serve him well.

Jack slung the Enfield musketoon rifle over his shoulder and unwound a length of rope. He looped it around the trunk and started to walk up the tree by sticking the triangular gaffs into the thick bark and pulling himself upward with the rope.

Slim and tough, supple as a cat, he'd learned to translate his skill at stringing telegraph wires along the Florida railway line into a more harrowing job. He avoided catching the rifle or his equipment in the protruding boughs. He crawled onto a substantial branch, and sitting astride, settled his back against the main trunk. Judging his seat secure, he didn't need to tie himself to his perch. He shifted to unsling the rifle and cradled it in his arms.

The gray of his uniform jacket blended in with the shadows cast by the foliage. He stared through the leaves at a battery a couple hundred yards away. Crack shots from his regiment had been selected to silence those destructive guns. The blue-clad artillery crews swarmed around the cannons, loading them with the exploding shells that had been creating havoc on his side. His

1

job was to disrupt their effectiveness.

Jack's Enfield two-bander, equipped with a telescope to help focus on targets and a shorter barrel to make it easier to handle in close quarters, was the most practical rifle the Confederacy had so far found to equip its marksmen. In the hands of a skilled shooter it proved deadly accurate.

Jack was such an expert.

He watched the blue-coated soldiers for a moment, studying their placement and movements. The situation required haste but not at the expense of wasting ammunition. He estimated the distance and considered trajectory. Then he lifted the stock to his shoulder and braced for the recoil, taking into account the three-inch space he needed between his eye and the telescope. Too close, and the rifle's kick would ram his face and give him a black eye. Artillery horses made big, inviting targets, but he hated to kill them. They had not volunteered to pull the caissons for the Union army.

He singled out an officer who paced behind the cannon, barking out orders, his arm chopping. Jack sighted through the telescope, tracking him with the muzzle of his rifle. He pushed aside a fleeting thought of his Yankee brother. *Dan isn't an artillery officer.* He led a little ahead of the center of the man's body and gently squeezed the trigger.

The bark of the black powder explosion spewed out the muzzle, sparing his ears. The recoil bumped hard against his shoulder. He peered through the plume of stinking smoke, reloaded and assessed the effect his handiwork had wrought. Handling the muzzle-loader was an awkward process that would have been simpler on the ground, but he was well-practiced.

The blue-coated officer lay on the ground. Two crewmen rushed over to their stricken leader, disrupting the sequence of firing the piece of artillery.

The crack of a rifle to his right reminded him he was not alone. Could be Bill, one of his messmates. A crewman fell across the barrel of the cannon and slid off.

It was a painstaking but effective process, keeping the artillerymen busy trying not to get shot. He contributed his part to render the battery harmless, and from the crack of rifle fire on either side, other skirmishers were on the job as well.

Jack lifted the rifle to his shoulder again and trained his weapon on one of the men who had run to the fallen officer. The Yankee whirled and froze like a pointer, looking in the sharpshooter's direction. Jack imagined the soldier staring into his eyes. He sighted the stationary target, ready to fire a bullet into the fellow's chest.

But the Yankee moved out of the scope's field. Jack swung the barrel by degrees until he found his target again. The uncooperative prey slipped in and out of view as Jack followed, then disappeared behind a field piece. Jack gave him up as a bad job and picked out an easier mark, a soldier carrying a rammer. Again he squeezed the trigger and felt the jolt. He didn't see the man fall, but his marksman's intuition told him the bullet had found its home. As the breeze drifted the smoke away he saw the artillerist had sat down and appeared to sag sideways.

He could do this all day, reload, aim and fire, occasionally swabbing the barrel to keep it clean, but it was time to move. The smoke from his rifle had given away his position and would bring fire his way.

He slid the rifle's sling back over his shoulder and unwound his rope to aid his descent. Then he widened his eyes in alarm. The crew of the first gun had jumped back to the task and had swung the barrel around. This time he stared at the foreshortened piece pointed toward his perch.

His hunter's blind had become a trap. Calculating that the drop would harm him less than a cannonball in his gullet, he grabbed a branch and tried to push clear. Something restrained him. He couldn't get free. His belt, hooked on a broken limb, had him stuck fast.

Jack swore and reached back to release himself from the jut of wood. From the corner of his eye he saw smoke blossoming from the mouth of the cannon just before he heard the boom. He jerked the belt upward with such violence he skinned his knuckles on the bark. He finally freed himself just as the world exploded in a blast of fire.

*

St. Augustine, Florida

Until recently, Martina Sanchez had never expected she would have to trade with the enemy for survival's sake. Dealing with Yankee soldiers, the same sort of people her older brother Francisco fought against, bothered her. Still, she bore responsibility for her younger brother, Carlo. She had no other means of supporting the two of them.

She looked over her shoulder at the boy. The fourteen year old lagged behind to play with a neighbor's black and tan terrier. "Hurry," she called out.

The little handcart held all she needed. The spicy fragrance of warm shrimp pilau filled her nostrils. She had cooked rice along with tomatoes preserved from her garden. Into the pot she'd added shrimp Carlo had caught in the tidewaters. Chopped datil peppers gave the pilau its distinct sharp flavor. She had tasted it beforehand to make sure it was just right so her customers would return for more.

Carlo trotted up, adjusting his straw hat. Like hers, his deep brown hair and eyes hinted at their Spanish and Minorcan heritage. "Did you throw in extra peppers?"

Martina laughed. "Of course not. Do you want me arrested for setting fire to those Yankees?"

"Ah, it won't hurt them. Just make them drink lots of water. And make their eyes run."

"Causing our customers pain would be bad for business."

"I don't want their business." Carlo picked up an oyster shell and skipped it across the sandy road.

"We have to live, Carlo." Martina brushed a stray strand of hair away from her eyebrow. "They are the only ones who have money."

"Who needs their money? I can catch all the fish we need."

"As much as you love the water, one of these days you'll sprout gills." She smiled at him. "What would I do without the mullet and shrimp you catch? As long as the soldiers are willing to buy my cooking, we can make a living."

"St. Augustine doesn't seem like home any more. It's a prison. What I really want us to do is to leave this place. Let the Yankees have it."

"Give up our home?" Martina shook her head. "Don't be foolish."

"You can stay here. I'd join the army, like Francisco, if you didn't need me."

"Hush. The wrong person might hear." She sighed, weary of the same old conversation. "You're too young, anyway. They wouldn't take you."

"I could catch a marsh tackie and join the cavalry, with Ramon."

Confederate cavalry prowled the woods outside the city, making the Yankee soldiers in the St. Augustine garrison jittery about leaving the town's defenses. Their cousin Ramon Andreu could be among them. Fearing retribution from the Union soldiers, he had moved his family from their home north of town, and she had heard nothing from them since.

Carlo could sneak out of town and meet up with the Confederates. He was small for his age. Would they let him join anyway? Surely Ramon wouldn't, but if they were desperate enough for recruits....

She pushed the cart through the narrow sand-and-shell street, greeting a few relatives and neighbors who watched from their balconies. Since the Yankee occupation, many townspeople had left, while some of those who stayed rarely left their homes, either out of fear or aloofness. Townspeople of Northern heritage or sympathies welcomed the invaders.

Although Martina disliked and feared the Union soldiers, huddling indoors and living off her dwindling savings was a luxury she could not afford. Some of her neighbors, like the elderly Miss Swingle, gave her disapproving looks for associating with the Yankees, but Martina was too busy to concern herself with their opinions.

Carlo ranged about, checking this and that, restless and impatient. Sometimes he acted just like a boy, quick to make mischief and cause her worry with his irreverence for the Yankees. Then he showed flashes of emerging manhood. He shouldered some of the burden of supporting them, and for that she felt grateful.

She turned the corner onto Cathedral Street, bordering the plaza. Off duty, blue-clad soldiers lounged about the grassy area. A few played cards or checkers in the now-unused slave market, a simple pavilion in sight of Matanzas Bay. A United States flag hanging from one of its pillars rippled in the breeze. The soldiers had placed it there because ardent secessionist ladies had chopped down the plaza flagpole in protest.

These men were far from home and lonely for female company.

Many of the women in town refused to acknowledge them at all. Martina worked at keeping her dealings with the soldiers businesslike and impersonal, despite their attempts at flirtation. She did not care to provide them with companionship.

She stopped under the broad shade of an oak tree next to the market and turned to Carlo. "Go tell the soldiers what we have to eat." She waved her hand toward the market.

He wandered off, and she prayed he would not tease or insult the Yankees. She arranged her wares then stood quietly, observing the scene. A cool ocean breeze wafted under her skirts, a welcome sensation after her hot walk through the streets.

Before her birth, the United States had annexed Florida from the Spanish and given the Castillo de San Marcos an American name, Fort Marion. Made from stone consisting of compressed seashells quarried nearby, the coquina castle overlooking the Matanzas River had never been taken by force. The Yankees had captured the gray citadel without firing a shot and used it for storage and barracks.

At the dock Martina noted the presence of a rickety transport ship she had not seen the day before. Rust stained its funnel and its wooden sides. The lettering on the prow read *Burnside*. She supposed it had brought in supplies, or perhaps more troops for the garrison. Truly the Yankee navy must be scraping deep in its barrel to commission such a worn and disreputable looking craft.

An officer, puffing a cigar, strolled up. He sported a fierce dark moustache and his eyes squinted, as though he were either shortsighted or bothered by the harsh sunlight. She recalled his name: Lieutenant Prescott.

"Good day to you, Miss Sanchez." He touched the brim of his fatigue cap. In his left hand he held a sheaf of papers. "Is that little brother of yours behaving himself?"

"He's a great help to me." She forced a smile. Lieutenant Prescott had a friendly, if forceful, manner. "Would you like some shrimp pilau?" She motioned to the pot. "I just made it this morning."

"Smells better than army rations." He removed the cigar from between his teeth and tapped off the ashes, which fortunately blew away from the food. "How much?"

She told him and he dug into his pocket while she spooned a

big helping into a bowl.

He stuck the cigar back in his mouth then handed her the money and one of the papers. "I've been posting these handbills," he said around the cigar. "Bad news for you, I expect."

She handed him the steamy rice dish and scanned the lettering. An order, signed by Colonel Bell, directed all civilians over the age of fourteen to attend a meeting at the Presbyterian Church. *Those who decline coming are to be treated as enemies.*

"What does this mean?" she asked Prescott.

He bent over and placed the lit cigar carefully on the grass, took a spoonful of pilau and chewed thoughtfully. "Pretty good. A man could get used to eating like this."

"What is the meeting about?"

"Don't you have a brother in the rebel army?"

She lifted her chin. "Like many of us."

"That doesn't help your case. We're sending all the rebel sympathizers away."

"Away?" Her hand flew to her mouth. "Where?"

"I suppose that would be your problem, Miss. Of course we will provide transportation to the rebel lines."

"But this is my home."

"St. Augustine belongs to the U. S. Government now."

He forked in the last bite and wiped his moustache with his fingers. "You might have an out, you know. Maybe you could stick around if you play it right." A smirk curved the corners of his mouth.

She crossed her arms over her chest, not liking the way he looked at her.

"We might let you take the oath and stay home. I say might. You being a rebel and all, it could be a problem."

CHAPTER TWO

A sulfurous odor filled Jack's nostrils, a chorus of demons rang in his head and every breath stabbed a pitchfork into his ribs. Sister Mary Joseph's prediction of his hell-bound fate had been accurate. He opened the eye on the side of his face not pressed into the ground. Instead of a Catholic school vision of a fiery pit he saw only forest floor.

The focus of torment crystallized and centered in his right side and arm, trapped under his body. With his free arm he pushed himself onto his back, shedding dirt and leaves that clung to his clothes, hair, and scorched cheeks. The movement brought no relief, only grinding pain. His mouth opened to cry out, but he could not hear himself. His vision darkened then returned.

Memory seeped back. He recalled the smoke bursting from the black maw of that cannon and the shock of an exploding shell. He did not remember falling.

Overhead what was left of the tree he'd climbed stood denuded of foliage and blackened. A branch dropped a few inches and swayed there, caught by a lower bough. Weren't there trees on either side, before? The one to the right was obliterated, in its place only open sky and piles of debris. It must have absorbed the main blow, a near miss that failed to kill him outright.

His Enfield. Where was his Enfield? He carried no sidearm. He needed the rifle as much as he needed his next shallow, agonized breath.

His right arm useless, he groped with his left hand, but all he found was a fallen limb, white wood exposed. Flat on his back, he had no hope of locating his weapon. He rolled onto his left side and elbowed up, again enduring the misery and blackness that washed over him. It passed, and he sought the weapon, which must be underneath debris from the destroyed trees.

Carefully he rocked to his knees, taking a chance the Yankees were not close enough to spot him through the brush. He supported his lame right arm with his left hand and paused, head drooping, gathering his strength.

He spotted the butt of the rifle a body's length away, beside the trunk of the tree he had just left. Leaves, sticks and dirt obscured the barrel. Unable to stand, Jack inched forward on his knees and one hand, sweat popping from his forehead at the pain and effort. When he finally closed his hand around the barrel he drew the cooling metal close and pressed his cheek against it as he would a lover. He sagged beside the weapon, spent.

Jack rested for a time, then pushed to a sitting position and propped his back against the oak's trunk, dragging the Enfield with him. The impact had broken the soldered telescopic sight fittings and the device sat cockeyed on the barrel, but the rifle appeared otherwise undamaged.

Unlike himself. He looked along his body, taking stock. His right trouser leg hung in shreds down the off side. Despite the blood and soreness, once he straightened the leg it functioned more or less as it should. He ought to be able to walk out of here, because his legs seemed sound enough. That is, he could if he didn't faint every time he lifted his head.

He touched his stinging cheek and found grit stuck in blood, which also matted his torn right sleeve. His arm was broken between the wrist and elbow. A piece of shrapnel stuck into the meat of his upper arm. He grasped the fragment, gritted his teeth against the expected jolt of fresh pain and pulled it out. A trickle of bright blood ran from the wound. He pressed it with his hand to slow the bleeding. The whole length of his right arm was soaked under the tattered cloth. Most likely splinters peppered his arm, but he couldn't manage removing the sleeve to pick them out.

He hadn't reloaded the Enfield before being knocked out of the tree, but he figured he could manage that one-armed though it would take longer. A single shot wouldn't do him any good against more than one Yankee. Besides, with only his left arm in working order, could he effectively aim and shoot the rifle?

He released his hand and discovered the bleeding had slowed. The ringing in his head had lessened. Sounds started to come through though they remained muffled.

His improved hearing allowed him to study the nearby boom of big guns he felt more than heard. Shells screeched overhead loud enough to penetrate his abused eardrums. Apparently he and the other boys had failed to silence the artillery. His hearing had not recovered enough for him to judge how far away or from what direction the faint crackle of small arms originated.

On his belt Jack located his cartridge box and canteen. He did not bother to try to locate his haversack and blanket, no doubt buried under bits of tree. Forcing himself to move calmly, he unbuckled the canteen and with trembling fingers pulled the cork stopper. A mouthful of water would do for now, just to wash out the dirt taste. Better hoard the rest for later, in case of dire need.

He reached down to remove the climbers from his boots, but unable to endure the bending of his battered body, he gave up. If the Yankees, the same Yankees whose fellows he had been killing, found him with his sharpshooter's telescope rifle and the gaffs on his boots, he expected them to exact swift vengeance on him.

Damned if he was going to let them.

He cradled the broken arm, but then he couldn't use his good arm to hold the rifle. Instead he let his wounded arm dangle straight down.

Holding the rifle upright, the stock to the ground, he braced against the tree and the weapon to rise to his feet. He stilled, sweating, waiting for the blood to return to his brain, the stab in his side forcing him to pant. His vision narrowed and he staggered, but steadied himself against the trunk.

He gritted his teeth and took another step, using the rifle as a walking stick. His knees buckled and he slumped to the ground, jarring his broken side.

Pain wrenched forth a racking sob. Dark closed in, threatening to steal his awareness. He knew how to fight and come out on top, but this was a different kind of battle, one he didn't know how to win.

New movement caught his attention. Jack froze and struggled to focus on the new threat.

A figure wearing a faded gray jacket similar to his came into view. Bill. The fellow sharpshooter slid to a crouch and gave him a ghastly powder-blackened grin. He must have said something because his lips moved.

"What?"

Bill leaned closer and shouted in his ear. "We're falling back."

"Get me out of here, will you?"

Bill cast a wary glance over his shoulder, probably realizing that lugging Jack would slow down his retreat. "Let's go."

*

Martina led Carlo into the Presbyterian Church. She had never before set foot inside the Protestant stronghold. The basic wooden structure boasted polished wooden pews, an altar, a speaker's podium and a stained glass window.

She scanned the rows of familiar faces and noticed the townspeople had arranged themselves roughly by political sentiment. The Unionists, such as the Northern-born Mrs. Anderson and the Farrells, who had moved from their holdings on the St. Johns River into town, allied themselves on one side of the church.

Most of her Minorcan kinsmen, the outspoken Mrs. Judge Smith, and other staunch Southerners filled the other side. Her neighbor, Mr. Toombs, slid aside to give her and Carlo more room. She crossed herself and adjusted her mantilla.

"Kneel," she said to Carlo. She pointed to the floor as she slipped off the seat onto the hard stone floor. "Pray."

"We ain't Presbyterian."

"Aren't. Do it anyway." Martina clasped her rosary and shut her eyes, leading Carlo through a Hail Mary and an Our Father. Whether Lieutenant Prescott had told her the truth she could not tell. For certain, the Yankees had not called a meeting of the townspeople to give them a holiday. "Holy Mother, pray for us," she murmured.

After ten Hail Marys and Our Fathers, she sat back on the bench and allowed Carlo to do the same

She recognized two of the Yankee officers who stood in front of the altar. Colonel Beard, who was in charge of the provost department, and Lieutenant Prescott.

She had little faith in churches that were not Catholic but this was a place of worship nonetheless, and the purpose of the town meeting seemed a desecration. The minister stood by, hands folded, looking gloomy, and why not? Armed Yankee soldiers at each door and a column of troops on the street had transformed his house of God into a jail.

More townspeople drifted in, subdued as though attending a funeral. A miasma of fear hung in the air.

*

Lieutenant Richard Prescott stood at the front near the pulpit and observed the citizens of St. Augustine straggle inside. A baby squalled, and the mother tried to hush it by placing it onto her shoulder and patting its back. An older boy curled up beside her on the bench sucking his thumb.

In a low voice Prescott said to the officer next to him, "Good riddance, I say."

Baker grunted in agreement. "Look at that Mrs. Smith." He nodded toward the dowager, her head held at a haughty angle. "Her son is a rebel general, for pity's sake. Besides that, she has a mouth big enough for a regiment of men. I've never met the fellow, but I doubt he can possibly be as ferocious as his mother."

"She has her nose so high up in the air it's a wonderment she didn't drown in a rainstorm," Prescott said. "Florida, land of snakes, traitors and alligators."

Baker snickered at his wit.

Prescott added, "The women in this town think they can say and do whatever treasonous act they please."

"They are in for a surprise."

"Comeuppance time," Prescott added, picturing the dismay that would shadow the faces of that pack of so-called ladies who had chopped down the flagpole in the plaza lest Old Glory fly. It was hard to work up any sympathy.

"To think we were handing out food to those ingrates. If it were up to me, they could have starved until they showed us a little respect. That ambush...." Baker let out a bitter laugh. "That tore it, didn't it?"

Prescott nodded agreement. An invitation for soldiers to attend a party at a house outside town resulted in the men fighting their way out.

He spotted the Sanchez girl with her kid brother and drew himself taller. She was easy to notice, with her sinuous movements, her long, braided hair half hidden by a lacy head covering, and her sultry eyes. Although reserved, she did not act openly hostile and would actually speak when spoken to, with the musical hint of Spanish coloring her Southern accent. "Now that one." He nodded in her direction. "She can stick around."

"Aha. Staking a claim, are you? A Papist Minorcan female? You fancy sugar cane and mullet," he snorted. "Lazy lot. Only way you can get the men to show a little energy is yell 'Mullet on the beach.' Then they scatter to fetch their nets."

Prescott cut his gaze back to Baker. "Just appreciating a fine specimen of womanhood. Besides, she's a good cook. Have you tried her shrimp pilau?"

"She'll probably have to go. Most of the Minorcans are Secesh. Don't you know her brother is in the rebel army?"

"Now that is a shame." Prescott tut-tutted and let his gaze rest on Martina Sanchez. She held her prayer beads and fingered them, her young brother perched sullenly beside her. Perhaps there were compensations to his being stuck in this backwater town.

Given time, he could win her over to his side, and not merely her political loyalties.

*

Martina watched Colonel Beard of the provost guard step up to the podium. He cleared his throat. The hum of voices did not abate, so he called out, "Attention!"

His face grim, he turned to the pastor. "You will lead a prayer for President Lincoln; then we'll have our meeting."

After the subdued clergyman, looking whipped, followed the order, Colonel Beard again stepped to the podium. "We've been generous and forbearing, opening our commissary to the wives and children of rebels. What have we received in return for our charity? Scorn, insults and treason from the citizens of this city.

"The treachery of a woman inviting soldiers to her house and getting them caught in an ambush is the sort of perfidy we can't tolerate. She would have been hanged if we'd found her.

"We've caught Confederate soldiers skulking about in the city, hidden and protected by so-called loyal citizens. We can't tolerate spies in our midst. If you cannot see your way clear to taking the oath of loyalty to the United States of America, you will be sent away. We reserve the right to decline the oath to those of you who have immediate relatives in the rebel army. Let the rebels feed their own."

Colonel Beard followed those hard words by explaining that a ship would take the Secessionists up the coast and leave them at the rebel lines. He extolled the benefits of loyalty to Old Glory. "You've all prospered under that flag, and it's time you admit the

United States is the best nation in the world." He went on in that vein, long enough for a bored Carlo to start squirming and making irreverent faces mocking the Yankee officer.

"Stop." Martina elbowed the boy, and he settled.

Colonel Beard pointed out three areas in the church where one could take the pledge. A Bible and stacks of paper rested on each table.

Lieutenant Prescott had moved to the table at the corner near the exit of the church and pulled up a chair. His gaze darted about until alighting on Martina.

She turned away from him and saw the stricken faces of the townspeople. The impact of the message clarified in her mind. She was being told to become a Unionist, if they even allowed it, or to clear out.

The Farrells appeared to take the news calmly. The gentleman rose to his feet, his wife joining him. Ignoring hostile glares from some of the people on Martina's side of the aisle, the couple made their way toward the back of the church.

Mr. Toombs swiveled around to watch and growled, "Look at that. Farrell has no trouble buttering both sides of his bread. You'd think, with his own son fighting for the Confederacy, he wouldn't be so quick to sell out."

"Just one son," Martina reminded him. "The other is with the Union army."

"To think he calls his Confederate son the black sheep. Ha. Doesn't he have that backwards?" Mr. Toombs frowned. "But it's true Jack has earned a bad name."

Carlo kicked at the pew in front of him. "I don't care what anybody says about Mr. Jack. He's my friend."

"Whenever Jack drove the stagecoach into town, he would let my brother climb up with him," Martina said. "He taught Carlo how to handle the lines and drive. Whatever else he did, he was always good to the boy." Her memories of Jack Farrell were distinct, as he had left a strong impression on her, one that had soured.

She recalled the last time she had seen him, at the Posey Dance, just before war broke out.

He bowed and presented her with a bouquet of fire-colored wildflowers. "I brought this for the most beautiful girl in the state."

He did not look as dangerous as the gossips implied. He was an attractive young man, slim and fluid of motion. She liked his smile, and the intensity in his blue eyes intrigued her.

"You flatter me." She accepted the Indian Blanket flowers and smiled back at him. "But I'm sure you say that to all the girls. I hear you've broken many a heart."

"I wouldn't deceive you with mere flattery." He held out his hand in an invitation. "Honor me with this dance."

On the floor he led with confident male power and apparent respect. He kept his full attention on her and she found his conversation interesting. Despite his backwoods upbringing, he was well-spoken and informed. He had traveled, installing telegraph lines from Jacksonville to Cedar Keys on the west coast. He charmed her into suspecting that the gossips were liars. Perhaps she would give him permission to see her again, if he should ask.

Then Francisco intervened. He told Jack to leave his sister alone. She had never seen her brother so angry. "I won't have Martina sullying her reputation by associating with a scoundrel like you, Farrell."

Jack balled his fists and drew himself taut, a set expression on his face, reminding Martina of the talk that his quick temper had gotten him into trouble. It was said he had killed a man.

He turned to her and asked in an even tone, "Is that what you want?"

Terrified the men would come to blows, or worse, she simply nodded.

Jack laughed bitterly. "Never mind. I know plenty of ladies who aren't too good for the likes of me."

He spent the rest of the evening proving it, and proving Francisco and the gossips right.

Both men were now somewhere in Virginia, fighting for the same side.

Although her allegiance lay with Francisco's commitment to the Confederacy, how hard would it be to follow the elder Mr. Farrell's lead? If they let her take the oath despite Francisco's service, she could cross her fingers behind her back. Was lying such a terrible sin if it meant she and Carlo could stay in their home and live unmolested?

As though reading her thoughts, Mr. Toombs leaned close

15

and whispered, "You don't have to keep the oath. Say you will, or they'll shut you up."

Carlo glared at the older man. "Martina, you can't do that. We would be nothing but traitors."

Mr. Toombs snorted. "Mind your manners, boy."

Martina thumped Carlo on the back of the head. "Don't be impertinent." Catching reprimands from both sides, the boy huffed and settled into a sullen lump.

She had tried her best to maintain her loyalties without antagonizing the Yankees because she depended on their good will. Apparently that strategy had failed.

She turned and watched Mr. Farrell hold the door for his wife as they left the church, free to live their lives in peace.

Rousing from his sulk, Carlo whispered, "You can't do it."

"God knows where we'll end up, where we can live and how we can make a living. What will become of our home? Somebody else will move in and steal it, just like they steal from our grapevines."

"I don't care. Think of our brother. What will he think of us?"

"He isn't here, and I don't know when we'll see him again."

Carlo crossed his arms over his chest. "I won't do it. I'd rather starve."

Francisco would expect her to be honest and strong. He would expect her to hold her head up and remain true to her convictions, whatever it cost. Once banished, could she somehow get word to him so he could help in some way?

Maybe it was only a Yankee threat. Maybe they weren't evil enough to banish women, children and old men from their homes. She rubbed her thumb over her rosary beads, reciting the prayers in her head. What advice would the Blessed Mother have for her? Receiving no answer, she looked up at the cross on the wall and nodded. "All right, then. No oath. Let them do their worst."

CHAPTER THREE

Prescott passed the Farrells through and let them leave the church for home because they had taken the loyalty oath weeks before. Other townspeople lined up to lay a hand on the Bible and avow their fidelity to the United States, though Prescott suspected that Toombs fellow lied.

After those few cleared away, he noted Martina kneeling quietly in the pew with her prayer beads running through her fingers. Her little brother – Pablo... Pedro... Carlo, Prescott remembered – met his gaze defiantly. That one bore watching.

Prescott walked over to her and cleared his throat. She slid back onto the pew and stared at him. "Miss Sanchez, you have a problem." He pursed his lips. "Some might say your brother being in the Confederate army disqualifies you from declaring yourself a good United States citizen."

He noted the fear in her dark eyes. He could use that.

"I haven't noticed you insulting our soldiers or acting rebellious." He smiled and lowered his voice to keep from being overheard. "I'm not making any promises, but it's possible I can fix the situation for you."

She looked down at her prayer beads. "I wasn't going to take the oath anyway."

"Good for you, Tina," Carlo said. "Me neither."

Prescott shot a stern look at the boy, who glared right back at him. "You should teach your little brother his mouth can get him in trouble."

"I hear that a great deal." Martina shook her head at Carlo, who folded his arms across his chest and looked mutinous. She turned back to Prescott. "Whatever the politics, I never wanted trouble."

"You only have a few hours to decide. After that, we will escort the unrepentant rebels to the *Burnside*, which is waiting in the bay."

"It's hard to believe our conquerors would be so inhuman."

"Take my word, it isn't an empty threat."

17

She shifted as if to leave. "Then I'd better go home and pack."

"You aren't allowed to go yet. Only those willing to take the oath can leave and do as they please." He swept his hand toward the people still huddled inside the church. "We have you rebels all gathered up, can't let you scatter until we take names and find out where you live."

The fear in her eyes deepened.

"Like I said, I believe I can fix that. You've always behaved yourself, you don't demand rations from the commissary. I don't see why you should have to go." He smiled and stroked his moustache. "Besides, I've gotten used to your good pilau."

"Thank you," Martina said in a soft voice. "But I can't accept your help."

"If you change your mind," Prescott pointed at the table where he had been working. "I'll be ready. I would strongly recommend you don't wait until you're on the boat steaming up the coast."

*

Martina gripped her crucifix so hard the sharp edges bit into her flesh. Could Prescott really help her keep her home?

She would likely owe him more than a dish of pilau. What would he demand in return for his intervention? A thought of how he might exact his price made her shiver. Although she didn't think him the worst of the Yankees, she could not bear to let a man like that touch her. Something about him bothered her deeply. Her dislike for him was instinctive and unreasoned.

Besides, her brother was offering his life for the Confederacy, and she must honor that.

"You shouldn't take the oath just because that Yankee lieutenant said so." Carlo stuck out his chin. "I wish Francisco were here. He'd just shoot him."

"Hush. Don't say such things. What if they overhear you?"

"I hate them." At least he said it under his breath.

"The ship will take us to Jacksonville. From there we can get word to Francisco." Martina shook her head. "I don't know what he can do for us, though."

"How far away is Virginia?"

"Too far to walk." Francisco had traveled partly by rail, and from what his letters said the trip took many days.

"At least we won't have to put up with Yankees any more." Instead of appearing frightened, the boy seemed excited by the prospect of a new adventure. "We'll be all right. I can still fish and you can still cook."

Martina sighed. Hadn't the boy noticed what a day-to-day struggle they'd experienced, even with a roof over their heads?

The only slim chance to keep their home was through Lieutenant Prescott, and she could not accept a favor from him. Like it or not, her path was clear.

"Carlo, come with me." Sick of being made to feel caged, she left the pew and marched to Lieutenant Prescott's table. "We need to go home now and prepare to leave. Please don't try to stop us."

Frowning, Prescott stood up and leaned toward her, planting his hands on the table. "I don't have to stop you." He nodded toward the shotgun-toting guard standing at the door. "He has his orders. Anyone who won't take the oath must wait here until we release them to prepare."

"Am I a prisoner? What will they do, shoot me if I try to leave?"

"That's your final decision? It's yours to regret."

"Whatever we do will bring us regret."

"It's a big price for being a stubborn rebel. My offer still stands." His gaze dropped below her chin line. "I do have influence with my superior officers."

She took a deep breath. "I can't take such an oath."

Prescott rocked back on his feet without saying anything and walked over to the colonel. The two of them spoke in low tones, occasionally glancing her way. Prescott returned to his table. "Colonel Beard is directing everyone who won't take the oath to wait in the gallery."

Martina set her jaw. "Then I suppose we will have to stay here until the colonel decides to release us."

He laid his hand on her arm. "You can still change your mind. The colonel values my judgment."

She shivered as she withdrew from his grasp.

*

The stench of blood, vomit and human waste hung over the

19

hospital compound so thick Jack tasted it. His hearing, slowly strengthening, opened his senses to unwelcome sounds. Nearby someone wept. A shriek at a longer distance either signaled death or the persistence of torment. The continuous crack and boom of gunfire sent a constant stream of human wreckage to the hospital.

The crippling agony of his arm and side eclipsed the dull aches and sharp pains over the rest of his body. His long passage from the battlefront to the field hospital had used up his fortitude. Despite the horrors of the surroundings, temporary safety from attack allowed him to relax his vigilance. He shut his stinging eyes to rest and try to recover a shred of his usual vitality.

After a time thirst drove him to grope for his canteen and take a swig.

"Can I have some of that?" asked a voice at his elbow.

Jack turned his head to find the petitioner. The soldier's gray face nearly matched his uniform. His yellow sleeve facings indicated cavalry; the palmetto buttons showed he was a South Carolina trooper. A bloody rag covered his shoulder. "They haven't given you anything to drink?"

"Not yet." The fevered stare moved from the canteen to Jack's face. "What in God's name happened to you?"

Jack handed him the canteen. "Easy on it. That's all I have."

The cavalryman took a long pull. "Thanks, brother." He handed it back. "We might be here awhile."

Jack didn't make conversation as he took another swallow. Talk was too much trouble. The canteen felt lighter in his hand, holding barely enough water to slosh.

The man on his other side appeared to be quietly dying. Each shallow breath brought red bubbles from the man's mouth and nose. At first glance he looked familiar, but Jack didn't investigate. He had all the misery he could stand and didn't want to take on extra.

More men limped in; ambulance stewards dumped others among the pile of suffering bodies.

Finally a bucket-bearing orderly came through, stepping over living and dead, handing out water from a tin cup. Wounded men, thirst-crazed from loss of blood, clutched at the orderly's clothes as he passed through. He swore at them but continued to dip water and pass the cup from one man to another.

The orderly offered the cup to the cavalryman, who accepted it with a shaky hand, spilling some as he tried to drink. When it was Jack's turn, the orderly handed him the cup. Jack looked into it before he brought it to his mouth. Scum floated on top of the tea-colored water. He handed it back without taking any.

The dying man next to Jack, motionless on his back had completed the process. He no longer exhaled blood, his eyes half open and unfocused. Jack's dazed brain finally recalled the face of somebody he knew, someone he should have recognized right away if he had mustered the will to look closer. Francisco Sanchez.

He had let Francisco's young brother, Carlo, ride in the shotgun seat on stagecoach runs to the Picolata ferry landing on the St. Johns River. He had danced with their vivacious dark-eyed sister, Martina, a bittersweet memory from a warm spring night. Francisco told him to stay away from her, and Jack told him to go to hell. It appeared Francisco was well on his way.

It was Jack's turn to move on. After resting, he hoped he had rallied enough strength to leave. He pushed to his feet, breathing in the shallow manner his injuries required, and this time he didn't pass out.

The cavalryman said. "Where you think you're going?"

"Anywhere but here." Jack supported his broken arm with his good one, took a careful step, and another. Although lightheaded and wobbly, he could stay upright this time. He didn't intend to seek attention ahead of others who needed it worse. He simply needed to take charge of some part of his fate.

Jack made his way past scores of bloodied men to the tents where the surgeons did their work. A stack of dismembered body parts near the tent fly appeared to roil, animated by flies. He held his hurt arm protectively against his body. The same orderly who had brought water blocked his way. "What are you up to?"

"Sightseeing." Jack faltered on his feet and caught his balance. The demonstration of weakness angered him.

"What on earth happened to you?"

Jack glanced down at the blood covering his right side. His face must look just as bad. "Exploding shell."

"You have to wait your turn."

Jack fixed his gaze on the grisly stack, contemplating life with one arm, provided he lived. "While I'm waiting, got any opium? Whiskey? Anything?"

*

Martina crammed provisions into a carpetbag while Carlo dithered over what to take with him. "I'll need my mullet net." He picked up the heavy net constructed from knotted squares of string with lead sinkers sewn into its circumference.

"Yes, you need to catch fish so we can eat." The smoked mullet and cornbread she had on hand would feed them for about a day.

She went upstairs to her bedchamber and found the little bit of Confederate money and the U. S. bills she had hidden in a drawer. She unbuttoned her bodice and shoved the money under her corset, next to her skin. She tucked her silver bracelet into the carpetbag and added a change of clothing.

Martina returned down the stairs and walked out the back door, leaving it open. She breathed deep of the salt-tinged air. The stiff east wind brought a promise of heavy seas.

A few decades ago the Scottish physician, Andrew Turnbull, had lured Martina's forebears from the Mediterranean island of Minorca. They came filled with hope to the New World, only to find bitter disappointment. Most of the indentured farmers starved or perished from tropical diseases at the ill-prepared indigo plantation at Mosquito Inlet. Only after the hardy remnant fled to St. Augustine and took root here had they thrived.

She had lived in the Spanish-style house, built of tabby and wood, all her life. Her grandfather had added the upstairs and balcony for his expanding family. Though her father had perished at sea and her mother by yellow fever, she sometimes sensed their presence and took comfort. When no one was around to call her crazy, she spoke with them and it always helped. Like the Blessed Mother they returned no clear answers.

Her eyes misted over. She loved the little courtyard, with its lush twin orange trees that gave morning shade in the summer and fruit in the winter. Her trees had miraculously survived killing freezes and blight over the years. Green fruit hung from their boughs. Someone else would be eating her oranges come winter.

The natural fence of spiny Spanish bayonet bristled under the windows, discouraging intruders. Tomato and pepper plants grew in their urns. Grape vines curled up the trellises, the summer yield picked and gone. She and her brothers were born here, and she had never expected to stray far from home.

Now she was being banished as an undesirable. It was said that Minorcans removed from St. Augustine could not prosper.

She feared that might be true.

She had made a half-hearted effort to sell her house, but had found no buyers. Left vacant, her home would surely be claimed by Union soldiers.

Again she considered the lieutenant's offer to let her take the oath and stay home. She did not trust him despite the helpfulness his words implied.

Perhaps she was foolish not to accept his offer. Then she thought of Francisco, fighting Prescott's kind in Virginia, and her resolve hardened.

Carlo ran out with his carpetbag and the heavy net slung over his shoulders. "I'm ready." She gave him a hug. "You're much braver than I am, Chico." She looked around the courtyard, tears filling her eyes, and turned to leave.

*

"We're going to go on the ocean in that?" Martina's cousin, Mary Genovar, said. "They mean to kill us."

Martina, hugging her carpetbag, balked on the dock as she stared at the decrepit steamer. Next to her Carlo shouldered his net and paused with her. The timbers lacked paint, and some of them looked rotten. Rust stained the wood around salt-corroded nails. The deck rapidly filled with exiles huddled in a confused pack. She tried to reassure Mary. "Then the crew would die, too. Surely it's seaworthy."

Others besides Martina had either refused the oath or had been denied it due to close Confederate ties. Another cousin, Antonia Canova, had already boarded and sat on a bench on the deck, surrounded by her brood of four children. Her husband's army service condemned her to this fate. Little Elena curled against her mother, pale and unsmiling. In fact, Martina saw not a smile on any of the faces on the boat.

The breeze carried a sour odor from the hold, not the honest fishy smell of a shrimp boat like her father captained, but a taint of deeper decay.

The ship trembled at its hawsers as though fearful of its mission. Waves lapped hungrily at its sides. The choppy bay waters and the buffeting east wind suggested rough Atlantic seas beyond the inlet.

The Yankees weren't taking any chances on letting the

townspeople slip off, hide and avoid being sent away. A force commanded by Prescott had scoured the town and escorted the citizens to the boat landing.

"Move along," grumped a soldier from behind her.

Carlo bristled and turned to the man, but Martina grabbed his arm and propelled him toward the gangplank. "Don't do anything crazy and give him an excuse to hurt you. He has a gun and you have a mullet net," she said in a sharp undertone. Was the boy determined to make things even worse? His childish efforts to become a man would surely be the ruin of them both.

Carlo twisted to look back at the soldier. "He's the one who stole grapes from our vines. I saw him do it."

"Never mind. They'll get the oranges, too." Martina clenched her fist on the carpetbag handle. She turned to face the soldier, but he wasn't looking her way. He and his comrades moved toward the gangplank, herding the people who hung back onto the boat. Among the guards, Prescott met her gaze and raised an eyebrow.

Fury rose up in her chest. "Along with our house, they will steal everything we ever owned." She bit her lip, determined not to let them see her cry, and then marched across the gangplank onto the deck of the *Burnside*. The soldiers and crew ordered the confused and frightened passengers into the hold that smelled of mildew and brine. After descending into the gloomy space, Martina looked around. The open hatch and lanterns provided dim light. She took her place on a bench between Miss Swingle and a dazed-looking Mary Genovar, who cradled her youngest daughter in her lap. Martina looked for Carlo, but he had disappeared.

Martina realized the floor was wet and drew her carpetbag into her lap. "The boat seems to be leaking," she said to Mary.

"What are we going to do?" Mary dragged her skirts higher to keep them dry.

"Pray the bilge pumps work." Martina tried to be hopeful. "We shouldn't ever be out of sight of the beach."

Mary gave her a worried look.

"Do you have any relatives you can stay with?" Martina asked.

Mary shook her head. "If I get word to my husband, maybe he knows somebody. I think he's in Alabama now."

Miss Swingle cleared her throat. "Well, Martina, I'm surprised they made you come with us."

Martina turned to her, struck by the hostile tone. "I refused to take their oath, just like everyone else here."

"That surprises me, too. You've been mighty friendly with that Yankee lieutenant."

"He hasn't been unkind, and I don't hate him. Do you?"

"I certainly don't consort with Yankees." The schoolteacher inclined her head and looked away.

"What are you implying, Miss Swingle?"

"What would Francisco think? He's up north fighting Yankees and here you are cooking and sewing for them."

Martina sighed. "I won't accept Yankee charity by taking their commissary supplies, then turn around and spit on them."

"You seem to like them pretty well. Especially that one."

"Just because I don't refuse to talk to him? Just because I don't insult them or their flag?"

"I'm not the only one who's noticed."

"The conduct of some of the ladies in town is what's gotten us into this trouble. You think just because you're female they won't do anything to you. Now they've done it to all of us." Martina set her jaw and stood. "Excuse me, I need fresh air."

*

Carlo stood with his hands on the railing and the salt-laden wind in his face. The pilot headed the ship out at high tide, when the channel flowed oceanward and the water was deepest. His father had taught him to respect the inlet's strong currents and shifting sandbars.

Carlo had slipped back up from the hold while Martina remained below decks with the other ladies. The busy crew ignored him. When he thought one of the guards was about to order him below, he moved to the other side of the boat.

A steamship was a new experience for him as the local fishing vessels were powered by wind and oar. The deck of the *Burnside* thrummed with vibration from the propellers thrusting the craft through the water, into the wind. Black smoke from the twin funnels wafted away with the breeze. Porpoises escorted the steamer as it moved through the channel, possibly mistaking the ship for a fishing boat and hoping for a free meal of discarded trash fish. Their top fins arced through the water as they dove and powered along, outpacing the old tub. Seagulls came mewling in the wake and circled for a few minutes, then flew on.

Carlo imagined the steamship grounding on a sandbar. He would help the people below onto the top deck so they wouldn't perish as the water breached the hull. A strong swimmer, he would have no trouble gaining the shore. He could even carry others along through the undertow.

The *Burnside* cleared the mouth of the inlet safely and turned northward, hugging the shoreline of North Beach. Carlo would have to wait for another crisis before getting a chance to prove himself heroic.

The wide beach north of town rose to high sand dunes topped by sea oats, a bulwark against storm tides. He had often rowed across the North River and roamed that beach, hunting for pirate treasure and casting his mullet net in the surf. He had figured out fishing was a more profitable venture than treasure hunting.

Peaks and valleys of rolling waves rocked the steamer from side to side. Toward the shore, breakers churned white as they drove across the gray sand.

Carlo had dropped his carpetbag, his net and his wading boots at his feet. He didn't know where he and his sister would end up, but the chances were good it would be near salt water where he could fish for himself and Martina. He would see to it they had something to eat, just as he'd been doing all along.

From what he'd heard, Confederate soldiers now occupied Jacksonville. Perhaps getting out of Yankee-controlled St. Augustine would give him a chance to slip away and enlist. He could join Francisco in Virginia, and they could fight their enemies together. Martina and Francisco both had said he was too young, but he knew how to handle a musket.

Of course as the man of the family he would have to make sure Martina was all right before he left. For the past year it had taken their combined efforts to survive. Away from the Yankee boot in his face, he would finally feel free.

Martina came up from the hold and stood next to him. She stared at the passing shoreline. He put his arm around her, and she gave him a sad smile.

"We'll be all right," he said.

"I pray we will, Chico." She pressed her hand to her temple. "I pray we will."

CHAPTER FOUR

By nightfall Jack began to shiver, his resistance low. He hadn't eaten all day, but the thought of food made his stomach tighten into a fist. Although the sounds of battle had died down, dying men surrounded him.

Finally it was his turn to be seen by the surgeon. When an orderly came for him, Jack insisted on walking under his own power. Once inside the tent, he took in the dim lantern-lit nightmare. The surgeon, a saw-wielding madman wearing a bloodied apron pointed to a gore-stained board that served as a dissection table. The black shadow his body cast on the tent walls shifted, magnified to monstrous stature.

A team of stretcher-bearers jostled past, carrying out a man who was either unconscious or dead. Another orderly tossed a couple of detached limbs onto the pile. Jack held onto his broken arm, dreading the idea of seeing it added to the collection.

"Damn. Aren't we getting near the last of these?" The surgeon swayed, whether from fatigue or drunkenness it was not clear. His eyes widened. "Great God. What a bloody mess. What happened to you?"

"Exploding shell knocked me out of a tree. I took some shrapnel. My arm is busted, and some ribs besides."

Close at hand, the surgeon didn't seem so fiendish, merely jaded. Jack smelled liquor on the man's breath and regretted nobody had offered him any. Nor had they offered him anything else to dull his pain.

"You lost your eyebrows and your hair is singed. You spitting any blood?"

Jack shook his head no.

"Lucky for you." The surgeon turned to the orderly, "Clean him up first. I can't see what's under all that gore. And give him a dose of morphine. I'm damn sick of grown men hollering while I work on them."

The orderly told Jack to sit on a stool and handed him three small white pills from a bottle, then picked up shears from the nearby table. Jack gratefully swallowed the pills though he doubted such a tiny amount would do much good. Soon his shirt, trousers and undershirt lay in ribbons on the ground, leaving him only his drawers. The orderly wiped off blood with a wet cloth, exposing raw wounds and purple bruises to the flickering light. Mincemeat. Jack chewed his lip and endured the torture as best he could.

The surgeon ran his fingers over the swollen flesh. "Can't do much about the ribs besides bandage them up."

Jack fought faintness as the surgeon probed and picked out splinters and metal fragments from his right side.

The surgeon finally said, "The broken bones in your arm aren't exposed. Those are flesh wounds but I can't get to all the splinters under the skin. Maybe you can keep the arm if you want to take your chances with gangrene. I'll dress the wounds, set the break and splint it."

"Thank you," Jack managed to say. Apparently it wasn't his day to die.

*

Martina spent a sleepless night on the deck because she could not bear to stay in the dark hold with her fellow exiles. She feared the pumps would not stay ahead of the water leaking into the old hulk. If the *Vurnside* went down, she would rather take her chances in the open.

Annoyances also kept her from staying with the others. Besides Miss Swingle's criticism, the whining children, and the atmosphere of despair, the roll and pitch of the rough ocean swells made some of the passengers nauseated. The Yankee guards, including Lieutenant Prescott, suffered as well. She had seen him leaning over the rail. When he spotted her he acted nonchalant, but his sweaty, pale face showed his suffering. She almost felt sorry for him. Almost.

She and Carlo had escaped seasickness so far. Perhaps their seafaring ancestors had bequeathed them a degree of hardiness.

At dawn they stood on the port side of the steamer, looking out over the shoreline that yawned into the mouth of the St. Johns River. She felt the vessel start to turn as they changed course, the pilot negotiating the sandbar barriers and the river's outflow. The ship still bucked over the rolling waves, though morning had brought calmer waters.

Other ships rode the water in the distance, one lurking closer to the river's mouth. "Blockaders to keep out the trading ships." She pointed to the nearest smokestack. "The Yankees are determined to strangle our people."

"I wish they were Confederate ships that would capture this old wreck."

Martina nodded agreement.

"They're taking us to Jacksonville after all," Carlo muttered.

"The town is miles upstream," Martina said. "I wonder whether they'll steam the ship up the river or let us off sooner."

Coming from behind, Prescott's voice startled her. "The captain said they're going to take the people up the river in smaller boats. The sandbar is a problem, and he doesn't want to wait for high tide."

Holding onto the rail with one hand, Martina turned to face him. She hoped Carlo would hold his tongue around the Yankee officer. "Are you feeling any better, Lieutenant?"

He gave her a sickly smile. "You get to leave this tub. I have to ride it all the way back to St. Augustine."

"We should trade places."

"Miss Sanchez, you made your choice. Or are you willing to reconsider? Perhaps it isn't too late for you to return."

She looked away from him and stared out over the water. Thank the Blessed Mother that Carlo was busy ignoring Prescott. She recalled Miss Swingle's sharp words about her willingness to trade with the Yankees, Prescott in particular. She knew her own heart, and he had no claim on it.

The blockader had changed direction and was steaming toward the *Burnside*, smokestacks spewing, looming closer. Martina made out the U. S. flag flying over the ship, verifying that rescue by a Confederate warship was not possible. She pointed toward the ship. "Are they going to escort us in?"

Prescott squinted at the ship. "I'm sure they are expecting us."

As the vessel neared she spotted a signalman on the tower, signing with his flags.

"What does that mean?" she asked.

Prescott glanced up to the bridge and she followed his gaze. A sailor stood using his flags to sign an answer. The coded messages continued from one ship to the other.

"What could this be about?" she repeated. The *Burnside* started making a slow turn that steered it away from the river, toward the sea.

"I'm going to find out." Prescott headed for the bridge.

*

Prescott had not wanted to admit to her that he, a land-based officer, couldn't read the semaphores. He climbed the steps to the wheelhouse and saluted the other officers. "Captain, may I ask, sir, why the *Burnside* is turning?"

"Change of orders." The captain, holding his telescope in his hand, looked hot and bothered. "We've been commanded to return to St. Augustine."

"On whose authority?"

"General Terry's. That's what I'm told, at any rate." The captain waved his hand dismissively. "I'll let you know as needed."

The signalman poked his head inside. Prescott listened to the discussion long enough to assure himself the load of Confederate sympathizers was indeed returning to St. Augustine. Surely General Terry had approved the original. It was an odd vacillation by the high command.

He considered how the change of plans affected him. He had not been sorry to see most of the traitors leave, and had expected life to ease up once they were gone. Insults from the citizenry would diminish along with the annoyance of seeing them line up for rations. He would only regret losing the company of one particular rebel.

Now he had time to bring the obstinate woman around to his way of thinking. Best to consider her repatriation a fresh opportunity.

After the captain issued a series of orders, the *Burnside* steamed south.

Prescott sought out Martina, who gave him a questioning look.

"You got your wish. You're going home."

Her face, pinched with tension ever since the church meeting, lit with delight. "Is it the truth? We really are going back to St. Augustine?"

"Seems so. Some higher ups decided to go easy on you

rebels."

She wasted a hug on her sullen little brother and started to laugh. Prescott wished he were the one enjoying her embrace.

*

If the return trip was as miserable as the trip away from St. Augustine, Martina was oblivious. She was going home. It didn't matter that the waves threatened to swamp the *Burnside*, or that she and Carlo ran out of their little cache of food, or that the pumps barely kept the leaky craft afloat. Even the companionship of the ever-present Lieutenant Prescott seemed agreeable.

She forgave him his clipped speech, his frank stares, and the way he loomed over her in his overbearing way. He was not unpleasant to look at, and he conveyed a sense of command now that he had overcome his seasickness. While he didn't make her feel safe, he didn't make her feel threatened.

If only he weren't a Yankee who would as soon shoot her brother Francisco as look at him.

*

Jack didn't ride on an ambulance at first because he was marginally capable of walking. Besides, he couldn't stand the jolting of the wheels over ruts and rocks. He kept himself upright by hanging onto the side of the vehicle.

The surgeon had patched him up in quick and rudimentary fashion, rushed by an evacuation order. Thanks to the orderly who had replaced Jack's ruined clothes, he did not have to go naked. He suspected the previous owner wouldn't ever show up to claim the well-used shirt, jacket and trousers. They came from an Alabama soldier, judging by the eagle insignia on the jacket buttons. A sling supported his splinted arm, bandages swathed the cut-up flesh, and the shirt and jacket covered his shoulders like a poncho. An inadequate dose of morphine did little but dull the pain.

Apparently the foray into Maryland had ended badly, leaving the army to plod in an organized, if despondent, manner back toward the ridges of Virginia. The trains of wagons carrying groaning wounded stretched as far in either direction as Jack could see. He lugged one foot in front of another, ignoring the protests of his feverish body.

By mid-afternoon, Jack's legs turned to rubber under him. He fell out of line and collapsed at the side of the road.

"There's room for this un if we stack the deaders," a voice mumbled.

Rough hands lifted him, and he screamed when they bumped his injured chest and arm. Then they bundled him into the ambulance alongside other broken men.

Jack rolled onto his good side. The ambulance moved again with a jolt that forced a whimper from between his clenched teeth. Yesterday wasn't his day to die, but today death would be an improvement, unless Sister Mary Joseph's prediction of his descent into hell came true.

*

Prescott remained in Colonel Bell's office after giving his report. General Terry's ship had accompanied the *Burnside* back to St. Augustine, and now the general breezed in to explain the situation to the colonel.

The discussion wasn't going well. Colonel Bell was stiff-faced, his voice controlled, but his ears flushed purple. He jumped to his feet and paced, justifiably furious at having his orders reversed but plainly biting back his words. He couldn't very well express dissent to a general.

Politics aside, Prescott was almost as happy as the townspeople to leave the ocean behind and return to St. Augustine. He had resisted an urge to kiss the sand when he finally stepped off that rolling tub. Right away, once on solid earth, he felt the bouts of nausea plaguing him throughout the entire voyage fade away. He thanked the gods of war or whatever was responsible for his not enlisting in the navy.

"So you're telling me we are stuck with the three hundred Secesh, give or take a few of their brats, we thought we were well shut of?"

"That's so," Terry said. He sat relaxed in his chair, fingering a cigar, his voice bland. "Bureaucrats in the Department of the South considered the expulsion too harsh."

Colonel Bell strode back and forth like a caged tiger. "Are we still expected to continue to feed them while we endure their insults? Put up with their spying and hope they don't get us killed?" He shot a hard look at Prescott. "Lieutenant, you escorted the lot.

What of their attitudes now? Did they learn anything?"

"Perhaps," Prescott said. "However, I heard complaints from some of the ladies they had already sold their homes. They said they don't have anywhere to live now."

Bell waved his hand. "Never happy, are they? Let them go somewhere else, then."

"Problems with civilians shouldn't trouble you for long, Colonel." The general pulled an envelope from his inside pocket and handed it to Bell. "You have new orders. The 7th New Hampshire is going to replace the 4th, and we're sending you back to our post in Beaufort."

"We're being removed?"

"It's a rotation, merely a new assignment at your old South Carolina post."

While Bell read the order, frowning, Prescott wasn't much happier. He'd spent time in Beaufort, and it was another subtropical cooker as boring as St. Augustine. He'd even missed the assault on Charleston from James Island last summer. Had he participated, the ignoble outcome might have turned out better for the Union forces.

When would he see real action? When would he have an opportunity to prove his mettle and work his way up the ranks? Although garrison life was easy, his skill as a fighting man might never be tested and honed as long as he remained in the rear. He saw himself as a valiant leader of men taking the fight to the enemy, not a paper pusher marking time in the coastal backwaters.

Bell tossed the orders onto his desk. "Prescott, you are excused."

"Thank you, sir." Prescott saluted his superior officers then left the office, closing the door behind him. He took a deep breath and let it out, anticipating free time to relax after the unnerving and annoying day and night at sea. He had gotten no sleep, and his roiling stomach had accepted no nourishment. A dose of medicinal spirits would no doubt prove beneficial, and then perhaps he could manage a light meal. He considered Martina's pilau but decided he needed blander fare.

He made his way down the hall and into the lobby, drawing to a halt when he spotted the young woman who stood talking to the guard. Martina Sanchez turned to face him, her dark eyes wide and troubled. The guard said, "Lieutenant, this lady says soldiers have taken over her house and she wants somebody to run them out."

Prescott bowed. "It's a pleasure to see you again so soon, Miss Sanchez."

She offered a wan smile. "Lieutenant Prescott. Perhaps you can help me."

Those were pleasant words indeed. He clicked his heels together and bowed deeper. "I am at your service."

"Carlo and I went straight home and found two of your soldiers had already moved into my house, along with a Negro cook. I still own that house, Lieutenant, and they are trespassing." She clenched her small fists. "I asked them to leave, and they laughed and told me to make them."

Prescott smoothed his moustache. "Then I'll take care of it." He patted the handle of his pistol, showing her he meant business. He offered her his arm. "Take me there, and I'll handle this without delay."

*

Martina hurried home, escorted by Lieutenant Prescott. She hated asking him for help but had no choice.

Carlo still waited on the street as she had instructed, obedient for once. His face darkened when he saw Prescott, and Martina feared he would say something rash. But he held his tongue as Prescott strode to the door and swung it wide.

As Martina expected, it was no trick for him to evict her uninvited tenants. A few stern words from him, and the soldiers lost their swagger and sass. They gathered their baggage and hustled out, taking their cook or mistress or whatever she was with them.

Martina followed Carlo into the house then turned at the door to Prescott, who remained just outside. "Thank you, Lieutenant. You've done us a great service."

"My pleasure. Should you have any more trouble, you know where to find me, until I'm transferred."

"You're leaving?"

"You'll be losing your best customer." His gaze traveled to her chest. "And your fondest admirer."

"I'm sorry to hear that." She meant it, even though he made her nervous.

He stepped in closer, a cocky smile playing across his face. She ducked back reflexively. His smile hardened and he grabbed her wrist. "I thought you'd want to thank me properly."

"Lieutenant Prescott, please. Let go...." She twisted to get away, but his grip tightened painfully.

Carlo came up behind her. "Tina.... what's he doing?"

Prescott appeared startled. He dropped her hand and backed away a step. He cleared his throat. "I'll be back to say goodbye before I have to leave."

As she watched him walk away, she rubbed her abused wrist and shuddered at the thought of his lips pressing hers.

Carlo said, "If I had a gun, I'd shoot him."

Martina studied her little brother. He looked so much like a man, a grim, resolute man, growing up too quickly, with too much anger. Her breath caught in her throat.

"Chico, let it go. He saved us from an injustice, and he said he will be leaving St. Augustine soon. Then he won't bother us any more."

*

The next day Colonel Bell summoned Prescott to his office. "As you know, our regiment is being transferred back to Beaufort."

"Yes, sir. Do you know how soon the 7th will arrive and replace us?"

"I'll get to the point. Prescott, I've recommended you for a promotion."

Prescott suppressed an exclamation of delight. "Thank you, sir."

"As captain, you'll continue to be stationed in St. Augustine."

"Sir?" Perhaps the promotion would make continued service in this boring town bearable. Martina Sanchez could give him solace as well.

"I couldn't think of a better man for the job."

Prescott tried to look modest. Perhaps the colonel was pleased with the way he had handled his latest odious duty.

"Quite frankly, Lieutenant, your performance has been a monument to mediocrity. By transferring you to a new unit, we're giving you a chance to improve. As you know, we have adopted the strategy of raising colored units and training them to fight.

It's demoralizing to the rebels to see their former slaves taking up arms against them. You will be assigned to recruit and train a company of Negroes."

Prescott swallowed hard. Colonel Bell might as well have punched him in the gut. "I – I don't know what to say, sir. I'm no abolitionist. Are Negroes capable of fighting? Won't they only be good at digging ditches and mucking out stables?"

Colonel Bell gave him a hard look. "Your job is to *make* soldiers out of them."

"Sir, may I ask how I'm supposed to go about that task?"

"You can start by taking a mounted patrol into the countryside. You'll liberate the colored men and offer them enlistment. I suggest you select a dozen volunteers from your old company who can ride and prepare for your first expedition."

Prescott saluted and made a dignified exit from the colonel's office, his mind reeling. Except for a few impractical idealists, only the worst officers were assigned to lead colored troops. Colonel Bell had just relegated him to their number. Everybody knew Negroes wouldn't be any good at fighting. He didn't look forward to leading patrols through the rattlesnake-infested scrub, subject to pot shots from hidden foes. His would be a dirty, exhausting and unrewarding job.

He realized his men resented him because they didn't like taking orders. Surely that wasn't what caused such a bad turn in his career. He imagined his political opportunities evaporating. People back at home wouldn't think much of an officer who oversaw a crew of Negro laborers.

Prescott lit his cigar and puffed furiously. Colonel Bell always had it in for him. He no doubt wanted him out of his regiment, and this was Bell's first chance. What recourse did he have? He could refuse his promotion, but if he did he might find himself a noncom in a colored company instead.

He scuffed at a pile of horse manure as he crossed the street, then spotted a ragged Negro lazing under an oak tree in the plaza. He sized up the newly freed slave. How could he be expected to make soldiers out of such backward material? Wouldn't they turn and run at the least threat? He shook his head in disgust.

Across the plaza Martina Sanchez stood in her usual place selling lunch to the soldiers. Yesterday's teasing encounter had left him annoyed and frustrated. After the assistance he had given her, shouldn't she have been willing to favor him with at least a kiss? Now that he wasn't transferring to Beaufort with the rest of his regiment, he would seize his chance to collect on the debt, with interest. He smiled at the thought.

He closed the distance between them and when she looked his way, a flicker of fear crossed her face. Her expression increased his exasperation and his determination to have her whether she liked it or not.

"Lieutenant, did you come to tell me goodbye?" she asked.

He shook his head and pasted on a smile, hiding his growing irritation. "I'm not leaving. In fact, I've earned a promotion. I'm going to be a captain, and I'll be raising my own company."

"Congratulations. How wonderful for you." The fear hadn't left her eyes. He had not given her any justification, but perhaps he should.

"I'm sorry, but I've sold out." She opened the lid of the cast iron pot and showed him only a few rice grains stuck to the inside. "I'm just now going home."

"Then I'll escort you."

"You don't have to do that. It isn't far."

"I insist." He grasped the handle of her cart, heading off any further objection.

He told her how he planned to execute his new assignment. By the time they reached her door he almost believed he would do such great things with a Negro company it would further his ambitions. At any rate, he felt better about the situation.

He pushed through the yard gate, though she asked him to leave her there. He did her a service by taking the cart to the front door. Hidden from the street, he planted a forceful kiss on her mouth before she had a chance to pull away. Even under protest her lips tasted luscious and the softness promised even sweeter delights. He stole a brush of his hand up her front and imagined what it would be like to bury his face between her breasts.

He let her push him away but held her by the shoulders so she couldn't escape. He licked his lips. "I want you," he said in a low voice. "But I'd rather have you willingly."

"No." Her lovely eyes widened, showing alarm. He liked it. Unwilling would suit him just as well. Then anger replaced the terror in her eyes, and he liked that, too. He would enjoy a tussle on the way to claiming her. "I should remind you that a word from me, and you will be sent away. You have a nice house, you and your little brother. I wouldn't mind living here. Wouldn't it be better if you got to stay?" He nodded to the door. "Aren't you going to invite me inside?"

Her hand darted into her apron pocket and flashed up with a knife. She pointed the blade straight at his left eye. "Leave me now."

Prescott let go and stepped out of reach. Although he was stronger than she and could have wrestled the knife from her, she could still cut him. Released, she whirled and fled into the house, slamming the door behind her.

He stared at the solid wooden door, forming new respect for Martina Sanchez, the wildcat. She proved a challenge and called for a different approach. This could be fun. He'd have her sooner or later.

She would be worth the wait.

*

Martina pulled the door closed and threw her weight against it, breathing hard.

"What's the matter?" Carlo looked alarmed. "Why do you have your knife out? Did somebody try to rob you? Who was it? Did they steal anything? I'll get it back."

He tried to rush past her, but she held the door shut. If Carlo went after Prescott, the Yankee officer was capable of hurting him. The revolver on his belt might not be all for show. She shook her head furiously "No. Nothing happened."

Carlo's eyes narrowed. "Tell me."

"Never mind. It's nothing."

Carlo shifted on his feet, disbelief on his face.

Martina moved from the door and opened it a crack. Prescott had left. "You can go get my cart."

Carlo did as she asked. She slipped the knife back into her apron pocket.

She could complain to Prescott's superiors, but what was she to tell them? Why should they believe her word over the denials of one of their officers? If she became troublesome, they would send her away.

No, she must take care of herself, just as she had always done.

CHAPTER FIVE

Martina pushed her cart across the bridge, toward the wagons lining the road on the far side of the San Sebastian River. Already some of her neighbors were inspecting the contents of the wagons, and Martina hurried to see what produce could be bought or bartered.

The new St. Augustine garrison commander, Colonel Putnam, had decided to open the picket post on the bridge twice a week to allow trade between townspeople and inland farmers. No longer was St. Augustine an island of isolation. The word had spread, bringing a handful of country people to a ready market.

Although some of her neighbors and relatives had left, Martina was grateful to have kept her home. Carlo's fishing ability and her own cooking skills still sustained them. She maintained her peaceful coexistence with the enemy, her best customers.

Spirits high, Martina looked forward to the day's shopping trip. Depending on who showed up to trade and what they had to offer, she hoped to acquire Irish potatoes, sweet potatoes, corn, eggs, and maybe even a chicken. For the first time since the surrender of St. Augustine, she could supplement the seafood Carlo caught, her little garden, and the sparse goods available in town.

Carlo had run ahead carrying a couple of burlap sacks to harvest oysters on the newly opened west side of the river. She had given up on trying to keep him in school; his contribution to their living kept him too busy.

The cart's wooden wheels banged a rhythm on the bridge planks. The air smelled of salt marsh and a mullet splashed in the water below. Martina walked by the Yankee guards unchallenged. To her relief, she didn't spot Prescott among them. She had seen little of him since their last encounter.

Martina began at the first of the wagons and greeted the Negro driver, Isaac. She knew him, a freedman who had worked for the Farrells.

"I got some pretty sweet potatoes, Miss." He grinned at her, flashing strong white teeth as he plucked a plump, red tuber from the pile. He allowed it to drop with a soft thud before stripping the husk off a full ear of corn. "Nice fresh eggs too."

"Do you take Federal money?"

He nodded.

Martina filled a basket with produce from his wagon and paid him from her little hoard. Mr. Farrell came up and exchanged pleasantries with her. He seemed to have business to conduct with Isaac, so she moved to the next farmer's wagon. Miss Swingle had arrived ahead of her and refused to speak to her. Martina shrugged and picked out two heads of cabbage, three small onions and a watermelon.

The gentleman at the last wagon offered information along with vegetables. She knew Mr. Colee slightly. He used to own the stage line from St. Augustine to the river landing at Picolata, which had quit operating after the Union occupation. He showed her a Savannah newspaper. She glanced at the headlines, which promised news about the war in Virginia. "This is a month old," she pointed out. "Don't you have a more recent paper?"

He shook his head. "Ever since the Yankees have shut down the packet running to Jacksonville, we don't get much news. But a little mail has gotten through. Remind me of your name, please, Miss."

She told him, and he picked up a handful of letters from a basket. Martina held her breath as he shuffled through them, hoping he had one from Francisco.

He handed her an envelope. To her delight, it was addressed in Francisco's handwriting.

Mr. Colee picked up a second envelope and hesitated, a look of concern on his face. "Here's another." He gave it to her with visible reluctance.

The letter wasn't from Francisco. The return address was Captain Fleming, one of the officers in Francisco's company. Her hands turned icy cold. She knew of only one reason Francisco's commanding officer would have written a letter to her.

*

Carlo found Martina hunched in her chair, notepaper spread before her on the table, rosary clutched in her lap. When she turned toward him, he realized she had been crying.

He closed the door behind him and paused as realization closed in like a dark cloak. "Francisco," he breathed.

"Oh, Chico!" Grief cracked her voice. "He's gone. Our poor, dear brother is killed." She rocked forward and sobbed, brokenhearted.

It seemed the air had left the room. "No." He shook his head. "That's wrong. Somebody made a mistake. Isn't he just wounded? Or sick? He can't be dead."

Carlo crossed the floor and grasped her heaving shoulder, not knowing what to say or how to console her, unused to seeing his sister in this state. Tears came to his eyes, but he angrily wiped them off with his sleeve.

He picked up the letter Captain Fleming had written. Along with flowery words of condolence and praise Fleming stated that Francisco had died bravely, quickly, and with little suffering. Their brother had been given a Christian burial near the battlefield in Maryland. Carlo dropped the letter back onto the table and noticed another letter written in Francisco's own hand. He noted it was dated earlier than the captain's letter. He could not bear to read it yet.

Francisco had died in a faraway place and would not be coming home. The reality seemed unreal. How could that be? His big brother was too strong and brave to be killed by any Yankee. Or so it had always seemed.

He sank into the chair next to Martina, determined not to cry.

*

Jack sat on the hospital cot looking out the window. As readily as he would have accepted death during the torturous trek from Sharpsburg to Richmond, somehow he had survived. The army doctors had decided his injuries made him unfit for service during the time left before his enlistment expired, so there was no use keeping him. In a few hours he would be leaving, no pine box required.

With his right arm immobilized by plaster and a sling, he'd accustomed himself to doing tasks one-armed and left-handed. He sensed the bones starting to knit back together, though he had to take care not to move the wrong way. His chest still pained with every breath, and his persistent cough punctuated the misery. The doctor had diagnosed pleurisy and said in time he'd get over it on his own. With luck he wouldn't come down with pneumonia, too.

Splinters embedded along his right side were gradually working their way out and inflaming his flesh. He hadn't carried an ounce of spare weight before the shell struck; now he was down to skin and bones.

The flash burns, bruises and cuts on his face had healed enough to allow him to shave again. The cuts had left only minor scars, his eyebrows had grown back, and a barber had evened his undamaged hair to match the singed areas. He was ready to quit the confinement of the hospital and get on with his life.

He glanced down at the two haversacks on his cot. One contained his worldly goods, including his climbing gaffs and a supply of laudanum for the trip. The other held the scant possessions of Francisco Sanchez. Captain Fleming had asked him to deliver them to Francisco's family. The captain didn't have any suggestions as to how he might do that, considering St. Augustine was now behind Yankee lines, off limits to a Confederate veteran.

Letters to his father and stepmother had gone unanswered, either because Pop had refused to answer them, or because the mail service had failed. Captain Fleming had mentioned he sent a letter to Martina Sanchez, but whether it would ever reach its destination was anyone's guess.

Jack hoped the letter reached Martina before he talked with her. Then he wouldn't be responsible for bringing her the bad news. He hated the thought of causing her delicate features to buckle with grief.

He would rather remember how the appraising look in her eyes had given way to warmth as the evening progressed. Right before she had agreed with Francisco that Jack had no business associating with her. He had acted like a fool afterward, drowning his frustration in rum and with the first willing female he could find.

That sure made his case with Martina, didn't it?

Jack had already said his goodbyes to fellow convalescents and had one more stop to make on his way out. He found Mrs. Reid at her desk going through paperwork and waited for her to finish. The matron, trim and efficient, was about the age his mother would have been had she lived. Another Floridian, the widow had traveled to Richmond and personally founded a hospital for Florida soldiers in this sizable house. Her able management had made his stay bearable.

She looked up and smiled. "Mr. Farrell. I heard you're leaving us."

He nodded. "Yes, ma'am. I'll be making my way back home." He gave her a wry grin. "Going south to recruit my health in a warm climate like the rich Yankees used to do." He paused. "I credit you with saving my life. I came to thank you for all you've done and to say goodbye."

"I'll miss you. You've been one of my favorite patients."

"Thank you, Mrs. Reid. You are one of my few admirers."

"You were determined to get well, and your courage always made me smile."

"Most of that courage came from the laudanum."

"Are you sure you're well enough for such a long journey?" she asked. "I believe you should try to build yourself up first."

"Won't be hard. I'll take the rail line as far south as it goes and figure it out from there. Then I'll have to learn how to be a civilian again." He gave a one-shoulder shrug. "I guess it will be a while before I can climb another telegraph pole."

"I was surprised to hear about your discharge. You are coming along nicely. After you recover, do you plan to reenlist?"

"I figure I've done my duty." He reconsidered his abrupt reply. How could he tell this generous and patriotic lady he felt old, broken down and used up at 22 years of age? "Let's say I'm ready to try out a more peaceable life, at least until the conscription agents decide to throw me back into the fight."

"Mr. Farrell, I pray the war doesn't follow you home."

*

Martina could not afford the luxury of secluding herself for longer than a couple of days. She must continue her routine of cooking in the morning and taking her products to the plaza to sell to the Yankees. She donned the faded mourning clothes she had worn for her parents. She paid Father Aulance from her precious store of funds to say Mass for Francisco. Relatives and neighbors offered flowers and condolences. In her cousin Antonia's eyes she saw fear that her husband, who was in Francisco's regiment, would be next to die.

Staying busy should have helped her not to dwell on her losses. But her activities were the sort that allowed much thought, and her tears had little to do with the onions she chopped. The Yankees might find her cooking extra salty of late. Although the local troops had nothing to do with Francisco's battlefield death hundreds of miles away, they fought under the same flag and for the same Federal government. She could take their money, but she didn't have to like them.

After the initial shock Carlo seemed to take the news with stoic calm, but Martina sensed a smoldering rage lurking underneath. She feared one day his grief and anger would erupt like a lanced boil.

The same day she reopened her business, Prescott was among the first to show up for a dish of pilau. She touched the hard metal of the knife in her apron pocket. Fortunately she was not alone on the plaza with him, as other soldiers drilled nearby. Certainly Prescott would not insult her in front of them.

"I'm back." Prescott touched his cap brim and beamed at her as though nothing had happened between them.

His ebullience offended her. Did he not notice her mourning clothes? "Were you gone somewhere?" Focusing on his face she noticed welts like insect bites on his cheek and a fresh scratch under his eye.

"You didn't miss me?"

She lifted the lid on the pot of pilau, wishing she dared risk the consequences of throwing it at him. She hoped he didn't see her hand shake as she served him.

"We've been out recruiting Negroes for the past few days," he continued. "Ran into a few Rebels but drove them off."

She spooned the pilau into a dish and added a lump of cornbread as he always requested. "I've heard some of your soldiers talking, saying you didn't catch any of our soldiers but they captured some of yours."

"Your soldiers. Indeed." He took a long drag on his cigar. "The rebels came at us with overwhelming force, but we fought them off and prevailed. The scoundrels ran like rabbits, and I doubt they'll try coming around here again."

"I sure you terrified them," she said dryly.

He paid for his lunch. "If I may ask, why are you wearing widow's weeds?"

"You may ask." She handed him his dish, and he made a point of sliding his hand over hers as he took it. She moved her hand away.

"A near relative?"

She nodded. "My brother, Francisco."

"The one in the rebel army." He wiped his moustache. "Too bad for you. I should have said something before." He gave her a sympathetic but insincere smile. "I am sorry for your loss."

She did not respond.

He cleared his throat. "I also wish to apologize for my behavior last time I saw you. I regret appearing rude. I hope you will forgive me and allow me to make it up to you."

"Captain Prescott, it's too soon —"

"Later, of course. You're in mourning, and I respect that. I'll be away recruiting for a few days, at any rate. I'll call on you after I return."

An older, rugged-looking sergeant unwittingly rescued her by coming over and requesting a dish of pilau. As she served him, he expressed his regrets for her state of mourning. This Sergeant Owen was a rough man, but she could not fault his manners.

Apparently the sergeant belonged to Prescott's company. Between mouthfuls Prescott expounded his theories about the management of their Negro recruits. "They excel at hard labor," Prescott said. "The best thing is to put them to use doing menial work. Then our fighting men won't be wasted on such."

The sergeant held a fixed expression and said, "Yes, sir," often. Although Martina had little in common with the man, she understood how trapped he must feel.

At last the two gave back her dishes. Prescott promised to see her later and strode away.

If he did not return from his next patrol, she would not grieve. Martina silently prayed to the Blessed Mother, asking whether it was a mortal sin to wish ill on the man.

CHAPTER SIX

Jack surveyed the family homestead, cautious of riding in unannounced. The overgrowth of the yard leading to the house caused him concern. His father liked to keep the area grazed down so varmints could not hide in the weeds. Jack had not taken the time to visit any of the scattered neighbors to inquire about his family; he had been out of money, out of provisions, and in a hurry.

His rail journey from Richmond had terminated in southern Georgia at the end of the north-south track. Trying to walk a hundred miles further in his weakened and pain-wracked condition would surely have finished him off. He had bought the only horse he could afford, an aging marsh tackie equipped with well-worn saddle and bridle. Ladybug lacked fire and her easy gait suited Jack, as he had used the last of his laudanum.

At Jacksonville he had learned the territory along the west bank of the St. Johns River was under Confederate control, but his family's home was in the disputed land between the river and the ocean. Federal gunboats ruled the river and had used the homes of known secessionists for target practice.

From his war experience he expected surprises and tried to remain alert. It would have been a nasty disappointment if a trigger-happy Yankee ended his journey, so he had rolled up his gray jacket and tied it behind the saddle. After crossing to the east side of the St. Johns by ferry, he took a roundabout route to avoid swimming half a dozen tributaries. Eventually, he had made his way home to Picolata.

Jack dropped the reins onto Ladybug's neck and steered with his knees so he could keep his left hand close to the revolver on his belt. Fennel, milkweed and pokeberry, having grown taller than the grass, brushed the belly of his horse and trembled in the slight breeze from the river. The bay's unshod hooves picked through the damp growth, perhaps making enough noise to scare off rattlers hiding there. Large insects, roused by the disturbance, whirred from their hiding places, causing the horse to toss its head.

When Jack looked out over the orange grove, it appeared to enjoy a degree of order. Perhaps only distance obscured the weeds. Nip, the rangy red hound he had trusted to the hired man's care upon joining the army, did not run out to announce him as he hoped.

Jack had assumed his family received his letters and expected his return. He had also imagined his father would allow his castoff son to convalesce at his home. All Jack asked was sustenance and the chance to recuperate enough to make his own way. He was prepared for a strained reunion, not a deserted house.

He nudged Ladybug toward the pine log house, built of sensible Cracker design. Boards blinkered the windows, and from the outside the house appeared sound.

Jack halted Ladybug in the shade of the sweet gum and pecan trees dominating the front yard. He wearily dismounted, careful of his fragile right side, and tied Ladybug to a branch. Cedar piers elevated the house, sparing the wood floor from rot and discouraging snakes from taking up residence. He stepped up to the porch, his shoes scraping on the floor, and caught himself on the support post. He was too tired to lift his feet.

A roof connected the pair of two-room buildings, which created a shady dogtrot between them. The open-air kitchen was located behind the house, under an extension of the roof. He and his elder brother, Dan, had added the front porch, more shelter from the fierce Florida sun. Jack opened the unlocked front door to the north wing and stepped inside. It took a moment for his glare-accustomed eyes to adjust to the darkness. He inhaled the smell of mold and dust. A sneeze sent a fresh stab of pain through his ribs, followed by a coughing fit.

A pine table and four chairs made from the same rough wood remained as he recalled. He checked the back room and noted the rope bedstead, stripped of its mattress, was still there. Everything else portable or valuable had been removed. He hoped his father had done the removing, not a thief.

Jack resisted the urge to flop onto the ropes and let his worn-out body rest. He opened the door leading from the bedroom, stepped out into the dogtrot, and studied the back lot. Under the shade of pecan trees, the tool shed and the smokehouse appeared intact. A wagon stood empty beneath the overhang of the shed's roof. Beyond those outbuildings lay Isaac's cabin. With his family missing, what had become of their hired man? As a free man of color, Isaac could stay or go as he pleased within the limits of the law. In a corral beyond the buildings grazed a mule and a few runty scrub cows, signs of habitation.

Hand on the grip of his revolver, Jack walked across the yard to Isaac's cabin. A sizeable vegetable garden flourished in the plot beside the cabin, still bearing late-season tomatoes, beans, squash and melons. Chickens scattered at his approach. While the area in front of the main house had gone to jungle, the productive part of the homestead seemed well-ordered. He would not starve.

Jack knocked at the door. When no one answered, he opened it and stepped inside. The one-room cabin contained a bed, a table and chair, a lantern, and other household items that might have been salvaged from the main house. Full sacks of grain were stacked in a corner, and a quantity of jars and jugs. He needed to find Isaac, who could tell him where his family had gone.

He returned to the tool shed, where he found the full stock of farm implements, oiled and free of rust. A cow hunter's whip was coiled on a nail. Shovels, hoes, an axe and other items were stored in an orderly fashion. Jack hefted a crowbar and made his way back to the house. After he toured the property he could pry off the boards and let light inside. Then he could rest.

*

Easy, old gal," Jack murmured as he climbed into the saddle, using the porch edge as a mounting block. With a twitch of the reins, he set Ladybug toward the river, which comprised the west boundary of the Farrell land. Beyond the orange grove, corn stalks stood drying in the sun. Peas grew among them, supported by the stalks. A stand of sugar cane flourished on the swampy ground close to the river. He crossed the spring run that provided drinking water and passed through the trees to the riverbank. Along the way he came upon a sow ambling along with a half dozen piglets trailing her.

Jack rode along the water's edge to the dock he, his father, Isaac, and Dan built. He gazed out over the expanse to the other shore two miles distant. Here the tannin-brown river widened into a cove. He looked forward to soaking the travel dirt from his tired body in the cool water.

A muffled bark sounded close by. He whipped his head toward

the sound.

"Mister Jack."

Jack squinted into the brush, searching for the voice. Though it sounded like Isaac he kept his hand on his revolver grip. When he made out the half-hidden form behind the underbrush, he relaxed and cracked into a grin. "Well, Isaac. I thought you might be around somewhere."

"Bless my soul, I am so glad it's you." Isaac stepped from his hiding place, his movement cautious. Ahead of him bounded Nip, dragging a rope. "Any other soldiers with you, Mister Jack?"

Jack shook his head. "Who are you afraid of?"

"I thought you might be one of the regulators."

"So what? Everybody knows you're a free man."

"Don't matter to them. They give folks trouble just for meanness."

Jack dismounted and extended his good hand to Isaac. "I'm glad to see you, too. I was wondering if we had squatters."

Isaac shook his hand. "I been taking care of the place for Mr. Leon." He nodded toward Jack's lame arm. "Yankees shoot you, Mr. Jack?"

"Sort of. Then the army let me go." Jack knelt to greet the panting, wagging hound and grabbed the scruff of Nip's neck to prevent being bowled over. At least his dog was honestly glad to see him. He glanced up at Isaac. "Where are my folks?"

"Secesh boys troubling some of the Union folks. They came around after Mr. Leon. He fought 'em off but was afraid for the missus. He thought she'd be safer in town. She wanted him to come, too. After a while he did."

"Ah. They're all right, then?"

"They all right."

Isaac's reassuring words relieved the worst of his fears. "My brother? Do you know anything about him?"

"They say he got a promotion. He a lieutenant now."

"I'll be damned. A lieutenant." *Dan, the good son, the one who was going to amount to something. Dan, the damned Yankee officer, who always did outrank me.* "They never answered my letters, so I wondered."

"I been seeing Mr. Leon now that the Yankees let people in and out across the bridge. He takes what he and Miss Margaret wants. I sell the rest and settle up with him. The Yanks open the bridge twice a week, but I only goes once on account of it takes so long to get there and back."

"How are things in town since the Yanks took over?"

"Tolerable, I hear. Some of the Secesh folks get in trouble with the Yanks now and then. Sometimes they get run out of town. Since they took over St. Augustine I keeps to this side of the bridge."

"Aren't the Yankees friends of yours?"

"The Yanks been tryin' to recruit me. I don't want to be in no war. Besides, if I stay in town, I won't see Lacey and the babies."

Jack nodded, understanding. Isaac's wife and two little boys lived at the nearby Miller plantation. As a free man, he couldn't stay there, and Leon Farrell's efforts to buy Isaac's family had failed. It was an ongoing feud, tangled up with disputes over boundaries and who owned which scrub cattle. Miller was an irascible fellow, and Jack's father wasn't the most affable man in the county, either.

Isaac shifted, standing straighter. A stocky man, he'd been made strong by a life of hard work. "Mr. Leon lets me keep half the money from whatever I sell. I been saving up, and I almost have enough money so maybe Mr. Miller will let me buy them."

"I hope so."

"It's been lonesome around here. I don't get to see Lacey and the babies except on Sundays. I'm right glad to see you, Mr. Jack."

Jack looked off toward the river, blinking, so Isaac wouldn't see his emotion.

*

Revived by a lunch of watermelon, tomatoes, and pecans, Jack unsaddled and hobbled Ladybug, leaving her to graze the overgrown yard. Then with Isaac's help, he pried the boards free, opening the windows to air out the stagnant space.

Jack fingered a bullet hole in the doorframe. "Remember how we fought off that Seminole raiding party? Just you and me?"

"Hard to forget," Isaac said. "They left us our scalps but took the cows."

It was the first time Jack had fought for his life, at fifteen years of age. During the winter of '55, when the third round of war with the Seminoles broke out, Pop and Dan had gone off to south Florida hunting Indians with the army. Pop had taken Jack's stepmother to town for her safety and left him and Isaac in charge of the homestead.

Nobody had expected the Indians to strike this far north, but attack they did. Warded away from the house by shotgun and rifle fire, the raiders had abandoned their murderous intent and contented themselves with stealing the cows and chickens.

Those damned cows. Jack shook his head, remembering his father's displeasure.

Nip trotted alongside him. His stepmother had a strict rule against dogs in the house, but she wasn't there to enforce it. He let his hand drop onto the dog's silken head and stroked the long, soft ears.

When Jack explored the other side of the house he found the trunk where he had left his old clothes. Now he had something besides somebody else's uniform to wear.

He considered the problem of communicating with his family. He figured showing his face in the Federally occupied town would only get him arrested by the soldiers. Unless he turned his back on his loyalties and swore Federal allegiance, he would be considered an enemy of the United States. On the other hand, his father, a pledged citizen, too old for conscription, his elder son a Union officer, was safe with his Yankee friends behind the city walls.

For all practical purposes, Jack and his father were avowed enemies.

He ought to be used to it. They'd always been at odds over one thing or another. Still, he wanted to make sure his family was all right and let them know he had come home. He did crave news about them and his brother, the Yankee lieutenant.

Isaac's weekly excursions into town offered Jack a solution. He could maintain a correspondence through the hired man. Isaac could also smuggle Francisco's personal items to Martina through Jack's father. Still, he would rather deliver it personally, if that were possible.

"Let's store the lumber and nails inside, in case I have to board up the house again." He walked back onto the porch to help Isaac carry the wood to the shed. Mostly he used one arm to stack the boards on Isaac's outstretched arms. He hated being semi-useless but held hope someday the pain would go away, his strength would return, and he would regain the use of his bad arm.

"How tight do the Yankees have St. Augustine sewn up? Do you think I could slip in and see my folks?"

"They's that picket post up on the San Sebastian Bridge. The days they open it up to let folks trade the soldiers are watching everything. They threw up a big old wall across the north end of town. They's only one gate on it and they got guards."

"How about the San Sebastian marsh north of the bridge. Could somebody wade across it at low tide, maybe at night, and avoid the picket posts?"

"Maybe somebody get shot."

"When are you taking another load to town?"

"Day after tomorrow."

"That's about right. I'll come with you." His aching body demanded rest after his two-week journey. In a couple of days he ought to be ready to scout out the situation.

*

Isaac took the next day off to visit his wife and children. His mule knew the way to the Miller place, a couple of miles south. Sunday the Miller people had the day off. Isaac always took a path that avoided Mr. Miller's house. Lacey's owner only tolerated him because the fine strong children added to his wealth.

Jack's return had caught Isaac by surprise. He had been doing fine running the farm by himself, maintaining a smaller area than he and Mr. Leon had cultivated together. His side business making corn whiskey created more profit than vegetables ever could.

What it meant to have his employer's son on the place was yet to be seen. He was not used to taking orders from white men any more, though he had to keep his head down and stay in his place whenever in their presence. Jack had never been inclined to bully him, yet he used to be one of those Confederate soldiers. Isaac went out of his way to avoid soldiers from either side because every last one seemed to want something from him. Only their long association reassured him Jack wouldn't cause him more problems.

With the Confederates it was always up to him to prove he was a free Negro abiding the restrictions a freedman had to obey. Weary of having to produce his papers and prove he was on the right side of the law, he had taken to hiding whenever they came around. The regulators were the worst, so suspicious they didn't much care what papers he could show.

The Yanks wanted him to join up so he could help them kill the former masters. But he was not in a mood to kill anybody, and he did not have a master. If he went off with the Yanks, he would give up his limited freedom to come and go as he pleased.

Lacey had her own cabin she shared with the boys. Simon ran out to greet him and Isaac swung the boy up into his arms. Little Micah wasn't grown up enough to do any running, but from his perch on his mother's hip, he held out his arms to his father. Grinning, Isaac shifted Simon to one side and gathered the younger boy with his free arm. He had no arms left with which to hug his wife, so they settled for a kiss. He followed Lacey into her cabin for their precious private time together.

Lacey kept a neat, sparsely furnished one-room cabin, built from pine and palmetto logs felled to create fields and pastures. Her cabin shared walls with adjoining slave quarters. Isaac had laid down boards to create a wood floor. The boys had their own cots and in a trunk Lacey kept their clothing and treasures such as her sewing kit.

They sat on her cot and he reacquainted himself with his family, as was his custom every week. After a while they sent the boys outside to play while he and Lacey enjoyed their private reunion.

Lying together on the cot, Isaac told her about Jack's homecoming and his own progress in saving money. "I'm almost there, Lacey," he whispered into her ear. "I been selling all kinds of truck to the folks in town, and it'll only be a few more trips before I can go to Mr. Miller and make him an offer."

Lacey gave him a sad smile that shadowed her fine sepia features. "I sure hope he'll let you buy us, Isaac." She shook her head and buried her face in his shoulder, like she didn't really have much hope.

"What else we gonna do? You won't run away."

"You know I can't do that. I got the boys to worry about. Where would we go? Your house is the first place they'd look for us."

He patted her back. "If Mr. Miller wasn't such a hard case, he'd a sold a long time ago. Maybe he done changed his mind. Things is different now. With the Yankee boats steaming up and down the river, and the Yank patrols riding around, maybe he'd sooner sell you to me than wait for the Yanks to carry you off."

"I wants you to carry me off." Lacey gave him a wide smile. "Not some Yankee soldiers."

"Won't be long, sweetie. Won't be long now."

CHAPTER SEVEN

Jack watched Carlo fishing in the San Sebastian River from the cover of a huge palmetto bush, as close as he dared approach the Yankee picket post. He was amazed at his luck at finding the boy alone and out of sight of the Yankees.

Carlo had located a school of mullet in a channel between the muddy islands of marsh. Jack caught the strong scent of saltwater fish from where he watched. Each good cast Carlo made brought in at least one.

He wore a black band on his arm. If the mourning emblem honored Francisco, Carlo had already gotten the news.

Jack took another look around for unwanted company then slung Francisco's haversack over his good shoulder and slipped away from his hiding place. He had decided to scout around hoping to find a way to deliver his messages personally if possible, rather than entrust them to Isaac except as a last resort. It didn't seem right to put that job off on the hired man.

Carlo spread the net on the marsh grass. It jerked and throbbed with struggling fish, and the boy turned his full attention to extracting them from the net.

"I see the mullet are running."

Carlo jumped to his feet at the sound of Jack's voice and stared at him, dark eyes wide with alarm under his straw hat.

"I didn't mean to startle you." Jack gave him a disarming smile.

"Mr. Farrell." Carlo broke into a wide grin. "Isaac didn't say you were back."

"I asked him not to noise it around. Don't tell anybody, especially the Yankees, hear?"

Carlo shook his head. "I don't tell the Yankees nothing. I don't talk to them if I can help it. What's the matter with your arm, sir?"

Jack looked down at the loose shirt that overhung his imprisoned arm. "Fell out of a tree."

Carlo furrowed his brow. "You were climbing trees?"

"Shooting at Yankees." Jack cracked a rueful smile. "Unfortunately, they shot back, and their gun was bigger than mine. Speaking of bigger, you've grown some. You handle that net pretty well."

"Francisco taught me how. He and I made the net together." The boy sobered and looked away.

Jack pointed toward the black band on Carlo's arm. "That is to honor him?"

Carlo's face contracted, and he made a fist. "His captain sent a letter. The Yankees killed him."

"Captain Fleming asked me to deliver his personal effects." Jack drummed his fingers on the haversack. "You'll give them to Martina?"

Carlo stared at the haversack. "Yes, sir. Captain Fleming wrote that he was brave. Said he was a hero."

Jack nodded. "That's right. You're right to be proud of him." He handed Carlo the haversack.

Carlo took it but didn't look inside. He hefted it onto his own shoulder and looked at the ground, his lips a tight line, apparently struggling to hold back tears.

Jack gave him time to regain control then said, "Where's Martina?"

"King Street bridge." Carlo nodded in that general direction. "Today the Yankees let us out to trade. St. Augustine is like a prison ever since they came. Our jailers loosen our chains from time to time." The boy set his jaw, then continued. "She is buying whatever she can so she can cook it up."

"She's doing all right?"

The boy shrugged. "She's sad and scared." He pointed to the bucket of fish. "We smoke the mullet and she sells those, too. I catch as many as I can for her. The Yankees like her cooking, and they pay her for it."

"Best to stay on their good side, I suppose."

"I don't like what she does." Carlo gave him a bitter smile. "I pray they'll choke on a bone and die."

Jack rubbed his chin. "I hadn't thought of that strategy before. We'll have to suggest it to our generals."

Carlo stood straighter. "I want to join the army and kill Yankees. I can take Francisco's place."

"Nothing wrong with your spirit, but you're a minnow. They'd throw you back to let you grow bigger."

"I can shoot a gun. Francisco taught me how. I can ride a horse, too. You showed me how to drive a team, too."

"Do you have a horse?"

"I could steal one from the Yankees."

"Good luck with that," Jack snorted. Was the kid determined to get himself shot?

"Aren't you afraid the Yankees will see you and catch you? You aren't going to take their stinking oath, are you?"

Jack shook his head.

"They tried to make Martina do it, but she wouldn't. They put us on a boat and sent us off. Then they changed their minds and brought us back. She's afraid they'll send us away for good."

"Then you'd better not provoke them. Act like you respect them no matter how you feel."

"That's what Martina said. It's not easy. Mostly I stay away from them."

"Yeah, I'd rather stay away from them, too." Jack took a long breath. As a sworn Unionist, his father was safe from the Yankees. On the other hand, he felt unsafe. "Tell me about the Yankees. How many are garrisoned in town? Do they send out patrols?"

*

Carlo had been watching the Yankee comings and goings ever since they marched off their boats into St. Augustine. He told Jack Farrell what he knew about them, naming units and officers. He recounted what he had overheard the Yankees say about the skirmishing outside town.

"You've been paying attention, Carlo." Mr. Jack looked thoughtful. "I suppose some of the boys on our side would be interested."

"Do you really think it would help?" Carlo was thrilled to renew his friendship with a man he had always admired. He had never understood what Francisco had against Mr. Jack besides his killing somebody in self-defense. Since the war had started, that was what men had to do.

"I'm sure they'll want to know what the Yanks are doing. Somebody in town would be able to find out things they can't from this side of the picket line. I've only been back a few days and I haven't seen any of our soldiers yet. It's only a matter of time."

Carlo felt proud that a soldier who had seen action, and had wounds to prove it, said he had something important to offer.

"Instead of thinking about stealing Yankee horses or shooting at them, you can do something really useful. Help me keep an eye on them," Mr. Jack said.

"I come here to fish and gather oysters Mondays and Thursdays, when the Yankees let me out of town."

"I'd like to meet you here again, but not until next week. It's a long haul." Mr. Jack looked toward the bridge, then back at Carlo. "Think Martina would be willing to come? I'd like to talk to her, too."

"You said not to tell anybody about you."

"Don't you think I can trust her?"

"I'll bring her now." Carlo picked up his bucket and net. Balancing the heavy load, he trotted back to the bridge.

*

"Jack Farrell is here?" Carlo's excitement almost brought a smile from Martina. It was good to see something shake him out of his gloom. "Why should I want to speak to him, of all people?"

When Carlo handed her Francisco's haversack, her smile died and her eyes filled. She hugged it to her chest. She had no remains to view or bury, only this last keepsake from her lost brother. Later, after she gathered the strength, she would open the haversack and cherish its contents.

Carlo set down the bucket. "He saw me fishing and came over to talk. He's waiting for you. He can't come here because of the Yankees."

"Why is he back from Virginia?"

"He was wounded."

"Jack Farrell wounded?" Although she shared Francisco's bad opinion of him, she felt a tug of compassion. "Does he need help?"

"He didn't ask for any. He got hurt at Sharpsburg. The same battle where the Yankees killed Francisco."

She looked around at the soldiers and the few remaining traders. She had finished her marketing and was ready to start home with a laden handcart. "How far away is he? What shall we do with everything?"

"I'll ask Isaac to give us a ride," Carlo said. "We can put our things in his wagon. They'll be safe." Before she could answer the boy ran over to the Negro. After a quick exchange, Carlo waved her over. "He'll take us. He'll even bring us back as far as the bridge."

Leaving with the free Negro without an explanation would certainly arouse curiosity, but what did that matter? She was already a topic with such as Miss Swingle.

*

Jack returned to where he had concealed his horse. He had planned to wait for Isaac anyway, so he might as well give Carlo a chance to fetch Martina if she could bring herself to speak to him.

As far as Jack knew Carlo had no reason to betray him to the Yankees, but they might still follow the boy. Jack used a log for a block and mounted Ladybug in case he had to make a hasty retreat. Strain from his long ride and the use of one arm made everything difficult. He didn't want to have to mount the horse in a hurry.

He used to climb and run with little thought or effort. Truly he missed the agility and strength he had taken for granted until that exploding shell laid him low. He also missed the pain-deadening effect a dose of laudanum would have provided.

Jack settled into the saddle. He kept a wary eye out for blue uniforms and listened for boot or hoof tread.

He didn't have long to wait before hearing the creak of wagon wheels and the soft thud of hooves on sand. "Mr. Jack," Carlo called out in a stage whisper. Jack nudged his pony forward and satisfied himself that no enemies accompanied Isaac's wagon.

Isaac halted the wagon and Carlo jumped off. Martina, slimness hidden by her mourning clothes, sat in the back of the wagon. Even the dowdy black dress, faded brown in places, and the dreary hood could not hide her finely chiseled beauty. Her long, dark eyelashes framed large, expressive eyes. The sight of her made his throat catch. Shyly she rested her gaze on Jack, then looked down as though unsure how to greet him.

Jack removed his hat and bowed his head. "Thank you for coming."

"Isaac was good enough to give us a ride." She lifted her gaze to his face. "Carlo said you wished to talk to me."

Jack kneed Ladybug closer, alongside the wagon. "I am deeply sorry about Francisco."

"Thank you. I know you had your differences."

"He wanted to protect you. I can understand that."

Her dark eyes shined luminous with unshed tears. "Carlo said you're home because you were badly wounded. I'm glad to see you are up and about. I hope you're recovering well."

"Better than some." He smiled. "Docs didn't saw anything off, at least."

"You aren't going back to the war?"

"I'm out of the army now. They said I'm disabled."

"Disabled?" Her troubled gaze searched his face.

"I'm betting they are wrong."

"I'm glad the Yankees didn't kill you." She said it as though she meant it.

"That makes two of us."

She clutched the haversack. "Thank you for going to the effort—"

"I believe Francisco would have done the same for me. How are you faring?"

"Carlo and I have each other, our home, and enough to eat." She gave him the merest of smiles. "We're grateful for that."

"Do the Yankees give you much trouble?"

She shook her head and the smile went into hiding. "Please. Tell me about Francisco."

He summarized what he had told Carlo.

"In his letter Captain Fleming said they buried him in Maryland."

"Near the fighting. We had to retreat. I'm sure it wasn't possible to bring him home."

"Of course not." She bit her lip. "What you brought me is all I have."

"I have a favor to ask of you and Carlo," he said. "I gave him a letter for my father. If he should care to answer it." He nodded toward the boy. "Can you meet me here next week?"

Carlo spoke up. "I'll be here. The Yankees gave me a pass to fish and gather oysters this side of the creek whenever the bridge is open."

Martina said, "I have no such pass, and I'd better go back now." To his surprise she held out her warm hand. He held on a moment longer than he had any right, but she didn't object. Most likely she felt sorry for him.

Isaac turned the wagon on the path with some difficulty, and Jack watched Martina until he lost sight of her in the scrub.

*

Martina thanked Isaac for taking her to meet Jack, gathered her purchases and set them back onto her handcart along with Carlo's catch. He wasn't through fishing and would no doubt bring more home. She set the strap of Francisco's haversack across her shoulder and carried it over her heart.

During the walk home she recalled the short exchange with Jack. She gave him credit for bringing her Francisco's earthly possessions all the way from Virginia. Jack's appearance had shocked her. He looked gaunt, his features sharp, pain etched around his eyes. Ruddy lines marked recently healed cuts on his face and hinted at deeper wounds hidden by his clothing.

His diffident manner bore no resemblance to the cocksure swagger she remembered from the year before, when he had confirmed Francisco's opinion of his sorry character.

Could this be the same man who had called her a snob and told Francisco to go to hell, right before he left the dance arm in arm with a snuff-dipping country girl as drunk as he was? It was a blessing she had seen that side of him and taken it as a warning. Otherwise he might have fooled her with his show of respect and consideration.

Once inside her house she set Francisco's haversack on the pine table and reverently inspected the contents. An unfinished letter to her, a little Confederate money, his watch that had stopped at 5:35. Whatever she thought of Jack, he was not a thief.

She touched her finger to a bloodstain on the back of the haversack, Francisco's only earthly remains within reach. She stacked the papers so she could reread every word at her leisure and went outside.

Martina went to work cleaning the fish she had brought home.

Neighborhood cats came yowling to her courtyard drawn by the powerful scent. A big yellow tom jumped down from the wall and strolled toward her meowing, his tail an upright banner. She tossed him a fish head and he pounced on it as though starved. A gray tiger kitten approached as he crunched his prize, but when the tom growled, the younger cat backed off. Martina threw him a second fish head, and peace prevailed.

She started a fire on the *orno*, an outdoor charcoal grill protected from rain by a thatched roof. Mullet, along with potatoes, carrots and green beans would make a good supper with enough left over for breakfast. The opening of trade had provided her new prosperity and more variety for herself, Carlo and her blue-coated customers. Perhaps she would soon be able to save money in case her fortunes worsened.

Carlo brought home three more good-sized mullet and set to work cleaning them while she prepared the vegetables. Scales flew as he skillfully scraped his knife backwards over the freshly killed fish.

He seemed quieter than usual. Carlo had always idolized Jack. Perhaps the same vices that repelled her fascinated the boy, and she saw danger in Jack's influence.

She told Carlo what was in the haversack. "I left the letters on the table so you can see them yourself. He would have wanted you to keep his watch. I'm going to bury his haversack beneath the shrine we made for him."

"Don't do that," Carlo said. "I want to use it."

"If you wish." She couldn't begrudge him the memento. "Did you deliver the letter to Mr. Farrell?"

"He gave me a nickel." Carlo wiped a scale off his cheek with his sleeve.

"You have a business delivering mail now?" Martina poured water into the pot and set it on the *orno* to heat. "Was Mr. Farrell glad to hear from his son?"

"He didn't say much."

Martina had heard much said about Mr. Farrell's disgust with his younger son, and she could hardly blame the man, though she wondered how the feud could progress now. She picked up a potato and started to peel it.

"That isn't all. Mr. Jack and I are going to fight the Yankees without firing a shot."

She looked up, alarmed. "How is that, Chico? Should I be worried?"

"Mr. Jack says I can find out what the Yanks are up to and let him know. He wants to pass it on to the Confederates. He says it's the most valuable thing I can do for the cause."

"He's asking you to spy for him?" A loose strand of hair tangled with her eyelashes, and she swept it aside.

"It'll be easy." Carlo threw a fish head to the cats, which had increased in number.

"And if you get caught? What will he do for you then?"

"I won't get caught." Carlo gutted the fish and tossed the insides to the waiting felines. "Mr. Jack told me not to provoke the Yankees so they won't suspect me of anything."

"Chico, the Yankees aren't stupid."

"I wish they hadn't brought us back home. Even if we didn't have anywhere to live, at least we wouldn't be living in fear."

"We'd be free to starve. Would that suit you better?"

"You can help. The Yankee officers talk to you. Captain Prescott likes to brag. You can find out a lot from him. All you have to do is listen to what the Yankees say and I'll tell Mr. Jack."

"All I have to do?" She stabbed the next potato. "Why should I?"

"Don't you like Mr. Jack?"

"He thinks I'm a snob, and I know he's a scoundrel. I really will despise him if he gets us in trouble with the Yankees."

"He likes you."

She glared at Carlo. "Jack Farrell told you this?"

Carlo looked up from his work, his eyes bright. "Just the way he looked at you."

"Ha. From what I've seen of him, he likes every young woman he sees, and liquor best of all." She picked up a carrot and hacked it into small pieces. "Carlo, it's dangerous for him to come this close to town, and you must not be caught with him. That man is trouble."

CHAPTER EIGHT

Jack lifted the jar of clear liquid up to the light and tasted it. He savored the burning sensation and licked his lips. "Why didn't you tell me you've been making this painkiller?"

Isaac's closed expression relaxed. "I been sellin' it to the Yankee soldiers. I got cane juice to sweeten it with."

"Quite a setup. I congratulate you on your enterprise." Jack looked over the still, ingeniously rigged from barrels, washtubs and pipes, hidden deep in the woods. A fire pit heated the closed kettle, boiling off the spirits. A tube ran through a barrel filled with cool water tapped from the spring run. The finished product dripped through a funnel into a jug. "You're doing the Lord's work here, Isaac. Drunken Yankees can't shoot straight. Does Pop know about it?"

Isaac shook his head. "I figure what he don't know don't hurt nothin'. I sell it kind of quiet-like."

Jack recalled yesterday's trip to town, when burlap sacks hid some of Isaac's produce from view. "At a good price, I'll bet. Explains how you've been able to set a little something aside."

"Yes, sir, Mr. Jack. I grows the sugar cane and corn. The mill over to the trading post at Tocoi is still running, so I get the corn ground there. I can sell everything I make."

Jack savored another sip. It clawed down his throat and warmed him all over. Maybe a good dose at night would relieve his aches and coughing fits, allowing him to sleep. "Keep it up, then. I'm not my father, and I won't interfere with your business. In fact, I'd like for you to show me how you do it." Continuing their tour of the homestead, they made their way to the orange grove. He kept the jar of popskull to enjoy later.

A brief rainsquall last night had given way to a stiff northern breeze that swept away mosquitoes and freshened the air. To Isaac he said, "This cool snap will help sweeten the oranges."

Isaac nodded agreement. He lovingly examined a hard green orange where it dangled from a branch. "It'll be a fine crop for sure, Mr. Jack."

"I ought to have my arm back in action by then." Jack reached down, uprooted a clump of milkweed and tossed it aside. "I'd like to hold up my share of the work around here." He looked forward to the day his broken bones mended and his cough went away.

A warning bark caught his attention. Nip ran toward the road, continuing his intruder alarm. Jack set his hand on the grip of his revolver and watched two cavalrymen approach, their horses' hooves quiet on the sandy soil. They wore the right uniforms so he relaxed but kept his hand close to the holster.

"It's all right, Isaac. They're Confed." But when he turned to the black man, he was not there. Jack caught a glimpse of Isaac's back as he beat a hasty retreat between the orange trees toward the dense woods. It struck him that his view on who constituted the enemy differed from Isaac's.

"Come on in, Nip," he called.

The dog ran alongside the horses, escorting them down the path. Jack recognized one of the men, a St. Augustine Minorcan, and walked over to meet the pair. The shadows from Ramon Andreu's hat-brim deepened his well-tanned features. On his jacket were corporal's stripes. Jack did not recall knowing the other soldier, a lanky young private with a short, sandy beard.

Nip trotted over to Jack, and he gave the dog a rough pat on the head. "Good boy. You did good."

Ramon nodded a greeting. "Jack Farrell. Didn't know anybody was home. You in a scrap? Appears you got the worst of it."

"I was at Sharpsburg with General Lee."

Ramon's companion smirked. "We're in Florida with Captain Dickison."

"Jack, this here's Russell Cates," Ramon said. "From over Moultrie Creek way. We were in the neighborhood, just left George Colee's place."

Jack had not yet gone to visit any neighbors, and it would be good to catch up on their doings. He held up the jar. "Y'all come on inside and let's share a smile."

"Now you're talking." Ramon dismounted, and Cates did the same. They tied their horses to trees in the front yard. Jack led them inside and set out cups for the liquor. He diluted the popskull with water and cane juice so it would taste better and go farther.

The newcomers sat at the table. Ramon took a sip and said,

"We're scouting this side of the river, seeing what the Yanks are up to."

"Just got back a few days ago." Jack uncovered a plate of cornbread left over from breakfast. From his experience, soldiers were always hungry. Then he sat down with his visitors and told them what he knew of the Sharpsburg battle, how he ended up in this condition, and about the long retreat back to Virginia. He also mentioned what he knew of other Florida men. "Wasn't Francisco Sanchez your cousin?" he asked Ramon.

"First cousins. Our mothers were sisters. I heard he got killed."

"The other day I delivered his belongings to his brother and sister."

Ramon sipped his popskull.

"My sister's husband was killed at Perryville. They keep sending our Florida boys up north to meet their maker." Cates picked up a chunk of pone, wiped up syrup with it and wolfed it. "After you heal up I guess you'll go back north with the 2nd Florida to meet yours."

"I've been discharged on account of disability."

"You stove up that bad?"

"Doctor said so."

"You figure on staying here?" Cates raised an eyebrow.

"I don't have any other plans, not for the time being."

Cates shook his head. "Yanks won't leave you be. Not on this side of the river."

"Haven't seen any so far."

"You will. They've been sending out raiding parties from St. Augustine. Besides that, their boats have brought troops in through the Picolata landing, just around the point."

Jack knew in his soul Cates was right. He lifted his cup in a toast. "'Til then." He tossed back a mouthful and felt the pleasant burn work all the way down.

Cates swirled the liquor in his cup before taking another sip. "Where did you get this stuff?"

"Know who made it."

"Pretty raw."

Jack nodded. "You boys are lucky they haven't transferred you out of the state. Better to be close to home."

"Somebody has to stay here and fight," Cates said. "President

Davis doesn't seem to think Florida's worth defending."

Ramon rejoined the conversation, his voice glum. "When the Yanks took St. Augustine, I had to send my wife and little girl away. They're in Lake City."

Jack recalled the Ramon holdings were just north of St. Augustine. Ramon's house probably sheltered a Yankee picket post by now, if it still stood intact.

"Kind of glad I don't have a wife to worry about," Cates said. "The Yanks want to clear our people out. You're lucky a gunboat hasn't blown up your house. They only want to let Unionists stay this side of the St. Johns. It's easier to protect our people on the west side."

"I'll look to myself for protection." Jack guessed he sounded tougher than he felt, and he especially did not like the part about getting blown up. "I did some scouting over toward St. Augustine a couple of days ago. Got an idea what the Yanks have going on there." He told them what he had learned through his own observation and the inside information gleaned from Carlo.

"You heard that from somebody in town?" Cates asked.

"Who is it?" Ramon finally rejoined the conversation.

"Cousin of yours," Jack said.

"Then it could be anybody," Ramon said.

Jack grinned. "Yeah, all you Minorcans are kin one way or another. I don't guess there's any harm in telling you it's Francisco's brother Carlo."

Ramon cracked a smile. "Carlo's a pistol."

"Yeah, he's busting to join the army" Jack said. "I hope this will keep him from slipping off when Martina isn't looking."

"Yanks might catch him talking to you," Ramon pointed out.

"Even the Yanks won't hang a fourteen year old," Jack said. "I'll be seeing him again soon, find out what else he's learned now that we know y'all are interested."

"Our company could use another scout," Cates said. "You said you were a sharpshooter?"

Ramon joined in. "You ought to know the country pretty well. After you heal up, why don't you join the cavalry?"

Jack looked away, letting the idea gel in his mind. He didn't want to admit to these troopers he'd had enough fighting to last the rest of his life. But it seemed the war was impossible to ignore. "It's something to consider."

"You always were a scrapper," Ramon said. "Even at the academy, when Pons tried to push you around, you whipped him so bad he never bothered you again. He was bigger, but you were quicker."

"I got myself expelled. Best thing ever happened." Jack smiled wryly. "Pop gave me the licking Pons couldn't. It was worth it. Mr. Colee took over my education after that. Saved me from being a complete ignoramus, I guess."

"Three of his boys are in the army, and Charlie is going to join up with us." Ramon said. "His mama wants to nail his feet to the floor, but he's almost eighteen."

Ramon looked thoughtful. "Didn't I hear out you killed somebody in a fight over Lake City way?"

Jack poured the last of the corn liquor into their cups, not liking the reminder of his jail time and of the shadow of disgrace that still followed him. Or did it? Killing had increased in respectability of late, if these affable fellows were any measure.

"I heard he beat up a woman then came after you," Ramon said.

The jury had ruled in his favor. Afterward some people still blamed him and called it murder. Even the woman he saved from Sloan hated him for killing her boyfriend. "Until I can use my arm again, all I can handle is this navy Colt. Left handed."

"After the Yankees run you out, you'll want to join up." Cates snorted. "Unless they drag you off to prison."

"I'm keeping my head down." Jack drained his portion and turned the empty cup longingly. *Better not raid Isaac's still for more. Not yet.* "Tell me more about your Captain Dickison."

Cates said, "We're Company H, 2nd Florida Cav. As for Dickison, he's a real gamecock." Cates told of how the agile cavalry troop had been operating between Palatka and Jacksonville, rounding up deserters, catching runaway Negroes and snatching any Yankees who dared venture from their fortifications.

Jack gathered the style of fighting in sparsely populated Florida differed from the murderous slugging between huge armies he had experienced in Virginia. Without a large force, Dickison specialized in lightning hit-and-run raids. "Just last week we got into a sharp little fight south of town," Cates said. "Picked up some prisoners and ran off the rest."

Jack tapped his fingers on the cup, recalling what Carlo had told him. "The Yanks claim they ran you off."

"You know them Yanks are all brag," Cates huffed. "They didn't hurt us a bit."

Jack figured Cates was all brag, too. He didn't doubt the truth lay somewhere between the two versions. Nor did he bother to point out their little skirmish sounded like a holiday dance compared with the bloodbaths he had seen. He would rather keep his jaded opinions to himself.

"Tell you what, boys. I'll help as much as I can, try to keep you informed. We can set up a system if Captain Dickison wants to send a courier by every now and then."

*

"What did they want, boss?" Isaac had waited until the cavalrymen were well gone before he came out of hiding. He had no use for the Confederates, and it worried him that Jack Farrell was on their side. He wasn't ready to fight alongside the Yankees, but he didn't mind giving them a word up when he heard something they needed to hear.

Jack gave him a searching look. "I told them to leave you alone."

"That's good, Mr. Jack." Isaac didn't put much stock in such promises.

"I told them to get the word out to the rest of the soldiers not to bother you. I told them you're a free man working for me."

"I reckon you doin' what you can."

"I reckon no matter what you'll still go to ground the second you hear anybody coming." Jack let out a harsh laugh. "Can't say I blame you." He looked out toward the road. "Whenever anybody comes around, I kind of get the urge to do the same thing."

"Yessir," Isaac agreed. "These is sure enough uneasy times."

CHAPTER NINE

Jack met Carlo at the riverbank a week after their first meeting. The boy eagerly handed him a sealed envelope. "I gave your letter to Mr. Farrell, and he answered you."

"Did you tell him where I'd be meeting you?"

"He wanted to know, but you said I shouldn't tell anybody but Martina."

Jack touched his hand to his hat in a salute. "You're a good soldier."

Carlo grinned. "You think so?"

"It's an important service you're doing right here, better than fighting somewhere else."

The boy glowed at the praise.

"Some of Captain Dickison's men were interested in what you had to say about the Yanks."

"Really?"

"Your cousin, Ramon Andreu, is a scout. He and a fellow named Cates came by, and we talked. They can use any information you have."

Carlo said in a confidential tone, "A Yankee officer, a Captain Prescott, likes to brag to Martina. I've been listening."

"Your sister sees this Yankee officer?"

Carlo grimaced. "She doesn't like him back but won't tell him so. I think she's afraid of him."

Jack rubbed his chin, wishing he could do something about the Yankee officer. But the last time he had come to a woman's rescue, it had ended in a disaster. "What has he been saying?"

Carlo repeated the brags Prescott had made and mentioned the Yanks had set up a picket post at the Fairbanks place. Apparently Fairbanks, who lived near Ramon Andreu, had also abandoned his holdings north of the town's fortifications.

"I'll take a scout up the river," Jack said. "Low tide. Now is a good time to find a place to cross in case anybody on our side is interested."

"I'll go with you." Carlo glanced toward where Jack had hidden Ladybug. "Can't we ride double?"

Jack considered the possibility of running into Yankee pickets. He would rather not endanger the boy more than he was already doing. "Nope. You'd better stay here and tend your net."

He started for the ford at the headwaters, a couple of miles north. The opposite shore was not far away and clearly visible. He kept to the woods to avoid being spotted from the embankment the Yankee had built on the other side. When he cleared the north end of town, he cut back along the riverbank seeking an easier path. Fiddler crabs scuttled along the wet mud, popping into tiny holes. Wading birds ran from the horse's approach and took flight.

The river widened into a sea of marsh grass veined by a network of shallow channels. He studied the opposite bank but did not see any signs of a Yankee outpost. Probably they expected attack more likely from the Jacksonville road than from the swampy creek.

At the ford, the riverbed appeared clear of oyster shells that could injure a horse's legs. Jack urged Ladybug through the stream, the water never higher than the bottom of the stirrup. The sure-footed marsh pony crossed the first island without sliding or bogging down, though the mud was deep and slippery. Ladybug snatched mouthfuls of the salty, musty smelling marsh grass and munched as they crossed to the other side of the stream.

"Nobody shot at us," he told Ladybug. "If we could cross here, so could a cavalry troop."

Jack turned around and backtracked to where Carlo continued to fish. There he dismounted, tied the horse, and unfolded the letter from his father.

Leon Farrell assured Jack he and his stepmother were well and his brother was so far unharmed in the Union service. The rest of his message consisted of the usual lecture, dripping with criticism. Jack could not recall a time when his father showed pride in him or simply acceptance. Pop expressed hope Jack had learned from his mistakes and repented the error of his ways. He wanted his errant son to come in through the picket post, surrender and take the loyalty oath.

Jack wadded the letter in his fist and threw it on the ground.

Why had he been so trusting as to let Leon Farrell know he had returned? Now his own father was in a position to get him killed.

Although Carlo had not told him how and where they met, Jack's father could figure it out on his own or simply follow the boy. Jack glanced in the direction of the bridge, half expecting to see a blue-clad crowd running his way. Worse, his doting sire could tell the Yankees where he lived and send them after him.

He stared down at the crumpled paper at his feet. His temper had gotten the better of him before he read the rest of the letter.

Reluctantly, he picked it up and smoothed the paper flat across his thigh. His stepmother's part of the letter expressed dutiful concern over his injuries and about his welfare. She would come to the homestead and see him, but Leon had deemed it too dangerous because of the partisans ranging about. She was agreeable enough, but they had never been close.

He turned the letter over and penciled his brief reply. "Sir, I may be out of the service but I have not changed sides." He wrote a longer note to his stepmother, signed it and slipped it back into the envelope. He took a match out of his saddlebag, lit it and re-melted the wax seal.

*

Martina expected to make her purchases quickly and leave them with Isaac until she returned from meeting Jack. Isaac confirmed Jack had ridden toward town with him and intended to talk with Carlo. She planned to catch them together and make it clear she would not let Jack involve Carlo in his dangerous games.

The Yankee pickets, playing cards at their post, seemed unconcerned with the traders. She hoped to escape the notice of Prescott, who stood smoking a cigar and idly observing the market activities.

Jack's father had taken his share of the produce Isaac had brought. While she picked out what she wanted from the wagon bed, she overheard their conversation without intending to eavesdrop, something about Isaac having enough money. Mr. Farrell said, "Get Jack to go with you. He might have better luck with Miller than I did."

"Yessir. I'll ask him."

"The only way Jack could have given that letter to the

Sanchez boy was to come near town. Why didn't you tell me he was here?"

"He said he wanted to tell you hisself."

"Did he come with you today?"

Isaac didn't answer.

"If he wants to see me, he'll have to come into town and give himself up."

Despite her irritation with Jack, Martina felt a stab of pity for him. How must it feel to be alone, hurting, and cut off by one's own father? When Mr. Farrell turned and noticed her, he tipped his hat and gave her a searching look. He was a fine-looking man. Although graying and more severe of aspect, by his resemblance he could not have denied Jack was his son.

"Miss Sanchez, I regret your recent loss. Is there anything I can do for you?"

"Thank you, sir. I can't think of anything. We are managing."

"I presume you know Carlo has been delivering messages between Jack and me."

She chose her words carefully. "I did hear Jack had returned."

"Isaac tells me he was wounded more seriously than he let on in his letter. I suspect you overheard my harsh words, and I don't want you to get the wrong impression. Please understand despite our differences he is still my blood and I do care about him."

Martina had always been taught to keep her opinions to herself when addressing men or her elders. That lesson had lately outgrown its usefulness. "Mr. Farrell, if you truly care about your wounded son, perhaps you'd better go see him for yourself."

"Well now." He blinked as though she'd struck him, then scowled. "I don't see how it's any of your business, young lady."

She should have apologized, but she continued. "He may have angered you for whatever he did in the past, but he is not an outlaw for joining the Confederate army, any more than my brother Francisco." Surprised at her own vehemence, she lifted her hand to her mouth. Could she really be defending Jack Farrell to his own father?

"Miss Sanchez, Jack's joining an unworthy cause is only the latest of a score of disappointments. I want him safe. He would be better off in town if he would declare his loyalty, just as your situation would be more secure if you did the same thing."

Prescott sauntered over, bowed to her and greeted Mr. Farrell. Hiding her exasperation, she managed a tight and insincere smile.

Prescott said to Isaac, "How'd you like to join the army and fight the rebels? We sure could use a big strapping boy like you."

Isaac hunched his shoulders, his face blank. "Not today, boss."

"I've been promoted to a captaincy; in charge of raising a company of you Negroes. Join up now, or I'll be coming to get you by and by."

Mr. Farrell said, "Isaac has his own business to tend right now."

"Huh. Business?" Prescott snorted. "What more urgent business can a Negro have but fighting his oppressors? Where's your courage, boy?"

Turtle-like, Isaac drew further into his shoulders.

"Next time you come around, you'd better think about volunteering. It'll be easier on you than if I have to resort to conscription." Prescott took a dime out of his pocket. "In the meantime, I'll take that watermelon."

Hefting the melon under his arm, Prescott turned to Martina. "You look fetching as usual, Miss Sanchez. I hope you've found some tasty items." He smoothed his moustache and cast an up-and-down look over her. "I'm looking forward to sampling what you have to offer. After you finish shopping, I'll walk you home."

"No, Captain Prescott. I'd rather you didn't."

"I promise to be a gentleman this time. I'll wait right here until you're ready to go."

Trapped, she glared at him. Prescott would not let her out of his sight. The man was harder to get rid of than an infestation of chiggers. There went her plans to confront Jack. She moved to another wagon and angrily stuffed turnip greens into her croaker sack. She glanced to where Prescott leaned against Isaac's wagon chatting with Mr. Farrell.

If she must spend time with Prescott, she would do her best to make good use of it. Perhaps she would do a little information gathering of her own, sparing Carlo the risk. She paid for the greens and marched back to Prescott. "I'm ready to go home now."

Martina was not used to putting on an act, but now seemed

the right time to practice. She smiled at Prescott and pretended to be fascinated with his every word, not an easy thing to do.

So far he had lived up to his promise to behave, which certainly must have been an effort for him, as he pushed her cart down King Street.

He told her about his last foray outside the city toward Palatka. He bragged about his success at bringing in a half dozen stout Negro men. "For the time being we have them reinforcing our defenses. They are well-suited for that sort of work."

"Where do you plan to go next time?" Surely the Confederates would want to know whatever the Yankees planned. "Up toward Jacksonville, or back to Palatka?"

"We'll be patrolling along the St. Johns River, from Tocoi, around the swamp to Picolata, maybe as far north as New Switzerland. I'll take the troops out day after tomorrow."

He told her about Sergeant Owen, the regular army man she had met a few days before. "He's rough, but he knows his business. He spent part of his career out west fighting Indians. He'll be good at whipping the Negroes into soldiers if it's possible. He says those rebels better not come after us or they'll be sorry."

"Do you expect to run into more Confederates soon?"

"Oh, we can't predict when they'll turn up unless the country folk let us know like they did last time. Some partisan bands are operating around here, under a Captain Dickison and a Captain Hough. In any case, we're most likely to see their backs as they run away from us."

"Which country people are telling you about the Confederates? The Negroes?"

"Certainly. After all, they have the most to gain. Some of the whites are friendly to the Union, too. We'll be clearing the area of rebel sympathizers. We have to run them out, or they'll keep on giving us trouble."

She said in a teasing voice, "Rebel sympathizers like me?"

He laughed. "Not like you, my dear. I believe I can tame you. Be warned, I haven't given up on persuading you to change sides."

"What will you do to them? The people you want to clear out?"

"Burn them out, confiscate or slaughter their stock. Force them to get out or starve."

75

Her own problems hadn't left room for her to worry about others until now, but his words appalled her. *What sort of monster was Prescott?* She tried to hide the depth of her revulsion. "That's terrible. I know what it's like to be forced to leave my home."

"The expulsion wasn't my doing, and it turned out all right for you."

"Would you harm them? I mean, you are surely harming them if you destroy their homes. Would you shoot them?"

"Only if they resist."

"Even if they aren't soldiers?"

"Some of the worst ones aren't soldiers. They're crazy fools who shoot at us from the scrub. We'll hunt them down, and it'll be the last thing they ever do."

She knew her dismay showed on her face, but she couldn't help it. Francisco had said Jack's quick temper and readiness to fight had caused his trouble with the law. Was he hotheaded enough to invite his own destruction?

Why should she care if he did?

"Am I upsetting you, Miss Sanchez?" Prescott harrumphed. "If people behave themselves, they have nothing to fear. If they're Unionists and take the oath, we'll let them stay. Of course we do make exceptions, like yourself."

And never let me forget you can clear me out as well, whenever you want.

Prescott raised an eyebrow. "I saw you talking with Mr. Farrell. He told us about his son, Jack. He used to be in the rebel army, but they sent him home because of some disabling wounds or such. He's living on Farrell's land, and the old man asked us to go easy on him."

"I should hope so. How could one wounded man cause you any trouble?"

"Colonel Putnam is inclined to be lenient. Too lenient, in my opinion, but he's the colonel and I have to follow orders. We could arrest Farrell's son, but I will let him know he'll be all right as long as he behaves himself." He gave her a sharp look. "Don't you know him? I saw you talking with his father."

She answered with care. "I've lived here all my life, Captain Prescott. I know most of the people in the country around St. Augustine, at least by name."

"He's a friend of yours?"

She shrugged and gave him a beseeching look. "I simply know the family, and it would break Mrs. Farrell's heart if her stepson is harmed more than he has been already. Jack's brother is an officer in the Union army you know, and the family has had enough hardship...."

"Of course. Your concern is understandable."

She forced herself to show a bright smile and hoped he didn't see through her deceit and flattery. "Showing mercy to a poor, helpless wounded enemy is really noble of you, Captain, isn't it? I admire that in a man."

He preened like a rooster. "Rest assured, Miss Martina, if he's really a poor, helpless wounded ex-rebel and doesn't cause us any problems, we won't harm a hair on his head."

*

Prescott congratulated himself. His new strategy with Martina Sanchez was working admirably. Friendly and smiling, she hung on his every word, actually flirting with him. The girl presented a true challenge, and it would take longer this way, but perhaps offering her honey instead of vinegar would get him into her bed.

She stopped at her gate and paused. He took her hand, saying, "May I come in?"

"You promised to be a gentleman."

"I did ask your permission, didn't I?" He checked his annoyance. He'd resolved to proceed with patience though his needs demanded results.

"Please, Captain Prescott. You promised."

The outline of her knife showed in her apron pocket. He could confiscate it in an instant, but the rules of the game had changed. They were his rules, and he would abide by them. "As you wish, Miss Sanchez. I enjoyed our stroll and look forward to next time." He touched the brim of his cap and walked away frustrated.

*

Martina wrestled the handcart through the gate and shut it behind her. She listened to Prescott's footfalls as he moved away from her home.

Pretense had worked a terrible strain on her. Listening to his smug talk about how he planned to destroy people's lives had sickened her.

She rolled the handcart into the house to protect her purchases, then went back outside and opened the gate just wide enough to make sure Prescott had left. She slipped out to the street and started toward the bridge, walking as quickly as she could without arousing undue attention. Maybe, just maybe, it wasn't too late to find Jack on the far bank of the river. She had to tell him the Yankees knew about him and Prescott would be taking soldiers to his home.

Before she reached King Street she spotted Carlo walking her way, net slung over his shoulder, a heavy-looking croaker sack hanging from his hand.

"Where's Jack?" she asked. "Is he still by the river?"

"Yankees closed the bridge. I had to come home, and he left."

"He's gone?" Martina wanted to weep in frustration. "How long ago?"

"You'll never catch up with him on foot, even if the pickets let you through."

"I have to tell him about the Yankee patrols."

"He knows about them," Carlo said.

In her distress she had forgotten how much about the Yankees Carlo might be passing on to Jack. "They know about him, too, but they have orders not to harm him." If only she trusted Prescott to keep his word. "Captain Prescott wouldn't leave me be, and he insisted on walking me home."

They started back toward their gate. "Did you find out anything else?" Carlo asked.

"You think I'm going to join your spying game?"

"You want to get rid of Captain Prescott, don't you? The more our soldiers know about him, the better they can fight him."

Carlo's blunt answer caught her by surprise. She stared at him. The boy returned her gaze levelly. He continued, "Before the Yankees killed Francisco I just wanted to join up and help our side win. Now I want to get even with my brother's killers, too. I've found a way to do it."

She sighed. "As a matter of fact, Captain Prescott told me a great deal. After we get home we'll talk about it."

*

On the return trip, it seemed to Jack that the reserved Isaac was in an ebullient mood, singing softly to himself, handling the reins gently.

Jack set his jaw in annoyance at the cheerful intrusion into his morose mood. His father's hard message had set his teeth on edge. What a fool he had been for contacting him. Isaac had mentioned a Yankee officer had walked Martina from the bridge, adding to Jack's disgust.

As usual, the long ride inflamed his injuries and he wanted laudanum to sooth his miseries. He took the next best thing, a flask of Isaac's finest, out of his saddlebag and slugged down a mouthful.

The stagecoach trace connecting Picolata and St. Augustine cut through low, swampy areas, the worst of them reinforced by cross timbers. Dense forest bounded most of the route except for a few tracts settlers had cleared and cultivated. During Jack's stagecoach driving days, he had often asked the passengers to get off and lighten the load so he could unstick the wheels. He had no such trouble on horseback, but the wagon crawled along at no faster than a walk.

He and Isaac had risen before dawn so they could reach St. Augustine by noon. As they did last week, soon they would find a likely spot and spend the night in the wagon. Considering the time the trip took, once a week was all they could manage without spending their lives on the road.

Jack said to Isaac, "You sure seem happy. Did you have a good business day?"

"Yessir, Mr. Jack. I done real good the past three weeks. The popskull went fast and for a good price. Even after I settled up with Mr. Farrell, I have plenty of money left over."

Jack admired Isaac's thrift. He hadn't seen him buy any nonessentials. "You have enough to satisfy Mr. Miller?" Having to buy one's own wife and children was a strange business, one Jack did not have a liking for. That was one of the few opinions he and his father had in common. Still, it was the way things stood unless the abolitionists got their way. He suspected Miller's unwillingness to sell had as much to do with disagreement over politics as with territorial disputes.

Isaac smiled broadly. "I go see him tomorrow."

"You want me to come along? Maybe if I wear my gray jacket Miller will think better of us."

"Sure, boss. Maybe he listen to you. Mr. Leon thought so."

"I'll handle it if you want." It seemed likely his difficult neighbor would be more willing to deal with a white man.

"Thanks, Mr. Jack. I be taking the wagon so the babies won't have to walk. Lacey will want to bring all her stuff along, too."

"Appears to be plenty of room in your cabin for all four of you."

"I made a little bed for the babies. Don't need no extra bed for Lacey. She be sleeping with me."

"You'll sure be warm this winter."

Isaac grinned broadly. An unbidden thought of Martina, and how warmly she could fill his own lonely bed, crept into Jack's mind. Carlo said she didn't care for the Yankee officer, but how good a judge of such matters was that pup? He let out a long breath, knowing that more than a mere bridge separated them.

CHAPTER TEN

Halfway home, the thump of hoof-beats coming from behind made Jack glance back. He eased the revolver from his holster and turned to face the riders, a dozen or so, all wearing red shirts and straw hats. *Not regular troops from either army.*

Isaac looked over his shoulder. "Regulators," he spat.

"We'll never outrun them," Jack told Isaac. "Better see what they're about." He reined in Ladybug and sat waiting for the band to overtake them. He held his weapon down by his side, where the partisans could not see it right away.

Jack flashed a grin. "Howdy, boys," he hailed as the pursuers reached the wagon. He noted their belts bristled with knives and pistols. They resembled pirates more than Confederate soldiers, but he figured them to be more or less on his side of the conflict. Unless they were confirmed outlaws, in which case he and Isaac faced serious trouble.

The riders seemed most interested in whatever remained in Isaac's wagon but must have been disappointed that it was empty. Isaac sat hunched and submissive, keeping his eyes downcast.

The man who appeared to be their leader looked Jack over, taking in his crippled arm and said, "Who are you and what's your business?"

"I'm Private Jack Farrell, with the 2nd Florida Confederate Infantry. This is my man, Isaac." Let them think he was still attached to the army and that Isaac was his property. The less they knew, the better. "Who might you fine fellows be?"

"I'm Captain Hough. Raised this company of partisan rangers myself. You live around here?"

"Down the road."

An especially rough-looking bearded fellow said, "You kin to Leon Farrell?"

"Might be."

"I got a bone to pick with him." The bearded man spat.

"Damned Unionist. Where is that bastard? Last time I looked for him, he wasn't to home."

"Haven't seen him in over a year," Jack said. "I've been off in Virginia fighting the Yanks."

"Boys, we got us a patriot." Captain Hough nodded approval. "Farrell, you could just as well have been fightin' 'em down here."

"So I noticed, Captain. Blue targets everywhere." To the bearded man he said, "What's your quarrel with Leon Farrell?"

"You kin to that bastard?"

"He's my father, and I understand his parents were legally married," Jack said in an even tone.

"My pard, Lester, and I went to his house to arrest him for bein' a Unionist. He shot Lester in the arm."

"That sounds like the Leon Farrell I know," Jack said.

Somebody in the crowd snickered.

"You think it's funny?" growled the bearded man.

"Actually, I thought he was a better shot than that." Jack offered a no-offense grin. "He must be slipping."

"You on wound furlough?" Hough said.

Jack nodded. "Yes, sir." While that was not quite true, he did not want Captain Hough to know he was discharged. The partisan leader might want to conscript him, and Jack wanted nothing to do with this rough-looking band.

"You get a notion not to go back with the 2nd, you can ride with us."

"Well, now, Captain, I am honored you suggested that, and I'll sure keep it in mind." He glanced down at his bad arm. "As you can see, it might be a little while before I'm in fighting form."

"Remember us, Farrell."

"I will do that. By the way, Captain, you might consider having your men wear some other color. Red makes a fine target. I spotted y'all a long ways off."

Captain Hough narrowed his eyes, then said, "Good day." He gave an order, and his company flowed around the wagon and down the road.

"Good thing they were friendly." Jack returned the revolver to his belt. "I'd sure hate to meet that set in an unfriendly mood."

"Mr. Jack, you mighty sassy to them regulators." Isaac shook his head. "How much popskull you been drinkin'?"

Jack laughed out loud. "Oh, those boys are all right. Not that I'd want to kick in with them. They do look better from a distance, don't they?"

＊

The Miller plantation seemed oddly quiet when Jack and Isaac turned into the drive. Jack thought it unusual that nobody was working the fields during the cool of the morning, the most productive time of day. The cornfield was picked clean, the stalks dry and broken. The winter crops of cabbage and other greens were still young and not ready for harvest. Isaac, driving the wagon, eagerly scanned the fields as they rode toward the house.

While Isaac parked the wagon in front, Jack dismounted and tethered Ladybug. He led Isaac onto the porch but didn't need to knock because Miller opened the door a crack. He held a fowling piece in the crook of his arm.

"Howdy, neighbor." Jack extended his hand.

Miller stepped outside and shook Jack's hand. He gave Isaac an unfriendly look. "What brings you out here? It ain't Sunday." Miller glanced at Jack's disabled arm, took in the gray jacket and moved the plug from one cheek to the other. Miller had always been a mean-looking fellow, who appeared to have hardened over the years.

"Might as well get to the point." Jack pulled the bills out of his pocket. Grasping them in his sling-bound hand, he riffled through them with his free hand. "We're here to make an offer on Lacey and her boys."

"They're gone." Miller spat a stream of tobacco juice past the porch boards onto the dirt.

Jack sensed Isaac tensing up behind him. "Where'd they go?"

"I sent my people across the river, inland before the Yankees could steal them."

Jack glanced back at Isaac, whose burly arms were crossed. He was looking down, probably so Miller couldn't read his eyes.

"Who'd you sell them to?" Jack asked. "We don't mind making an offer to whoever's got them."

"Never you mind. They're not for sale to you, never have been. I told your nigra lovin' papa as much, and I'm telling you the same."

"What'd you do with them?" Isaac growled. "Tell me where you sent my woman and my babies." The floor creaked as Isaac stepped forward.

Miller raised his shotgun and pointed it past Jack. "Tell your boy to keep his distance or I'll blow him in two."

Miller made the mistake of poking the barrel too close. Jack snaked out his hand, thrust the weapon aside and rendered it harmless.

"Don't do that," Jack snarled. "I've killed better men than you." Miller tried to yank the gun away. If the cast had not imprisoned his right arm, Jack could have drawn his revolver. He could not reach it, nor could he continue to hang on to the shotgun's barrel against Miller's two-handed grip. To Isaac he snapped, "Get his gun."

Isaac wrested the piece away from Miller, whipped it around and turned it on him.

"No!" Jack hit the shotgun's muzzle. Both barrels blasted a pepperbox in the front of Miller's house.

Isaac stood, the smoking shotgun in his hands, blowing like a bull. Jack reached for the gun and locked eyes with Isaac. For a moment he feared he was in for a fight with his friend, but fortunately Isaac relented and let him have it without a fuss.

The money still clasped in his off hand, Jack turned to the white-faced Miller. "The offer still stands."

"Go to hell." Miller took a step back. "Get off my property."

Jack turned to Isaac, "We're done here for now. Need to go at this another way."

"Tell me where you took Lacey and my babies, Miller." Isaac's face contorted, and his voice choked with grief and rage.

"I ain't tellin' you nothing, nigra. I'll see you lynched for tryin' to kill a white man." He spewed another arc of spit-laden tobacco juice, which splattered onto Isaac's pants leg and dripped in a nasty glob.

"This is useless. Let's go." Jack stepped off the porch to his horse. He was relieved to see Isaac turn with him and follow him toward the wagon. It had shaken him seeing the normally good-natured Isaac fly into a murderous rage.

"Give me my shotgun back," hollered Miller.

Although it had been discharged, Miller could still find

ammunition, reload it and come after them. Jack set it in the wagon and mounted his horse. "I'll leave it down by the road."

"I'm gonna get the regulators on you, nigra." Miller shook his fist. "They'll hang you higher'n Haman! I ain't through with you either, Farrell."

"Go to hell yourself, neighbor. I've already met your regulator friends, and they are all brag." Jack turned to Isaac to make sure he climbed into the wagon. He pressed his heels into his pony's sides and got the hell away before he lost control and personally murdered Miller or else turned Isaac loose on him like he wanted to do.

*

When Jack asked him what he was going to do next, Isaac kept his thoughts to himself. He was used to keeping his mouth shut because his opinions were too dangerous for a white man's ears. By force of habit he had obeyed Jack and had given him the gun. If he had that to do all over again, he wouldn't.

"He won't let this rest." Jack said. "You meant to kill him, and he'll have you strung up for your impudence."

"What about you, Mr. Jack. You gonna help 'em do it?"

"You know me better than that," Jack snarled. "Hell, I felt like killing him myself."

Isaac mumbled an apology.

"When a crowd comes for you, I won't be able to hold them off," Jack said.

"No, I don't reckon you can."

"You're going to need this." Jack handed his money back.

Isaac understood Jack was telling him to run.

Miller had stolen the sole reason for his careful hoarding. Instead of weeping for the theft of his family, Isaac felt a cold, hard rage. He had to act, but what could he do?

Miller knew where he had sent Lacey and his two little boys. Yes, his boys. By what right did anyone claim his children as their property? By what right did any man keep from him his own woman and children?

He would make Miller tell him where they were, and he would take them back from whoever was holding them. Tonight he'd slip away, and he didn't care if he ever came back to his cabin, unless he could bring Lacey and the boys.

He watched Jack riding a little ahead of him. Although he'd grown up with Jack and had always considered him a friend, the white boy was on the side of Isaac's enemies, just like those other rebel soldiers.

That night Isaac waited until well after dark before he saddled the mule and headed toward the Miller place. A full moon, filtering light through the pines, showed his way, though he and the critter knew the path well enough to find it blind. No watchdog had announced their earlier approach; he believed he could sneak in without warning. He hoped the old widower was alone.

He tied the mule well away from Miller's house and stalked to the door, knowing if Miller heard him coming he would use the shotgun without asking questions. Isaac's only weapon was a freshly sharpened fish-cleaning knife, useless against a scattergun.

He tried the door and found it locked or barred from the inside. He crept around the side of the house and discovered an open window. Peering inside, he saw Miller, revealed by the moonlight, lying on his back in bed, covered to his neck. He heard the man snoring. He raised the window all the way. It made a noise, so he rushed inside. Miller sat up, but Isaac was on him before he could reach for a weapon.

Isaac grabbed Miller by his greasy gray hair and held the knife blade to his throat. "Where'd you send Lacey?" he growled.

"I – I had a trader pick them up. I don't know where he's taking them." Miller's voice quavered

"You lying. Where are they?"

"Maybe Georgia. Maybe middle Florida. Don't know."

"What trader?"

"Fellow named Bass. Works out of Jacksonville. I'd tell you more if I knew." Miller's voice gathered strength and authority as though it would work on Isaac. "Put down that knife, nigra, and let me go."

As though acting beyond his will, Isaac's hand moved, quick and hard. Miller gave out a short squeal.

Still sitting, held in place by Isaac gripping his hair, Miller held his hand to his neck, gagging, blood gushing from between his fingers. Isaac released his hair and let the dying man sag. He held up the knife and examined it in wonder, as though it had a life of its own. Blood, black in the dim light, smeared the blade and dripped down his hand. He trembled in an agony of fright.

Isaac whispered, "Lord, lordy lord." Panic rushed through him, and he froze in place. He had taken his fill of pain and humiliation and had lashed out in a single knife thrust. Then he reasoned he had only done what he had to do. Like Jack had said, Miller wouldn't let his threat go unpunished. It was Miller or him.

Miller collapsed, jerked and twitched as blood gurgled in his throat. Finally, he lay still on his back on his gore-soaked quilt, eyes wide open, mouth a gaping hole, no longer capable of telling Isaac another thing.

Isaac wanted to run but forced himself to think it out, though he could not control the shaking. Was anyone else in the house?

Miller had died quietly. Surely his struggles had made no more noise than his snoring. Holding his breath, Isaac picked up the shotgun Miller had left on the bedside table. He prowled around the house, checked each room and found no one else home.

Isaac went back to Miller's bedroom and studied the dead man, repelled yet fascinated. He wasn't sorry Miller was dead. He was just sorry he didn't find out where Lacey had gone first.

He looked out the window but didn't see anyone. He glanced back at the dead man. How soon would the body be found? How soon would the hunt for freedman Isaac begin? Maybe he could slow down the manhunt if nobody missed Miller for a while.

He could torch the house with the body in it, but a log house might not easily catch fire and burn to the ground. Besides, a fire would not go unnoticed.

Steeling his nerve and resolve, Isaac unlatched the front door and peered out. He still didn't see anybody coming, so he jogged outside to where he'd tethered the mule and brought the beast closer to the house. He returned to the bedroom and bundled Miller in the quilt. He ripped the bloody sheets from the bed and tied them around the corpse. Good thing Miller was a scrawny devil.

Grunting with the effort, Isaac heaved the swaddled body over his shoulder and carried it outside. He talked in a low voice to calm the mule and draped the bundle over the saddle. Holding the dead man on the saddle, he led the mule to the riverbank. Miller's place had a boat landing, making it possible for Isaac to carry his burden out to the deeper water at the end of the dock. He dropped Miller into the St. Johns, causing a splash and a gurgle as bubbles rose from the sinking body. It bobbed just under the surface. With any luck the fish and crabs would have their way with Miller, and his death would remain a mystery.

At the shoreline Isaac washed the blood off his hands then nerved himself to return to the house. In the dark he couldn't tell whether he'd left any of Miller's blood behind. He picked up the shotgun, stepped out of the house, and closed the front door.

He quit the Miller place as fast as his kicks could urge the mule and tried to slow his fevered mind to think things through. He could row across the river and blunder around the vast land that lay on the other side hoping to find his family. Getting caught by the regulators or Confederate soldiers was just about a sure thing, especially if anyone connected him with Miller's killing. He would be a wanted man, and they would shoot or hang a black man without question or trial.

Maybe there was another way.

The Yankees had already told him they wanted to recruit him to fight Confederate soldiers. Just yesterday he had put off that Yankee officer who tried to talk him into joining up. They wouldn't know what he had done tonight. Isaac suspected they might not much mind his killing Miller anyhow.

Maybe the Yankees could somehow help him find his family during one of their raids into the rebel-held land. He was better off with numbers and authority to back him up. He could imagine himself filling one of those blue uniforms.

It was time to move up from his fishing knife to a rifle and bayonet. Best not to stop by the cabin he used to call home. Although Jack would not cause him grief over this morning's argument with Miller, he might try to stop him from joining the Yankee army.

Isaac turned the mule down the road toward St. Augustine.

CHAPTER ELEVEN

Jack sat on the edge of the porch cleaning his revolver so it would be ready the next time he needed to use it. Earlier that day he had killed a rattlesnake that slithered too close to the chickens. Nip, full of rattlesnake meat, lazed alongside him, twitching in his sleep as though animated by the snake's spirit.

He took a swallow of Isaac's brew from a jar. Sweetened with orange and cane juice, it helped soothe the nagging pains dogging his heels and gave him a pleasant sense of wellbeing. After helping Isaac create the last batch he knew how to make more.

"No lynch mob yet," he told the snoozing dog. "I'm kind of surprised at old Miller. Anyhow, they don't worry me. I'll just tell 'em Isaac took off and they're welcome to look for him. Most likely he went hunting for his family. I'd do the same thing if somebody stole my woman."

His thoughts meandered to Martina. He oiled the barrel of the revolver, imagining what it would be like to make love to her. Most likely he would never find out. He set down the weapon and downed another swig.

The hound roused then leaped to his feet. Nip chuffed, tail held in high alert, stared toward the path leading toward the house, and let out a full-blown bay.

Jack set down the jar and focused in the same direction. Dickison's scouts had been making regular visits, but this was more than the two or three men he was used to seeing. Could it be the lynch mob coming for Isaac? Captain Hough's band?

No. A line of blue-coated soldiers rode straight toward his house. He grabbed the barrel of his unloaded, disassembled revolver, then remembered it was useless.

They'd caught him in the open, unarmed, outnumbered and a little bit drunk. He saw no escape route and no means of defending himself. Inside or outside the house they had him. If he ran toward the woods, they would ride him down or corner him at the riverbank. He had no choice but to face them and hope they hadn't come to kill him.

Lydia Hawke

He stood and grabbed Nip by the scruff of the neck. "Let's not give them an excuse to shoot either one of us." He hauled the unwilling dog to the front door, shouldered it open, shoved Nip inside and slammed it shut. Nip scratched at the door and howled in protest.

Jack gripped the porch support so his hand would not shake. He studied the leaders, a captain and a sergeant, as the party filed into the front yard and halted. The officer, sweating and florid faced in his fancy uniform, frowned through his drooping moustache as he looked down his nose at Jack.

The sergeant, an older, more workmanlike-looking fellow, gave Jack a measuring stare, taking in the popskull jar, the disassembled revolver by Jack's feet and the arm sling. When their gaze met, Jack realized he had made a mistake letting the man see into his eyes, revealing too much of himself.

Jack collected himself. The liquor he'd downed was no longer muddling his brain. The Yankees had shocked him sober.

"You're Jack Farrell?" snapped the officer.

Somebody had told the Yankees he lived here. Pop. Jack forced a smile. "Captain? I don't believe I've had the pleasure of making your acquaintance."

"I'm Captain Richard Prescott, of the 7[h] New Hampshire. We were in the area and thought we'd drop by."

Prescott was the Yankee officer courting Martina. Jack did some measuring of his own. He hadn't heard from Martina's own lips what she thought of Prescott, but at first glance Jack wasn't impressed with the pompous New Englander.

The party consisted of twelve soldiers and a couple of Negroes in civilian clothes. No doubt they would force him to saddle his horse and accompany them back to St. Augustine under guard. He set his jaw, angry at the thought of becoming a prisoner and unable to do anything to prevent it. *Thanks for turning me in, Pop.* He affected a casual demeanor. "Just a neighborly call?"

"A warning call."

Jack inclined his head. "I'm listening."

"We've been told you were discharged from the Confederate army."

"I was." Jack shifted his broken arm. "Lost an argument with an artillery shell. The docs said the war is over for me."

"The smartest thing you can do is take the loyalty oath to the

90

United States of America. Think of it as an insurance policy."

Jack didn't comment. He glanced at the formidable sergeant and noted his steady gaze.

"Well?"

Jack returned his attention back to the captain. "I'll think about it."

"You'd better think hard. Behave yourself, or we'll come after you. Keep in mind we know where you live."

Jack exhaled, just now realizing he'd been holding his breath. They weren't here to arrest him but to make it clear they had him lined up in their sights. "I hear you."

The sergeant said to the officer, "Sir, I suggest we disarm him."

"Make it so," Prescott said. The sergeant told a man to dismount and fetch Jack's revolver.

"I need it to kill snakes," Jack said.

"Use a stick," the sergeant said.

The trooper picked up the revolver and the detached cylinder from the porch and handed the parts to the sergeant.

"We're going to take a look around," Prescott said.

"I can't stop you."

He watched them ride away from the house but didn't follow. They were going to do whatever they pleased, and if he got in their way they could use it as an excuse to kill him.

He heard shouts and a gunshot. He flinched, expecting more. That was all, just one shot. He held hope they weren't slaughtering every animal in the pasture. After some time had passed the Yankees came back around on their way out.

Four chickens flopped from a trooper's saddle. One of the young pigs, dripping blood from a bullet hole through its head, lay across the pommel of another saddle. Each set of saddlebags bulged, likely with the garden's best produce. One of the troopers was peeling a green orange with his knife.

Clearly, they wanted to make the point they were free to take whatever they pleased, whenever they liked, in whatever manner they chose.

Prescott reined in and turned his horse to face Jack. "We went easy on you today, just took what we need to feed my troops. As long as we remain friends, we won't burn you out."

"Is the U. S. Army going to pay for the livestock and produce you just confiscated?"

"Consider it a tax in kind."

"I need that revolver. Would you be so kind as to return it?"

"We can't be sure how you'll use it."

"When I shot that rattlesnake going after my chickens this morning," Jack pointed to the snakeskin hanging on the porch rail, his temper overtaking his judgment, "I didn't know friends like y'all were coming over for supper. I should have let the rattler take them instead."

"You are an insolent bastard." Prescott straightened in the saddle. "One more remark like that and I'll have you dragged away in chains."

Jack compressed his lips. *And you are merely an ordinary bastard.* "I got your message. You can do whatever you want and I'd better like it. Right?"

"Watch your step, and we'll leave you be. But mark my words, if you cooperate with the rebels we'll shoot you as dead as that rattlesnake." Prescott nodded toward the drying snakeskin. "Understood?"

"Clear as glass." Of course he hadn't seen the last of them. They'd be back again and again like malarial chills and fever.

He watched the bluecoats ride away then sank down onto the step, weak with relief.

*

"I believe he knows where he stands with us," Prescott said.

"Well, sir," Sergeant Owen said, "too bad we can't bring him in while we have the chance. Save ourselves the trouble later."

Prescott stared at him. "Why? He seemed harmless enough, except for that bit of sass he threw our way. Wasn't he drinking in the middle of the day? Scrawny, weak, and he's got a bad arm. Our boys in the Army of the Potomac did a fine job taking him out of action."

"I fought Indians out west. That boy is a brave. I know the kind, and there ain't no taming them. I wish he was on our side, but he ain't. Once he heals up he's going to cause us problems. He may be out of the army for the time being, but he'll soon be dangerous."

"We had our orders," Prescott shrugged. "The colonel said to give him conditional immunity on account of his daddy pleading his case."

"His daddy is a tough customer." Owen shook his head. "And his brother is a career officer in our army. Blood tells, sir."

"We let him know if he takes up arms there will be consequences."

"Somehow I don't think he will give a damn."

"Then we'll have to keep an eye on him." Prescott adjusted his cap. "Once he steps out of line you can have him shot."

"I'll be watching," Owen said.

CHAPTER TWELVE

"He's not here." Carlo's voice trailed off in disappointment.

Martina peered in the direction from which she expected Jack to appear, but she only saw green underbrush, trees and sky. Prescott's soulless recital of how the Union troops treated outliers echoed in her mind. She had failed to get word to Jack that the Yankees planned to pay him a visit, and now he was absent from the usual meeting place.

Although she did not consider Jack a friend, she owed him for bringing her Francisco's belongings. She wished to reassure herself the Yankees had not harmed him. Perhaps something she had learned from Prescott would help Jack stay out of danger.

Had he fallen sick? Did he do something to goad Prescott's men into harming him? Or did he simply decide not to come today? If he failed to show, she had no way of knowing why.

She tied up her skirts, unfastened her shoes, and pulled them off along with her stockings. The soles of her feet were tough because she spent much of the time at home barefoot, but oyster shells would surely cut them if she was not mindful. She picked up a croaker sack and a rake and carefully stepped into the ankle-deep water where she could see what lay underfoot. Dragging the sack in the water, she waded across the muddy river bottom avoiding stepping on shells, to the shelf of oysters. She raked them to her, examined them to assure their quality, and dropped them into the sack.

Martina glanced toward Carlo, who had ventured waist deep to cast his net, and again scanned toward the scrub at the river's edge for any sign of Jack. Tired of bending over, she stood straight and stretched, then returned to her task.

From the corner of her eye she caught a glimpse of a man approaching on horseback and recognized Jack. She left the sack full of oysters in the shallows where they would not spoil and picked her way out of the water.

Realizing her skirts were hiked up to an unacceptable level, she stooped to untie them. Jack rode up to her before she could finish. Two weeks had passed since their last meeting, and he appeared stronger, not as gaunt. He wore a blue and white check shirt and sky-blue uniform trousers. Although the broad-brimmed hat shadowed his eyes, it did not conceal his jaunty smile, and she felt a ripple of embarrassment that he had caught her in an immodest condition.

He took off his hat and held it over his chest in a kind of salute. His grin extended to his eyes. "Miss Martina. I am right pleased to see you."

She let go of her damp hem. "The pickets gave me a pass so I could help Carlo."

He glanced toward the bridge, out of sight behind the shoreline woods. "Nobody followed you?"

"Why should they be suspicious? The Yankees know Carlo has a routine."

He set the hat back on his head and dismounted. She noted the care he took with his actions. Clearly, his wounds still plagued him. She walked with him as he led his horse to the thicket, picking her way over the shoreline debris. Carlo rushed up behind her, empty handed because he had dropped his net next to the water.

She smoothed her hand over the horse's hot, damp neck down to its shoulder. The animal curved its head around to nuzzle her arm. She liked the soft tickle of whiskers and warm breath, smelling of fresh grass.

The cast and sling still confining his broken arm, Jack handed the reins to Carlo, who wrapped them around a limb. Carlo said, "Mr. Jack, Martina was worried about you. She heard the Yanks were going to your place."

"They did." Jack raised an eyebrow. "Worried about me, Miss Martina?"

She lifted her chin. In his boots he stood half a head taller than she did barefooted, and she had to look up to meet his eyes "Don't take it personally, Mr. Farrell. I just hate to see them hurt people."

Jack smiled sardonically. "Your Captain Prescott paid me a visit, in force."

"*My* Captain Prescott? Why do you say that?" Martina narrowed her eyes. "He is a monster. What did he do?"

"At least you didn't let the monster kidnap you like he did last time." Jack continued to smile, but his eyeteeth showed.

He was jealous of Prescott. She might have laughed if she didn't find one man frightening and the other exasperating.

"What happened?" Carlo asked.

Jack's smile drifted away. "I'm missing one revolver, four chickens and a pig, for starters. He didn't arrest me, hang me or shoot me. I believe if he catches me off the homestead, he will try."

"We would have warned you, but you'd left," Carlo said. "It was too late."

"Turned out all right. Did my father put him up to it?"

"Your father asked them to leave you alone," Martina said. "My *friend* Captain Prescott told me."

"I suppose Pop drew him a map and directions, just to make sure they could leave me alone even better."

"Your father does care about you, Jack." Martina was beginning to wonder if that was true.

Jack turned to Carlo. "Untie that sack from the saddle. I brought y'all something you could use." He gave Martina a sidewise glance. "Instead of a bunch of wildflowers."

Martina gave Jack a questioning look, surprised he would remind her of last year's disastrous Posy Dance.

"Sweet potatoes, squash, onions, cabbage, pecans and pole beans," Jack said. "I can't eat it all. Isaac's kitchen garden is yielding well, and it would be a shame to let it rot. He's nowhere to be found."

"Carlo saw him. He's in town," Martina said.

"What's he doing in St. Augustine? I figured he lit out west of the river to look for his family."

"He's with the soldiers." Carlo broke in. "I think he's joining the army. They have him digging fortifications north of town."

"Oh, hell." Jack clenched his jaw, glanced at Martina then away. "I'm sorry. I haven't been in the company of a lady for a while –"

"Thank you for the vegetables." Ignoring his outburst she took the heavy sack from Carlo and set it down. "It was thoughtful of you. How much do I owe –?"

"It's a gift. I can bring more next time."

"Mr. Jack, how are you going to sell anything from your farm without Isaac coming to town?" Carlo asked.

"It's Pop's farm. I just live there."

"I could help." Carlo gave Jack an expectant look.

"How, Chico?" Martina wanted to know. "You are making me worry again."

"I'll work for Mr. Jack. I'll help him pick stuff and bring it to market."

"It's too dangerous," Martina said. "Both armies are out there shooting at each other. If you're in the middle –"

"She's right, Carlo." Jack gripped the boy's shoulder in comradely fashion. "You're smart and ambitious. But listen to your sister. You're better off in town. Besides, she needs you."

"She could come with me. Both of us could stay at your place."

"Carlo!" Martina yelped.

"That would suit me fine." Jack ran his gaze over her face, a teasing smile playing across his lips. "I enjoy female company."

"So I've noticed," Martina snapped. "I won't be added to your list."

"Of course you won't." Jack's smile hardened. "Virtuous young ladies are well advised to stay away from sinners like me."

He gave Carlo's shoulder an additional squeeze. "Tell you what, Carlo, let's have a talk, just between us fellows. Excuse us, Miss Martina."

Thus excluded, she had no further reason to stay. Her conversation with Jack was over, and she planned to take his advice and stay away from him. She collected the sack of vegetables Jack had brought and the oysters she had gathered and started home.

*

Jack steered Carlo down to the water line where they stopped. An egret stepped through the marsh and waded into a channel. A turtle stuck its head up as it paddled along the surface. Jack inhaled the salty scent and noticed a deep breath did not pain him as much as it did even the day before. One fine day he would be whole again.

The boy hunched his shoulders as though expecting a reprimand. Jack said, "I know life's been hard on you and your sister lately. Don't you feel like you're trying to hold up the weight of the world?"

Carlo appeared open-mouthed astonished, probably grateful somebody made an effort to see his side of things. "I don't mind. We're doing all right, Martina and me."

"You deserve a lot of credit for sticking by her. Martina is probably too busy to tell you. She has a great deal on her mind."

Carlo nodded.

"But I have to ask. You aren't trying to play matchmaker, are you?"

"I want to get her away from Captain Prescott. He's nothing but a bully."

"You think I can protect her?"

Carlo nodded again.

"Hell's fire, boy." Jack scrubbed his hand over his face. "When they came to my house I couldn't even save myself if they had a mind to string me up. They'll always come in force, and I'm only one man. Until I get my arm back I'm not even the worth of that."

"There would be two of us." Carlo said. "You're a fighter. Everybody says so."

"Do they?" Jack let out a bitter laugh, amazed at the boy's naïve faith. He changed tack. "One other thing you have to understand. Martina won't want to come live at my home. She's a proper young lady and I'm an unmarried man. It would cause her problems because people would assume…. Well, they wouldn't be kind."

"She's got problems now, Mr. Jack."

"You'd better not bring it up again. It will only insult her. She doesn't approve of me anyway."

"Once she gets to know you she'll change her mind."

"If she wants to."

"But… the Yankees made us leave St. Augustine once. What if they do it again?"

Jack watched the egret stab its beak into the water and come up with a silver minnow, struggling, glinting in the sun. "In that case… in an emergency… you know where to come, straight west down the Picolata road to the river, and turn north. The door is always unlocked."

*

Martina struggled along the narrow strip of the riverbank, the heavy load forcing the wheels of her handcart to sink into the soft sand. Perhaps she should have waited for Carlo, but she could not abide another sarcastic comment from Jack. She could forgive Carlo for his youthful lack of understanding, but Jack knew better.

Just as she gained sight of the bridge she saw a blue-coated soldier striding toward her. Prescott. What if he caught Carlo with Jack? He would assume... he would know... Carlo had been feeding information to his enemies. She had to prevent him from blundering into Jack.

Making her slow, bogged-down way, she intercepted him. He removed his cap and said, "What a pleasant surprise, Miss Sanchez."

"I could have sworn you were pursuing me."

He chuckled. "Is there a law against taking a walk along a riverbank?"

"I suppose you can do whatever you wish. Nowadays your army is the law."

"So sharp of tongue you are today, Miss Martina. Perhaps because you are so heavily burdened? I can assist you."

She forced herself to smile and let go of the handcart. Anything to keep him from seeing Jack and Carlo together. "I would like that very much."

Prescott took over pushing the loaded cart across the deep sand, back toward the bridge, away from Carlo and Jack, while she walked beside him. Carlo was safe now, because he was not Prescott's quarry. She was.

Of course Prescott insisted on walking her all the way home. She pretended to listen to him brag about his progress with the colored troops. Once they reached her gate. Martina tried to head him off, but Prescott shouldered his way inside and to her door.

Cornered, she said, "Thank you for your help, Captain Prescott, but it's time for you to leave me now."

"Aren't you going to invite me in?"

"What would people say?"

He glanced around. "What people? No one can see us behind the fence."

Her hand slipped toward the knife in her apron, but he grabbed her wrist. With his other hand he withdrew the knife and held it blade up in front of her face. "Is this what you were after?"

"I will scream."

"No you won't. You have too much to lose." His mouth came down on hers, and the scream died in her throat. His bristly moustache scratched her face, and he tasted of cigars. She struggled to free herself and stamped her foot on his hard boot as he pinned her to the doorframe. He held her around the waist with one arm; with the other he opened the door and started to force her inside.

Her flailing arm hit something hard. Her hand closed around the handle of his sidearm. She dragged it out, pressed the barrel against his ribs and pulled back the hammer. He froze.

"Leave me," she said between her teeth.

He broke his hold on her and backed up a few steps, his eyes hot. "If you shoot me you will be hanged."

She glanced down at the revolver in her hand and noted the caps were in place. "I won't shoot you if you leave me now."

He held out his hand. "Give me my weapon."

She shook her head.

"Give it to me or I'll have you imprisoned for stealing government property."

"I'll trade your gun for my knife."

Scowling, he dropped the knife at her feet.

"Never speak to me again, Captain Prescott. You must never come near me, ever again. Go outside the gate and I will give you the gun."

Prescott turned on his heel and stalked down the short path to the fence. He turned to glare at her before he left her yard, slamming the gate behind him. Martina picked up the knife and used it to pry off the caps, dropping them into her apron pocket. She threw the revolver as hard as she could over the fence. It thudded onto the sand.

She spun into the house, shut the door and bolted it. Her temples pounded, and her breath came in gulps. She pressed her shaking hands to her hot cheeks.

Not for a moment did she believe she had seen the last of him.

*

Carlo brought home a bucket and a sack full of oysters but no fish. The mullet were not running. He was surprised to see Martina's handcart still outside the door, still full. When he tried the door he found it bolted.

"Tina," he called.

She opened the door. "You're back. Thank the Blessed Mother."

She hugged him, and he squirmed free. "Tina, what's the matter?"

"Carlo, you must not meet with Jack Farrell any more."

"Just because you're mad at him? I don't understand what you have against—"

"The Yankees are going to catch you talking to him. We almost got caught today."

Bewildered, Carlo said, "What else happened?"

She pointed to the door with her chin. "Let's roast the oysters before they spoil."

"I won't stop meeting Jack. It's too important."

She shot him a scathing look. "I forbid it."

Carlo shook his head, biting his lip. "You can't stop me, Tina."

She blinked at him as though shocked at the rebellion. "Carlo, you're only fourteen...."

"Mr. Jack won't let them catch us."

"You put too much faith in Jack Farrell. They can catch him, too. If he runs, they will shoot him. Don't you understand? This is life and death."

Carlo drew himself up to stand as tall as he could. "He isn't afraid, and neither am I." He saw the fear in his sister's eyes. "We don't have to stay here. We have a place to go."

That didn't seem to help. Martina slumped into a chair and buried her face into her folded arms on the table. He moved closer and rested his hand on her back. He stayed with her until she shook off her despondency, raised her strained face to him and said, "We have work to do."

*

Jack sat on the porch with the dog by his side and his jar of popskull in hand. He felt naked without his revolver, but the knife in his boot was better than nothing. The advancing fall season promised a pleasant drop in temperature after sunset. It was a good night to get rousing drunk.

"How 'bout that Isaac," he said to Nip. "Now the whole damn family is on the other side. Are you going to join them, too?"

The dog lolled his tongue out and yawned.

"No, you're a faithful hound." He took a swig. "I could turn into shiftless no-account white trash, sitting around here as long as I'm stove up. Pick something from the garden to eat, cook a fish or an egg. Guess I have it good, huh? This place is a regular Garden of Eden. Without Eve."

In fact, a chance to rest and the abundance of fresh food had no doubt sped up the healing process. Jack set down his drink, removed his arm from the sling and flexed his elbow. He clenched the fist and worked the fingers. "Don't need this any more." He ripped the sling from around his neck and threw it aside then pulled the knife from his boot. He carefully cut and pried away the plaster splint.

He examined the healing punctures and rubbed the sore places where the plaster had been chafing the skin. Soap and water would help. The broken arm had lost muscle, appearing noticeably smaller than the left and not quite straight between wrist and elbow. With use, it should improve.

He ran his fingers up and down his shrapnel pitted arm, searching for new splinters that had worked their way out of his flesh through the skin. Finding none, he draped the shirt over his shoulders against the chill.

Now that he had his arm back, maybe he would be better able to defend himself next time somebody picked a fight.

Nip whipped around and dived at his hind leg, chewing industriously. A flea must have gotten in the first bite.

Jack's thoughts moved on to Martina and to Carlo's artless suggestion that the two of them come live with him. No doubt she would rather starve in the street.

Still, if she were within reach, would he be able to muster enough gentlemanly self-restraint to let her sleep alone?

"Well, Nip." He gave the dog a thump on the ribs with his newly freed right hand. "It's been a long time since anyone accused me of being a gentleman. I suppose I'd just have to keep on living down to their expectations."

CHAPTER THIRTEEN

Jack had just finished setting corn out for the stock when a detachment of Captain Dickison's company rode into the yard. They arrived early enough in the day to find him sober.

Relieved the invasion was friendly this time, he invited the troopers to fill their canteens and water their horses in the spring. Their commanding officer sat with him on the porch. The conversation quickly turned from polite pleasantries to business.

"It's getting harder to defend the country between the St. Johns and the ocean." Dickison, a trim man in his 40's, wore a neat moustache, and his soft, low-country accent reminded Jack of the South Carolina men he had met in Virginia. "The Yanks have been conducting raids against our civilians on this side of the river."

"A party of mounted infantry paid me a visit," Jack said.

"You're lucky they didn't clean you out."

"Just left me a little poorer. A Captain Prescott led the party. I understand he's looking for colored men to recruit. He's put them on a work detail for the time being."

"We're aware of their intent. We've been rounding up runaways. Folks have been sending their people across the river to keep the Yanks from getting to them."

"Yes, sir," Jack said dryly. "Fellow named Miller sent off the family of the free Negro who lived here and wouldn't tell him where they went. Upset Isaac so much he ran off and joined the Yanks. Before that Isaac wasn't military minded at all."

"Miller, you say? Planter just down the road?'

Jack nodded.

"Fishermen found his body in the river, down at the end of his dock."

Jack stared at Dickison. "When?"

"Couple of days ago. Must have been him, though I understand it wasn't easy to be sure. You know how it is. Crabs."

"Anybody know what happened to him?"

"Somebody slit his throat and wrapped him up in a quilt."

Jack's mind raced. That explained a few things, such as why no lynch party ever came for Isaac; Miller was in no condition to complain. Could the easy-going Isaac have murdered him before he lit out?

"I made it a point to stop by and talk to you," Dickison said. "My scouts say you have been giving them valuable information about the Yankee garrison in St. Augustine."

"I've been riding toward town once a week, finding out what I can, passing along whatever I hear." Jack mentioned the Fairbanks place, where the Yanks had set up a camp, north of the city fortifications. He sketched a map in the dirt and gave Dickison the names of officers he'd learned. "I rode up to the north end of the San Sebastian and scouted it out. I believe you can cross there and surprise them if you think it's worth your trouble."

"My local men tell me you know St. Johns County and you've already volunteered to assist us," Dickison said. "I'd like for you to guide us over that way and help us plan an attack strategy."

"Ramon used to live near there. He knows that area better than I do."

"He thought you'd want to ride along. Are you well enough yet?"

"I've been getting around, making the trip to St. Augustine, but I have to take it easy." Jack flexed his weak arm, considering the request.

"How long has it been since you've seen a doctor?"

"Over a month ago, up in Richmond. Army gave me a disability discharge."

"Our company surgeon can take a look. Save you from having to report to our camp for an examination."

Jack knew what that was about. The army was hungry for recruits, and a medical discharge was not a free pass. Once healed up, he would be ripe for conscription.

He endured the medical examination inside the house. He told the surgeon what had happened to him, and that some of the deep-seated shell fragments and splinters had never been removed.

Dr. Williams confirmed his suspicions that the checkup was not entirely for humanitarian reasons. "You still have lung congestion from your injuries. I'll tell the captain you are fit only for light duty. Maybe in a few weeks you'll be ready for cavalry service. In the meantime I can prescribe laudanum for the pain."

"That will help." Jack buttoned his shirt. "I'm willing to ride with the troop to St. Augustine today. I'll get ready."

He stuffed cold cornbread and ham he'd been planning to eat for supper into his old haversack. He took the uniform jacket he'd worn home out of the trunk and shrugged it on. Without his arm in a splint, donning a shirt and jacket took less care.

If the Yanks captured him fighting in civilian clothes he wouldn't be an ordinary prisoner of war; he'd be considered a spy fit for hanging. If Prescott caught him either way it might bring the same result. Maybe he could catch Prescott instead, a satisfying thought.

He grabbed his wide-brimmed hat and his haversack, then rushed out the door to saddle his horse.

Jack, Cates and Ramon scouted ahead of the troop, watching for enemy soldiers along the Picolata-St. Augustine stagecoach trace. The captain had provided Jack with a serviceable Colt revolver to replace the one the Yankees had confiscated. Equipped with a small civilian saddle and light load, he hoped Ladybug could keep up with the younger horses. Most of the men rode small Florida cow ponies of the same type as his, descended from the original Spanish horses. They weren't much to look at but were hardy, agile and adapted to marsh and scrub.

Fortified with drugs, Jack felt in rhythm with his surroundings. The jingle of spurs, equipment and weapons created a counterpoint to the rattle of brush being pushed aside and the huff of equine breath. Aware of the soft thud of hooves on dirt, or occasional clatter across corduroy, he might as well have been taking a pleasure ride.

Ladybug balked when a deer leaped across the path ahead of him. Forbidden to discharge firearms, the soldiers let the tempting meal on hooves run away in peace. Overhead a hawk dipped and circled.

Cates pulled alongside. "How do you like riding with the cavalry, Jack?"

"Always had to jump aside whenever the critter soldiers shoved lowlies like me off the road. Then I got to step over their manure. I prefer the view from atop the horse's back."

"You'll need a better horse when you join up," Cates pointed out.

Jack squashed a horsefly on Ladybug's neck, contemplating

the probability of having to reenlist in the future.

"You can appropriate one off a Yank," Cates offered.

"Hell, you're talking like I've already joined up."

"We'll get you by and by. Soon as you're through malingering, you can join the fun."

"I always did enjoy risking my neck." Jack grinned. "It beats hanging around the house waiting for the Yanks to raid my chicken coop."

Hours later he, Cates and Ramon sat their horses, looking across the marshy headwaters of the San Sebastian River. Jack's injuries had reawakened, and he wanted another dose of laudanum. He slipped the flask out of the saddlebag to take a few drops of the soothing liquid.

"You say you came up this way last week?" Ramon asked Jack.

Jack nodded. "Not this far north, closer to town. I crossed and didn't raise an alarm. Nobody shot at me, so this far up should be clear."

"Good to hear," Cates grunted.

"My house is back that way, too, if there's anything left of it." Ramon took his Enfield out of the boot and loaded it.

Captain Dickison reined in next to Jack.

"We're a ways north of the Fairbanks place, so I don't think they'll observe us at this point," Jack told him. "If you want, we can cross here and slip on down through the woods. Don't know how much cover we'll have once we get closer."

"We'll cross and feel them out." Dickison studied Jack. "I appreciate your assistance, Mr. Farrell. You may leave us now if you wish."

Jack shifted stiffly in the saddle, wishing the laudanum had already taken effect. "I've come this far." He still had to face the trip home, but he hated showing weakness.

The troop crossed the muddy creek without getting any horses stuck in the mud, gained the far side and rode into the shelter of the trees on the east side. Riding along the bank would have left them exposed, so they worked their way through the woods toward the Yankee camp.

Jack heard the thump of axes on wood and said to Ramon, "They have a crew of woodcutters working."

"They better not cut down my orange trees." Ramon pointed

with his Enfield.

"Then let's get us some wood," Cates drew his revolver and checked the caps.

Jack recalled Carlo had told him the Yankees had put Isaac to work as a laborer. Could be his old friend was about to get a nasty surprise.

Dickison told a sergeant to have the men count off by fours. "Woods are too thick for horses. We're going in dismounted." He turned to Jack. "You're still a civilian, and you're looking poorly anyway. Stay with the horse-holders."

Jack reined aside while the troopers dismounted and headed into the woods. "Well," he said to the horse, "I won't have to watch Isaac get killed."

*

Isaac sank the axe into the pine stump, splitting out the resin-rich fat wood the soldiers would use for kindling. Today was wood chopping day for the new colored recruits. Yesterday he had wielded a shovel instead of an ax, helping to build up fortifications along the north end of St. Augustine. He had never minded hard labor, but this was not his idea of being a soldier.

He had found acquaintances among the other colored volunteers, including Zeke, who used to belong to Miller but had run to the Yankees before his owner sold his slaves.

Work details were not getting Isaac any closer to finding Lacey and the boys. Zeke had mentioned the Yanks were talking about shipping them someplace distant, up to the South Carolina coast, to train them how to be soldiers. Instead of helping him find his family, they were going to send him away. He had made a mistake enlisting in the army. He wanted to walk off, but Captain Prescott had told him they shot deserters.

A handful of rifle-bearing New Hampshire soldiers stood about to protect them from attack, with a lieutenant in charge. No doubt the guards would be just as quick to make sure none of the new recruits threw down his shovel and left. The army had not trusted the colored recruits with rifles yet, assuming they would not know which end to point at the enemy. The captain had never asked him what he knew.

Isaac set down the axe, picked up an armload of wood and

threw it on the wagon while the bored young private watched him. The boy didn't appear to be any happier with his duty than Isaac was with his. Isaac wiped sweat off his face with his sleeve, dipped a ladle in the water bucket hanging from the wagon frame and took a long drink. He returned the ladle to the bucket and stretched. Then he ambled back to the stump and yanked the axe out.

A flock of birds burst noisily out of the treetops. Isaac stood still, listening and peering into the woods. He caught a flash of movement, then another. He ran back to the guard and pointed. "Somebody's coming at us through the woods."

The private peered in the direction Isaac pointed and smirked. "I don't see nothing. You darkies have some kind of imagination. Get back to work."

Then the shooting started, along with yips and hollers and smoke-bursts from the woods. The young private's mouth formed an astonished O. He lifted his rifle, searching for somebody to shoot at.

Unarmed except for axes, the woodcutters sensibly took to their heels, racing past Isaac. He joined them, sprinting for the safety of the main body of soldiers stationed at the Fairbanks farm. Alerted by the noise, blue-coated soldiers swarmed out to meet the threat. Panting and sweating, Isaac ran into the thick of them, listening to their jeers.

"Give me a rifle, and I'll show 'em fight," he growled under his breath.

*

Jack followed the progress of the skirmish by ear. Before long the Confederates broke through the brush, bringing out a single prisoner, a private who either had too much courage or else froze in fright. Didn't matter, the result was the same. The terrified New Hampshire boy rode double with one of the better-mounted troopers.

Ramon and Russell Cates mounted their horses and led off. Jack joined them. Ramon said, "Infantry is giving chase. We'll outrun them as soon as we cross the creek."

The troop spread out and splashed through the marsh channels, the soldiers urging their tired horses to get a move on.

Cates grinned at Jack. "You should have joined the fun. We surprised them good, drove in the woodcutters and their guards until we ran into a company of infantry. Didn't lose a man."

Jack respected the logic of Dickison's tactics, adapted to the circumstances. The surprise attack inflicted damage to the enemy and threw a scare into them. Then the quick disengagement saved Dickison's troopers from heavy losses a standing fight would bring. The Yankees would brag how their attackers turned tail, while they licked their wounds.

"We're teaching them to stay nice and safe in their garrison," Cates said.

"Suits me," Jack said. "I don't want them paying me any more visits."

Later, Dickison rode up alongside Jack. "I'm told you were picked for a sharpshooter battalion in the Army of Northern Virginia. That so?"

Jack nodded.

"Doctor Williams said it shouldn't be long before you're well enough for cavalry service," Dickison said. "We could use a man with your skills. I want you to volunteer for my company, once you've got your strength back, of course."

Jack had figured out his future. If Dickison didn't get him, eventually the conscription agents would, and he would have no say in where they sent him. Given a choice....

"I'll be honored, Captain."

CHAPTER FOURTEEN

Fighting her dread, Martina ventured out to take her usual place in the plaza. She would not, could not let Prescott frighten her into hiding.

The first day he did not appear. Nor did she see him the next few days. The headache that had plagued her subsided. The fourth day she arrived late because she had done her marketing that morning.

Sergeant Owen bought his lunch from her and she asked him whether Prescott's company had been on patrol. "Yes, Miss. We're just back this morning."

"Where did you go this time?"

"Down toward Palatka. Did a little recruiting, liberated a few slaves. Going to make soldiers out of them."

Jack lived due west, while Palatka lay well to the southwest. Probably they didn't pay him a visit this time, although that was no concern of hers. Her main worry was that Carlo not be caught with Jack.

A corporal standing nearby said, "I'll have some of that rice stuff, Missy, if you please."

She smiled and lifted the lid from the pot.

While she served his dish, the corporal said to Sergeant Owen, "You missed a right sharp little tussle north of town yesterday."

"Were you there?" Owen asked.

"No, Sergeant. I heard all about it, though. The rebs took one of our boys from Company C prisoner."

"Wish we'd been there to help," Owen said.

"Drove in the woodcutters. I guess it's easier to ambush coloreds without rifles on 'em. Anyways, once our boys was alerted, they repulsed 'em straightaway. Don't know if we did 'em any damage, though."

"Must have been a recon," Owen said. "Otherwise they'd have come down in force."

"Wished they did. We'd a swatted 'em like flies."

The two noncoms finished their lunch, gave her dishes back

and moved on, still discussing the big news of the day. Martina inwardly rejoiced that they did not know of any Confederates killed or captured. Some of those soldiers were most likely St. Augustine men, her neighbors or relatives.

A sense of inevitability cloaked her when she spotted Prescott striding her way like doom itself. She could never free herself from him, and that must be the natural order of things. The throbbing at her temples reasserted itself. He would not tolerate her threatening him with his own revolver. She was only surprised that it had taken him this long to chase her down. *Probably too busy on army business to exact his revenge until now.*

She instantly regretted not making conversation with her two previous customers and persuading them to stay a moment longer. She did not want Prescott to catch her alone.

Soldiers loitered nearby, but none within easy hearing.

Although she had so far managed to fend him off, each encounter increased his aggressiveness, and last time he would surely have had his way with her if she had not defended herself.

His sidearm was back in its place on his belt. A reminder of their last confrontation, the sight of it terrified her. She felt for her knife, which was also in its place in her apron pocket. Her stomach knotted. Acid threatened to come up her throat.

Prescott leaned close, unsmiling, eyes hard as grapeshot. "You've been a very bad girl, Miss Sanchez."

"I am a bad girl for resisting your advances?" she hissed. "Captain Prescott, why can't you leave me be?"

"I've been kind to you. I helped you when you were in need. How do you repay me? By threatening me and spying for the enemy."

Martina blinked. "Spying?" she echoed. How could he know?

"Last market day one of our soldiers spotted a man riding away from the San Sebastian. Then he saw your brother walking back from the same place. Close to where I met you. Who was that fellow, Miss Sanchez?"

"How should I know? How could you think anything of that?" Martina folded her arms over her chest so Prescott couldn't see her hands shake. "On market day, all sorts of people came in from the country."

"You were returning from that place just before he was seen.

Certainly you know who your brother was meeting."

"I have no idea." She did not meet his eyes. She wasn't a good liar.

"Yesterday's rebel raid… I fear someone has been informing the enemy of our activities."

Martina shook her head.

"You seem mighty interested in military topics, my dear."

"Only because that's what you like to talk about. You have no case against me."

"I don't have to make a case. I can denounce you and your brother as spies, and Colonel Putnam will certainly deal with you."

Martina stared at him, knowing he spoke the truth.

Prescott reached into his pocket and pulled out two gold pieces. "Twenty dollars, Miss Sanchez."

She blinked at him, dazed, not comprehending. "Are you buying lunch for your entire command? I don't prepare that much food in a week."

"No, I'm offering you a bargain. Let's go to your house. Be sweet to me, and I won't tell Colonel Putnam about my suspicions. I will give you twenty dollars in the bargain. You are not only a bad girl, you are an expensive one."

Enough! She picked up the half-full pot of pilau and heaved it into his face. The pot hit him full on, plastering him with food. He reeled backward at the impact and caught himself as the pot thumped to the ground. Prescott stared at her through the rice, shrimp pieces and tomatoes clinging to his face and dripping onto his shoulders. His tongue flicked out like a lizard's as he licked pilau from his moustache. He rubbed his fingers over his face, wiping off the mess, never taking his hot eyes away from her.

Sergeant Owen and the corporal, still standing nearby, started laughing. Prescott whipped around to face them and they fell quiet, though the sergeant lifted his hand over his mouth to cover a cough.

Prescott brushed off his uniform coat and turned back to Martina, giving her a look of fury. Then he stalked away.

Martina picked up the pot, set it on her handcart and fled down the narrow streets to her house. She whirled inside the fence and closed the gate. She found Carlo in the back yard cleaning ashes out of the *orno*.

"Chico, come inside the house. We're in trouble now."

He gave her a questioning look but followed her.

She bolted the door and said, "Gather what you need to take with you. We'll have to leave at a moment's notice."

"What did Captain Prescott do now?"

She had told Carlo little of Prescott's harassment, but he seemed to know something about it anyway. "He suspects we've been giving information to the Confederates. He has no proof. He tried to blackmail me into doing him favors, I refused, and I humiliated him in front of his men. He will make me answer for it." She picked up her rosary from the table, looped it around her neck and fingered the wooden beads she had worn to a shine. "What shall we do? The pickets won't let us leave town. We have nowhere to hide. Must we wait for the soldiers to arrest us?"

"It doesn't make sense. Nobody caught us, and Jack didn't even come today. He only makes the trip once a week."

"One of their men saw him ride away the last time. I don't think they know who he is, though."

Carlo shook his head. "I won't tell them."

"No. We never saw anyone, did we?" She dropped into a chair and set her elbow on the table, trying to think through her problem. "What can they do to us? Do they hang women? Young boys?"

"Tina, we can't stay here. Even if they can't prove we were spying, Prescott will always make trouble for you. We can stay with Mr. Jack. He told me his door is always open for us."

"Did he?" She rubbed her aching temples. "Take refuge with that man? You can do that, but I couldn't possibly…."

"Where else?"

"I don't know, Chico, I can't think…."

"Whatever happens, you won't be alone, Tina." Her brother put his arm protectively around her shoulders. In her eyes he had grown taller, looking more like her beloved Francisco than her little Chico.

*

Prescott rubbed the sloppy wet bruise on his forehead and fought an urge to follow Martina Sanchez home to beat her senseless. Only the presence of witnesses forced him to exercise restraint.

He had tried to be kind, and he had tried to be assertive. For weeks he had suffered rebuffs, ingratitude and insults from her without taking action. When she pulled his own gun on him it was an outrage, but one that excited him as much as it gave him pause.

Apparently she, a Minorcan girl, a mere Creole or Spanish or Greek or whatever kind of peasant she was, thought herself too good for a Union officer. Sergeant Owen and other men in his command had laughed out loud when she plastered him with slop.

No longer was their game of chess a private matter. She could not be allowed to go unpunished for insulting and humiliating him in front of his men. Her continuing presence would only remind every private of how foolish she had made him look.

The time had come to get rid of Martina Sanchez.

He returned to his quarters, washed his face and brushed off his soiled coat. He sat down and wrote out a note, disguising his handwriting. He folded the note and placed it in his coat pocket. Well prepared, he called upon Colonel Putnam.

*

Martina offered no resistance when Prescott came for her, backed by two privates. She had made Carlo promise to do the same. "Colonel Putnam wants to talk with you and your brother," he told her. "Come outside while I look through your house."

She and Carlo waited in the yard with the armed guards, young men she recognized, as both had enjoyed her cooking.

"What did you do to get arrested, Missy?" the dark haired private asked.

"I made your captain mad."

He snickered. "That ain't hard to do."

Prescott emerged from the house and loomed over Martina. "This will make a comfortable quarters. I'm going to enjoy living here." He nodded to the privates. "Let's escort them to headquarters."

Colonel Putnam interviewed Martina first. She stood in front of the garrison commander, who remained seated at his desk. Prescott stood at his elbow, hands behind his back, a smug smile playing across his face. The raised red bruise on his forehead marked the spot where Martina's pot had hit him. The guards stood at attention at either side of the closed door.

"These are serious charges, young lady," the colonel said. "You have been accused of spying for the enemy and assaulting a United States officer."

"Sir, Captain Prescott made improper advances. I was only defending myself."

Colonel Putnam glanced up at Prescott. "Improper advances, eh?"

"I believe I've always conducted myself properly, Colonel. Perhaps Miss Sanchez imagines herself irresistible."

"Is that so?" The garrison commander turned back to Martina. "I'm not so concerned with the assault charge." He smirked. "I believe a captain in the United States Army should be able to defend himself from a slender girl armed with an iron pot."

Prescott shifted on his feet, venom in his eyes.

"However, the spying charge is another thing entirely. Captain Prescott, on what basis do you make this accusation?"

"We have reason to believe Miss Sanchez and her brother have been meeting with a rebel sympathizer from outside town."

"Reason to believe, Captain Prescott?" the colonel said. "What is your evidence?"

"One of our privates saw a rider leaving the area where Miss Sanchez and her brother were fishing on the other side of the San Sebastian. Private Dobbins is available to testify. I had a man watching for the rider the last market day, but he didn't show. Otherwise we would have captured him. Apparently he is a partisan scout."

"How can you be sure of that?" The colonel gave Prescott a skeptical look. "A rider on what sort of business? Can Private Dobbins identify the man?"

"Unfortunately, he wasn't close enough to see his face." Prescott plucked a folded paper from his coat pocket with a theatrical flourish. "However, upon searching Miss Sanchez's home, I found this." He spread out the paper and handed it to Colonel Putnam, who held it away from his face and examined it.

"Why, this lists our officers, unit strengths and details about our deployment, including our activities north of town, where the attack took place." The colonel glared at Martina. "Pretty damning, I must say."

She felt the room closing in on her. Could Carlo have written something down? Could he have been so unwise as that and to leave it for Prescott to find? "Sir. May I see the note?"

He held it up to show her but did not give it to her.

"I've never seen it before. Never in my life. This is not my writing and I can't believe it was in my home." She added, "It isn't Carlo's writing, either."

"Someone must have given it to you to pass on. Who was that?"

She shook her head. "No one." Then she thought of something and looked at Prescott, who was smiling in his self-satisfied fashion. So far she had kept quiet about his harassment, fearing the Yankee command as much as she feared Prescott. Now she had nothing further to lose by speaking up. "Captain Prescott must have written it so he could make a case against me. He has nothing else."

Prescott reddened and cleared his throat. "Colonel, you are familiar with my handwriting. Who are you to believe, one of your officers, or this Secesh trash?"

"Captain, I believe we can conduct this interview without insulting anyone," the colonel said. "Miss Sanchez, you may wait outside. Private, bring in the boy."

Martina exchanged a worried look with Carlo as they passed each other. The door closed behind him. She stood outside wishing she could hear anything from within the office. She believed Colonel Putnam was a fair man. But how could he discount the importance of the note Prescott produced? What would Carlo say? She prayed the boy had enough good sense to speak as little as possible.

Soon the door opened and the guard escorted her back into the office. She took her place next to Carlo and found his hand. He pressed it in a reassuring manner.

Colonel Putnam sat back in his chair. His gaze moved from her to Carlo and back. "A serious charge has been brought against the two of you." He glanced at Prescott, who stood with his arms crossed looking down his nose at her.

The colonel continued, "Information is moving freely between the lines now that we've opened the bridge for trade twice a week. Sadly, it would be a simple matter for anyone so inclined to pass information through. I'm afraid we're going to have to review the practice of allowing market days." He picked up Prescott's note. "However, this tells me you are one of the main informers, Miss Sanchez."

"The note is a forgery," she said.

"I find that hard to believe. I'm going to give you one more chance to tell me where it came from. After you tell me who wrote the note, you will be free to go home and pack. We cannot let you remain in St. Augustine."

"Captain Prescott forged it." Martina didn't look at him but could feel his hateful stare.

"She's lying," Prescott snarled.

The colonel turned his gaze from Martina to Carlo and back again. "Didn't the two of you come up with that excuse before we arrested you?"

"Why would we leave such a note out in plain sight?" Martina said. "Wouldn't clever spies destroy such evidence?"

"Maybe you aren't clever."

The room seemed to spin. Martina rocked on her feet, and Carlo counterbalanced her just enough to let her regain her equilibrium.

"I'll be lenient. Instead of locking you up in the fort, I'll keep the two of you on house arrest until you divulge your contacts."

"We don't have anything to tell you." Carlo's voice sounded unexpectedly deep. When had his voice started to change?

Martina lifted her hand to her aching temple. "Colonel Putnam, I have one request." She shot a furtive glance at the glowering Prescott. "Please do not put that man, Captain Prescott, in charge of us in any way."

The colonel smiled grimly. "I can grant your request." He issued orders to the two guards, who escorted Martina and Carlo back to their house.

*

Martina sank into the chair and gathered her rosary into her hand. Carlo paced around the room, his movements jagged with barely controlled rage.

"Who wrote that note?" Martina asked him. Because the guards were outside the door, they could speak in low voices without being heard.

"I didn't," Carlo said. "I never saw it before."

"Did you know a Yankee soldier saw Jack riding away?"

Carlo shook his head. "He's so careful, I never thought anybody would see him."

"Your friend isn't invisible," Martina said. "But they didn't know it was him. It's a blessing he didn't meet you today or they would have caught you both. You didn't tell them about Jack, did you?"

Again he shook his head. "I told them it must have been somebody coming to market. I told them we're innocent. It isn't Mr. Jack's fault we're in trouble."

She wanted to blame Jack but found herself agreeing with Carlo. "Prescott has been threatening me for weeks. He wanted another thing to blackmail me with, so he made up something."

"You haven't told me everything Prescott did to you."

"What would you have done about it? Something crazy that would have brought the whole Yankee army down on us?"

"You're the one hit him with a pot."

"You should have seen him." Martina giggled. She imitated Prescott's startled look and snaked out her tongue, lizard-like, to lick imaginary rice off her upper lip.

Carlo finally grinned. "I wish I'd been there."

*

The next day Colonel Putnam sent for Martina and Carlo. She was getting accustomed to the indignity of having Yankee soldiers escort her everywhere she was ordered to go. As before, the colonel interviewed them individually, but this time he spoke with Carlo first.

After a few minutes it was her turn.

Colonel Putnam sent the guard out. She was alone with the garrison commander.

"Have you decided to tell us who gave you that information?" he asked.

She crossed her arms. "I already did. Captain Prescott forged it."

"You and your brother are well-rehearsed." Colonel Putnam sighed deeply. "What could be his motivation for such a thing? Are you saying Captain Prescott is a spy? How absurd."

"No, sir. I'm saying he wants revenge. I humiliated him in

public, and he wants to get rid of me. He was the one who searched my house and claims he found the note there. I know he made it up."

"That is a serious charge, Miss Sanchez."

It was her turn to sigh. "Take it as you wish."

"I believe you two were having an affair of the heart."

"No, sir." She lifted her chin. "He was pursuing me, but I never asked for his affections. I discouraged him, but he would not leave me be."

"If what you say is true, why didn't you complain about him sooner?"

"You would have called me a troublemaker and sent me away. You send away everybody who is troublesome."

The colonel flipped the corner of a paper on his desk. "I'm afraid you have become a distraction. You cannot stay here."

"I was right, wasn't I?" Martina looked down at the floor. "I have no power. Do what you will." She shifted her gaze and met the colonel's eyes. He appeared bothered, as though he didn't enjoy making a decision about her.

"This is all very unpleasant," he said.

"Unpleasant for you. For us it's life or death."

"It is life or death for us as well," he said. "Our men are under constant threat of attack, and we just lost a man taken prisoner in a rebel ambush. We can't afford to let you people help the enemy."

"What are you going to do with us?"

"I'll give you until noon tomorrow to pack your things and leave town. If you haven't left by then, I promise I will imprison you both."

Martina bit her lip and nodded. "Then we'd better get started."

"You can hire a conveyance, or you can walk. It makes no difference to me." The colonel stood up, came around his desk and opened the door for her. "Escort these two home," he told the guards. He gave them further instructions to allow the prisoners to find their best way out of town.

As Martina left the colonel's office, she heard him say to his orderly. "Find Captain Prescott and tell him to report to me."

For a fleeting moment she hoped Prescott would get into some sort of trouble. *No, the colonel will probably give him a medal, instead.*

CHAPTER FIFTEEN

Jack set a chunk of pine upright on the stump and brought the axe down on it. Cleaved in two, the wood fell away. He chucked it onto the pile and picked up another length of wood. Isaac had told him oak was best for distilling purposes. He would use this lightwood for cooking and heat. The weather would be turning colder soon, so he'd best lay in an extra supply of firewood.

Still stove up from the forty-mile-long cavalry march, he had to work through the pain. He did not want to squander the small amount of laudanum the army surgeon had given him. Nor would he dose himself with popskull while wielding an axe. His arms and legs were still attached, and he liked to keep them that way.

Though early November, the warm afternoon sun had induced him to remove his shirt. Later he would take a swim; the river had not yet absorbed the autumn chill. He flexed his lame right hand. The scars down the length of his arm showed red and white. The arm had healed crooked, but the muscles were strengthening with use. Soon he would be using it to heft an army rifle if Captain Dickison had his way. Jack split another log and threw it onto the growing pile.

Nip's bark announced company. Jack looked toward the road and shrugged into his shirt. He picked up the Colt revolver from next to the stump and fastened the belt. He kept the shirttail out to make the weapon less obvious. Nonetheless, if the Yankees returned, they would steal this one, too.

Instead of a force of blue-coated horsemen, a single wagon approached. The mule pulled it toward his house through the path he and his horse had trampled out of the weeds. Jack made out the driver, a St. Augustine man. More importantly, Carlo walked alongside and the woman in a faded black dress rode in the shotgun seat.

He remembered telling Carlo they could come to him in an emergency. What disaster had brought them all the way out here?

Carlo ran toward him, followed by the capering Nip. Jack noticed Francisco's haversack slung over the boy's shoulder. Carlo turned and fell into step with Jack to meet the wagon. "The Yankees made us leave," the boy said. "You told me we could come to you."

"That's right." Jack rested his hand on Carlo's shoulder and switched his attention to Martina. She sat watching him in her guarded way, her head high and prim, letting him know she may be compromising herself by coming to him, but he'd better by God not try to take advantage.

Lord, he wanted to. Though she was dusty, travel-worn and not at all happy, she seemed to him the most desirable thing on earth.

Stifling a smile, he removed his hat and offered her a formal bow. "Welcome, Miss Sanchez."

She nodded, mirroring his decorum. "Mr. Farrell, I hope this isn't too much of an imposition."

"Never." Jack greeted the driver, an older man he knew only as Mr. Toombs.

The driver nodded. "Where you want me to park this rig?"

The wagon contained a couple of trunks, Carlo's mullet net, provisions and some household items. "As close to the porch as you can," Jack said. "We'll unload it there." He walked alongside the wagon, close to Martina, Carlo trailing behind.

After the driver pulled the wagon to a halt and secured the horse, Jack offered his hand to assist Martina. She accepted his help and dismounted, light as a bird wing. Her hands felt almost as work-roughened as his. She looked up at him and some of the defensiveness disappeared, leaving her shell-shocked and uncertain. He resisted the urge to wrap his arms around her.

"You want to know what happened," she said.

"I can make a good guess. Yankees wanted your house?" He nodded toward the porch. "I've been living in the right half. You and Carlo can have the other. It isn't ready for company. I apologize for that."

"You had no reason to expect us. I don't plan to stay long, just until we find a place of our own." She ran her gaze down his flannel shirt. "Your cast is gone. How is your arm?"

"Seems to work tolerably."

"I'm glad you're getting better."

"It's only a matter of time."

Carlo had started unloading the wagon and setting their worldly goods on the porch. Jack, Martina and Mr. Toombs joined him. Within a few minutes the transfer was complete and the driver was on his way back to St. Augustine.

While Jack helped them move in they told him a disjointed account of how they came to be ejected from their home. After a supper of smoked mullet Martina had brought and greens from his garden, the three of them rested on the edge of the porch. He heard the rest of the story, at least as much as Martina was willing to tell. He suspected she was holding back something about Prescott.

"It was a good thing you didn't meet me yesterday, because they spotted you the time before," Carlo said. "They might have set a trap."

"I was just back from a spin with Dickison's men." Jack idly rubbed Nip's ears, and the hound leaned into the massage.

Carlo's eyes lit up. "You rode with Captain Dickison?"

"I guided them across the marsh, that's all. North of where we were meeting."

"The raid?" Now Carlo was really interested. "You led the raid?"

"The captain was in charge, and I didn't join in the fight. I'm still a civilian, though they want to change that." Jack turned to Martina. "You're saying the Yankees accused you and Carlo of spying? Just because they spotted someone riding in the vicinity? Pretty flimsy, as evidence goes."

"Captain Prescott needed an excuse to punish me. He came up with a forged note of military information to make us look guilty." She smiled ironically. "None of them had any idea how guilty we really were."

Jack's jaw tightened. "I should never have involved you and Carlo."

"It would be easy to blame you," Martina said. "I told Carlo not to spy for you. Then I questioned Captain Prescott and passed on the information, too." Her dry smile deepened. "I did it because I wanted to. No one forced me."

*

Martina rested her head against the porch support, drowsy

after her ordeal and grateful to reach a temporary place of refuge. Carlo had insisted they come here, and she had given in because she had no better ideas. For the time being she was content to let others take charge.

A whippoorwill made its call, and somewhere near the spring run a bullfrog croaked. She had never set foot on the Farrell homestead before. The rustic house, along with the deep woods and rough fields, seemed just the kind of wild lair Jack would call home. She watched him from the corner of her eye while he and Carlo discussed the best places in the river to avoid the cypress knees and cast a net. The two of them had taken a swim earlier, and their hair was still damp. Jack had warned her and Carlo to watch out for gunboats in case the Yanks decided to practice on a moving target.

Jack was a good-looking scamp, with intelligent, far-seeing eyes and hard but even features. The fading scars on the right side of his face reminded her he could have died with Francisco.

Her opinion of her host was improving. Jack seemed a curious blend of contrasts. Well-bred gentility one moment, frontier toughness the next. His apparent decency seemed at odds with his orneriness. He had been genuinely considerate, and she was ready to forgive his behavior at last year's dance when he had acted like a common rowdy. She planned to repay his hospitality by helping him tend the garden and by preparing their meals until she found another place to stay.

She could comfortably tarry here until then, although she doubted she could avoid creating a scandal, living at the home of the notorious Jack Farrell. Did it really matter what anyone thought? She and Carlo had to survive somehow. Besides, she sensed that unlike Prescott, Jack possessed a shred of honor and would not cruelly force himself on her.

Martina shut her eyes, noticing her headache was gone, along with the threat of Prescott pushing, pushing, pushing. Of course she missed her own house. Would she ever live there again? The thought of Prescott moving into her bedchamber disgusted her. But she was free of that man and hoped he would never again torment her. She had implored Mr. Toombs to keep secret where he had taken her, and she prayed he would heed her plea. She feared Prescott would find her here.

She had held back from Jack and Carlo the intensity of

Prescott's assaults. No good could come of telling them. She could not predict what Jack would do, and she did not think she could stop Carlo from a disastrous attempt to defend her honor.

She must have fallen asleep, because the next thing she felt was Carlo gently squeezing her hand. Startled awake, she blinked in the darkness and realized it wasn't Carlo but Jack who had awakened her. "Do you really want to spend the night on the porch?" he asked. "A chill is coming on."

He helped her up. Half asleep, she didn't resist as he led her across the porch. His firm arm righted her, and she leaned into him. She remembered the dance, how assertive, supple, and strong he was. Then he and Francisco had ruined everything.

As she returned to wakefulness, it struck her how much instinctive trust she now granted in letting him escort her to her room.

"Good night, Martina," he murmured. "I'll do my best to keep you safe."

"I know." She slipped through the door and listened to him walk away.

*

Next morning Jack found Martina already at work under the kitchen roof. He paused at the end of the dogtrot and admired the sight of her setting the cast iron skillet on the grate over the wood fire. Her face glowed in the reflected flames, her fine features set in concentration. As always, her delicate beauty made his throat catch. Her bare toes peeked out from under her skirt, and he guessed she was not quite as prim as she made out. Her presence was a gift, one he must approach with care.

She noticed him and smiled. "You must have slept soundly."

"It's my clear conscience. It allows me to oversleep." He didn't add that his mending body craved rest. The laudanum he took last night knocked him cold, and most of the time he had little motivation to rise early – until now. Jack regretted not waking sooner.

"I brought some coffee with me." She picked up a pot, poured the hot liquid into a cup, and handed it to him.

He inhaled the aroma and took a sip of the strong brew. "Real coffee? Where did you get this? I haven't had any for months."

"I was able to buy it from the Yankee commissary. Carlo found some eggs, and I'm going to fry them. He checked your trotline and cleaned a mess of fish. I'm frying them, too. I hope you don't mind our raiding your chicken nests."

"Mind?" He chuckled. "I could get used to this. Seems you're in charge of the kitchen. I'm sure it'll be an improvement over my sorry attempts."

She smiled, obviously comfortable in her element. "I'd rather cook for the three of us than for a bunch of Yankees."

"Those Yankees are going to be sorry they kicked you out of town."

She laughed softly and then sobered. "I don't think Captain Prescott planned for everything to turn out this way. He wanted to keep me within reach. After I made his men laugh at him, he didn't want me around to remind him."

"He's a fool." Jack thought of more pungent words to describe Prescott. He curbed them in Martina's presence.

"At first I thought he was nice, but he likes to push people around." Martina cracked the eggs into the skillet. "Do you think he will be coming back here?"

"Most likely. If you see anybody that looks like soldiers, or if the dog sounds off, you and Carlo better hide in the house or in the woods."

A troubled look, real fear, shadowed her face. She had cause. How could he defend the three of them from Prescott and a dozen armed men?

"What did he do to you, Martina?"

"Nothing. I wouldn't let him. He was angry with me for defending myself." She heaped food onto a plate and handed it to Jack. "Let's not talk about him any more."

A breaded, crisply fried fish, an egg, and a big serving of grits adorned the plate. It looked and smelled delicious. "Keep on feeding me like this, and you're going to make me fat."

She rested her hand on her hip, cocked her head and gave him an appraising look. "You could use a little flesh to cover those bones."

Carlo jogged up, Nip at his heels, as though he'd sensed breakfast was ready. The three of them carried their plates and their coffee to the porch, where Martina insisted Jack say grace. Afterward he made short work of his breakfast.

"You are well off here," Martina said. "You have most everything you need."

"I can't take any credit. Isaac planted these crops, and I'm reaping the harvest. By all rights it belongs to Pop."

"Carlo wanted to help you market the produce," Martina said. "But we can't be seen near St. Augustine, either."

Jack shrugged. "If Pop wants anything, he'll have to come get it."

"We can sell it somewhere else," Carlo fended off the persistent Nip then threw him a bite of fish. "Aren't there trading posts near here?"

"There used to be one at Picolata," Jack said. "Along with a big guest house. When the Yanks shut down the ferry, the stage line and the steamboats, that ended the trading, too. Probably we'd have to go down to Palatka to find the nearest one."

"Don't you grow cotton?" Carlo asked. "I didn't see any."

"Pop liked oranges better than cotton. A cotton crop will bring bugs that ruin the oranges. Besides, he needed more workers to cultivate cotton, and he wouldn't own a slave. He had me, my brother Dan, and Isaac, until my brother and I left home."

"Show me what to do, and I'll help," Carlo said.

"I have to feed the animals now. Come with me and I'll show you around." Jack picked up his empty plate and said to Martina, "That was a fine breakfast. Don't you want to see the place with us?"

"I'd like that. The dishes can wait."

He offered her his hand and helped her to her feet, suspecting she needed no help but allowed it anyway.

*

Martina walked toward the river with Jack as Carlo and the dog ran ahead, full of energy and excitement. She missed her house, she missed the spirits of her departed family and would probably lose her legacy forever. At least she didn't have to worry every waking moment about Prescott coming after her. Jack treated her with respect, and his brand of male aggressiveness did not threaten her the way Prescott's did.

"You've been kind to take us in," she said. "I didn't know where else to come. We had no time to make other arrangements.

Carlo told me what you said, that it would be all right."

He smiled wryly. "We outcasts have to stick together."

"Of course I can't stay here." She chose her words carefully. "It's an unacceptable arrangement."

"I'm satisfied with it."

"Jack, you know what I mean."

"You're afraid of what people will say about you."

"Carlo hardly counts as a chaperone. Surely you realize –"

"What people, Martina? Are they going to offer you any help or just criticize you for doing what you must to survive?"

She didn't reply. Jack was the only person who had done a thing for her and Carlo lately. She had also noticed he did not fault her for trading with the Yankees, though some of the townspeople did.

"You're free to go wherever you want, and I'll help you any way I can. Let's think this through." He turned to face her. "Do you have relatives you can visit?"

She shook her head no. "Most of them are still in St. Augustine, or they left and I don't know where they went."

"Then they aren't any better off than you are."

She nodded, biting her lip.

"I have neighbors, the Colees and Mrs. Tanner. Would you rather stay with one of them?"

"I – I hardly know them." She stared at Jack. She hardly knew him either. "I suppose—"

"Jacksonville is half burned and has been invaded by the Yanks twice. They seem to be taking over the seaports, and our army hasn't stopped them. You need to go inland to get away from them. Would you go to Lake City? Waldo? Gainesville? Palatka?"

She didn't reply. She knew nothing of those towns. Her whole life's experience had centered around St. Augustine. Her mind flailed like an animal snared in a trap. She had never come up with any place she would rather live than her own home or perhaps this backwoods place on the river.

He pressed on. "Do you have enough money to live, wherever you decide to go?"

"I have a little money."

"Enough for how long?"

She raised her hand to her temple, feeling the familiar throb, regretting the five dollars in U. S. money she had to pay Mr. Toombs for her ride here.

"Once you decide where you're going, how do you plan to get there? Will you walk? How do you expect to cross the river? It's a couple of miles wide here and the channel is deep. As far as I know, there's no ferry left in operation within miles. I crossed the river at Jacksonville after dark, to avoid the gunboats. It cost me all the money I had left because the ferryman claimed he was risking his life. We used to have a rowboat, but it's gone. Isaac said the Yankees busted it up to keep our side from using it. I guess a ferry might still be operating down Palatka way."

"I – I'll think of something."

"Face it, Martina." A sardonic smile crossed his face. "Like it or not, you're stuck here with Jack Farrell, the scourge of East Florida womanhood. You might as well make the best of it."

"I didn't mean… You've been a perfect gentleman."

"A gentleman, you say? Darlin', it's been a strain."

Some of Martina's tension relaxed as she laughed with him.

"Look at it this way," he said, his eyes alight. "You have plenty to eat, a roof over your head, and if you get cold, I promise to warm you up."

She punched his arm, making sure it was his good side.

"Whoa." He took a step back. "Are you telling me you'd rather freeze?"

"Remember, I grew up with two brothers." She crossed her arms and tried to look stern although she couldn't help enjoying his teasing. "I realize men are beasts."

He flashed his jaunty grin. "They taught you well, and you'd best not forget it."

CHAPTER SIXTEEN

Leon Farrell halted the buggy near Isaac's cabin and climbed down. Surprised but not pleased, Jack swatted garden dirt off his hands as he walked over to meet his father.

"Well, Jack," his father said, looking him over with little warmth. "I was led to believe you had one foot in the grave. You are somewhat worse for the wear, but you don't look so bad."

"I'm glad to see you, too, sir. How is Margaret?"

"Your stepmother is content. She prefers the social life in town, you know." Jack's father scanned the landscape. Carlo had gone to the river, and Martina was at the house, so Leon probably did not yet know about Jack's guests. "With Isaac gone, the weeds will certainly take over," the older man said. "Unless you've acquired a taste for farm labor."

"I never objected to hard work," Jack said. "It was just hard to live here."

"How are my oranges? Are they turning yet?"

"Have a look. The crop ought be good this year if we don't have a bad freeze."

As Jack led his father toward the grove, Carlo returned from the river with his net. The boy waved at them and Jack waved back. "Isn't that the Sanchez boy?" Pop asked.

"You ought to know him. He delivered our letters."

"I heard Colonel Putnam banished him and his sister from town. Is she here, too?"

"I'm letting them stay in one part of the house; I'm in the other."

The older man let out a dry chuckle. "You never had any trouble finding a pretty girl for your pleasure."

Jack stopped short. "Let's get one thing straight. Martina Sanchez is a fine young woman, and I won't have you insulting her."

"Defending her honor, are you?" Pop turned to face Jack, an unusual degree of approval in his eyes.

"She does it pretty well on her own."

"Good. You could do worse than to settle down with that young lady."

"It has occurred to me."

"She and her brother were accused of spying. I suspect you had something to do with it."

"Is that what you told your Yankee friends?" Jack crossed his arms over his chest. "You already told them where to find me. You should present them with a claim for the four chickens, the pig and the produce they stole."

"They did? I went to Colonel Putnam and asked him to grant protection to my holdings and my reformed rebel son. He promised to do so as long as you weren't taking up arms against the federal government. They shouldn't have stolen my property."

"Take it up with Captain Prescott, then. He led the troops."

"If you'd take the loyalty oath, they'd leave you alone."

"I doubt that. Wouldn't they try to conscript me? Force me to enlist in the Union Army?" Jack took off his shirt, exposing the crooked, lacerated arm. "It's the same on this side down to my boot-tops. I earned this fighting for the Confederacy, and I can't change sides as easily as I change clothes."

Leon stared at the ravaged flesh. His Adams apple bobbed as he swallowed, then he said hoarsely, "Your own brother is a lieutenant in the Union Army."

"The men I fought beside, those are my brothers." Jack dragged his shirt back on. "Dan is with my enemies. I hope he comes through this all right, but I don't wish him victory."

Carlo wandered over, curiosity on his face. "Howdy, Mr. Farrell."

"Howdy, Carlo," Leon said. "Unhitch the mule, water it and turn it out in the pasture. I'll be spending the night."

Jack and his father walked in sullen silence until they reached the orange grove. "I have no way to get the fruit to St. Augustine," Jack said. "Neither Carlo nor I better show up there. Maybe Palatka."

"They would go to feed your *brothers* in the Confederate Army."

"Come to think of it...."

"I can drive over and get the produce once a week and sell it in town," Leon said. "It isn't as dangerous now that our army has cleared out most of the Secessionists from this side of the river."

"Cleared out? I heard about their methods," Jack snorted.

"Shall we compare methods? Your sham secessionist government threatened to confiscate my property because I am a Unionist. Rebel toughs threatened to hang me. They didn't have the cods to put on a uniform to fight for their sorry cause. I suppose they thought it more prudent to pick off supposedly helpless Unionists." Leon's eyes glinted. "I winged one of them, and the cowards ran for it."

"I met one of those boys," Jack said. "He wasn't happy with you. Now he's riding with a partisan band under a Captain Hough. Seems brave enough with a crowd to back him up."

"Friends of yours?"

"Not exactly, but we parted cordially enough." Jack shrugged. "They didn't offer to hang me."

"I thought it best to bring Margaret into town. Isaac stayed here because he wanted to remain close to his family."

Leon strolled between the trees, looking over his oranges as lovingly as he would a favorite child. "Isaac wouldn't tell me why he changed his mind and joined the army. He just left the mule tied up at my house and was gone before I had a chance to talk with him. Didn't he ask you to go with him to see Miller?"

Jack told Leon about their disastrous attempt to purchase Lacey and the boys. "I heard Miller was dead. Somebody found him in the river a few days later."

"Well, then." Leon cupped a green orange in his hand. "He won't be stealing any more of my cows."

*

After a tense supper, watching father and son spar like gamecocks, Martina sat with her mending on the porch while Leon Farrell smoked his pipe. Jack's father had descended like a hurricane to blow away her serenity. Jack had eaten little, then made an excuse of needing to take care of some chore or other, and Carlo had disappeared toward the river.

"I did what you suggested, Miss Sanchez," Leon said. "I came to see Jack, and I'm sorry to say not much has changed between us."

Martina took a pair of Carlo's trousers out of her mending basket and examined the split seam. The boy was growing out of his pants faster than she could alter them. "Both of you have your minds made up about one another." She wanted to add each brought out the worst in the other, but she stopped short.

Leon frowned at her comment and took a drag on his pipe. "I didn't expect to find you and your brother here."

"Do you object?" Martina was glad to find a needle already threaded, because her nervous fingers would not have guided the thread easily.

"I do wonder about the accusations Captain Prescott made about you."

"Carlo was meeting with Jack. You knew that. As for the rest…." She glanced up at Leon and met his gaze. "Captain Prescott forged his evidence."

"Why would he do a thing like that? He liked you. I noticed him courting you."

"Courting me?" She smiled wanly. "The man is a brute."

"Jack's reputation isn't spotless, either."

"I don't care about his reputation any more. I care about his actions. He's been good to us, letting us find refuge here. I hope you will allow us to stay until we can come up with another solution."

"I wouldn't be so heartless as to evict a woman and a young boy from their only shelter." He smiled dryly. "Besides, Jack would bring you right back here as soon as I returned to town. Whatever my orders, I can rely on him to do the opposite."

"We are trying to make ourselves useful." Martina lined up the seam and pinned it together. "Carlo is a good worker and Jack needs help. I believe his injuries are still a torment, though he doesn't complain."

Leon stared at her, barely smiling. "And of course there's no romantic attachment between you and Jack."

"Sir, he's been a friend to us. He helped us when no one else did, and he's been a perfect gentleman." She tensed her jaw and met his eye. "We are not living in sin."

"If that's the case, he's certainly reformed."

"Perhaps he has."

"I tried my best to civilize him, but he has always been wild and hot-headed," Leon mused. "You seem to be an industrious, level-headed young woman. I told him he could do worse."

"It's good you have such a high opinion of me, sir." She

allowed sarcasm to color her voice.

"I hope Jack doesn't disappoint you as he has me."

"He won't, Mr. Farrell." She threw the unfinished trousers into the basket. It was time to finish the conversation and retire to her side of the house. "I don't expect anything of him but his friendship."

*

Jack finished stirring the mash at the still, then carried a jar of sweetened brew from Isaac's last batch to the dock. He sat down in the dark, letting his feet dangle over the river. At night the far bank presented only a smudge of tree line. Somewhere in the dark he heard a splash, and night birds echoed across the water in full cry.

He gulped down a mouthful of popskull. It hit fast, edging a pleasant lightness into his head. Nip flopped down on the boards next to him, and he reached over to stroke the dog's head. Jack felt especially stiff and out of sorts tonight. He'd already taken a dose of laudanum but not enough to have much effect.

Between his father's disapproving presence, their usual rows, and the chronic pain from his injuries, he wouldn't be able to sleep without assistance. He took the flask of laudanum back out of his pocket and sloshed the small amount of liquid.

"Not much left, Nip. I can stretch it out with some of Isaac's finest brew. That ought to set me right." He took a slug and replaced the cork.

"How 'bout that. Pop came for a visit. Came to see his wayward son." Jack shook his head. "Correction. He came to see his oranges. Hell, I believe the Yanks were more amiable company."

He watched the lights of a Yankee gunboat flickered in the distance, downriver toward Jacksonville. If the boat came his way, the darkness would shield him from the crew's sight.

He took another sip of the liquor then pulled out the flask of laudanum again and regarded it in his hand. "I can get more. Doc Williams has plenty of opium in his medical supply," he told Nip. "I'll get it next time the troops come through." He drank the rest of the laudanum. Already the pain was easing. He yawned, a good sign.

The temperature had dropped steeply after sundown, but it was not too cold for him to sleep outside on the dock. He had slept in snow. What was a little cold snap? He was forbidden to bed down where he really wanted to – with Martina.

If he went inside he would have to share the house with Pop instead, and endure the drip, drip, drip of corrosive comment. Though Pop wouldn't dare lay a strap on him nowadays, his tongue flayed as effectively. Stomach tied into knots, Jack had eaten hardly any of the fine supper Martina had prepared. He still wasn't hungry.

He took another slug of the popskull. After a few minutes the lightheadedness went wrong, and his brain seemed to spin freely inside his skull. He shut his eyes hoping the bad feeling would subside. It didn't. He swung his legs onto the dock and lay on his good side.

A wave of nausea hit him, and he moved over to throw up into the river. He spat out the acid taste, groaned and buried his face in his arm. He had always been able to gauge how much drinking he could get away with, and he was nowhere near that limit. He rolled onto his back and felt the empty laudanum flask pressing his shoulder.

He sure was not up to struggling to the house to hear his father's lecture about the evils of drunkenness. The stars twirled dizzily over him and he closed his eyes. He would just have to sleep it off.

*

Next morning, by the time Martina started the fire for breakfast, Jack's father was already loading produce onto the buggy for the trip back to St. Augustine. He had asked her if she knew where Jack had gone. He grumbled about how his son disappeared when there was work to be done. Carlo had promised to pitch in after he checked the trotline.

She would be glad to see the older man leave and take his discontent with him. Besides, Leon Farrell's bothersome line of questioning made her feel defensive. Apparently he held the notion Jack ought to make an honest woman out of her. He had no right to imply she needed to be made honest.

Of course, people were going to make assumptions. She

had expected gossip from the moment she let Carlo talk her into throwing them on Jack's mercy.

Carlo ran to her empty-handed. "Tina, you have to help Jack. I think he's sick."

"Where is he?"

"He's lying on the dock. Um, Tina, I think he's had too much to drink. I had a hard time waking him up."

"Jack is drunk?"

"Don't be mad at him. He and his father were arguing last night."

"Is that his excuse?"

"He didn't say. I told you because I didn't want Mr. Leon to know."

She picked up her skirts and marched toward the dock, heedless of her bare feet. The dog met her and escorted her the rest of the way. Just as Carlo had said, Jack lay flat on his back on the rough boards of the dock, a small metal flask and a jar half full of clear liquid nearby. His eyes were slits, and his mouth was ajar.

"Jack. Jack, wake up." She shook his shoulder. He groaned, and his eyes opened wider then slid shut. He smelled of vomit.

Carlo whispered, "Is he all right?"

"He won't be." Furious, she gave a fleeting thought to kicking Jack in the ribs but remembered his injuries. Instead, she shook him harder. "Wake up. What is the matter with you? Carlo, get a bucket of water, a cup and a clean cloth."

After the boy left, she hissed, "How dare you let Carlo find you like this." She yanked Jack's shirt. "He idolizes you and wants to be just like you. How dare you."

Jack focused on her, blinking stupidly.

"You're freezing cold. Did you spend the whole night out here without a blanket? Are you trying to kill yourself?"

He elbowed up, then dropped his head back. He gave her a crooked smile. "If I don't succeed, I believe you are mad enough to do it for me."

Some of her anger drained away. She released her death grip on his shirt, took off her shawl and threw it around his shoulders. "Why, Jack? What makes you do this?"

"Must have been the opium." He stared down at the flask. "I took a dose so I could sleep."

"What about this?" She picked up the jar and sniffed the strong smell of alcohol and cane juice. "You were drinking, too."

"I ought to be able to hold a little bit of liquor." He struggled to a sitting position and glared at her. "You want to believe the worst?" he snarled. "Take a good look. This is the real Jack Farrell. Blind drunk, passed out like a cow hunter on payday."

She shook her head. "The Jack Farrell I know is decent and responsible. If anybody told him different, he would laugh at him. He wouldn't go off and drown himself."

He looked away and swallowed. "Believe me, I didn't get this way on purpose. Martina – I am sorry as hell."

Carlo brought the bucket and set it down. Martina dipped the cup in the water and handed it to Jack. He sipped it slowly. Then she wrung out the cloth and gave it to him so he could he wipe his face.

"We can't let your father see you like this."

"Why not?" Jack coughed. "He would find the sight satisfying. He knows I'm a reprobate, and he enjoys being right."

"Can you eat breakfast?"

He shook his head no.

She took the cloth from him, rinsed it, wrung it and gave it back to him. "You look better now. You smell better, too. I pray it was just the laudanum and the liquor making you sick."

Jack turned to Carlo. "Your sister is afraid you are busting to get into this shape. Any chance of that?"

Carlo shook his head.

Jack grinned at Martina. "See, I'm not such a bad influence. I'm teaching your brother how not to act. Forgive me?"

"I'll think about it." She couldn't resist a grudging smile. "Carlo, you'd better check the fire. See if it needs more wood." The boy didn't argue with her, but his departure was nonetheless reluctant.

"Martina, what you think of me is important." Jack looked off across the river then back to her. "The last thing I wanted to do was offend you."

"You have a peculiar way of showing it. Can you get up now?"

He nodded, and she helped him to stand. She didn't want his father to think worse of him, if that were possible. He wobbled, then righted himself. What she saw in his eyes made her understand what he tried to hide. "So many things inside you are broken," she said softly. "It isn't just your bones that need mending."

He closed his eyes but did not shut himself off from her completely. "Martina…." His voice was unsteady. "Do not let me run you off."

"Promise you won't get drunk again."

He met her gaze steadily. "I swear. Anything."

She realized what she should have known all along. This difficult and dissolute man was in love with her, and her attraction to him warred with her better judgment. What was she to do about him? For the time being, they needed each other.

Better prospects for husband material had vied for her affections, but the war had carried them off. Only Jack had washed back, resembling a shipwreck. He was worth salvaging, if only for his own sake. Was she up to the job?

She reached for his hand. "I believe in you."

He gripped her hand in return, and his expression softened. "Thank you."

She glanced toward the house. "If we don't show up soon, your father is going to be convinced we were up to no good."

His wry smile slid back into place. "If only he was right about that, darlin'."

*

By afternoon, Jack had recovered from the worst hangover of his life and regained his equilibrium. Earlier that day his father had left with his load of produce, and life had settled back to the way Jack liked it. That evening he returned to the dock to watch the river flow by. Instead of a jar of popskull, Martina and Carlo joined him. She sat tantalizingly close to him with her legs tucked under her wide skirts. Jack let his feet swing over the edge.

This morning she had lit into him like an avenging angel. Never again did he want to earn her wrath. Yet her words echoed in his mind.

I believe in you.

The dark-eyed Minorcan girl kept bringing him gifts he hardly deserved.

I believe in you.

He had earned the respect of employers, fellow workers and

army comrades, along with the affection of casual girlfriends. None of that mattered as much as Martina's opinion. Twice he had lapsed into disgusting behavior in her sight, and twice she had forgiven him. He must not show her a third episode.

I believe in you.

It was only a matter of time before Carlo found the still. Jack wanted to teach the boy how to tend the cooker, though Martina would most likely have a conniption at the notion. Considering this morning's humiliation, he had better consult her first.

In good time.

The light from the setting sun reflected on the ripples on the river's surface, creating a dazzling, jeweled effect. No Yankee boats were in sight this evening, adding to the scene's peace. He pointed to a log-like shape that drifted slowly, leaving a slight wake. "There goes an alligator," he said. "See his eyes sticking up?"

Martina leaned forward. Carlo, who stood at the end of the dock, peered into the glare. "I see him."

"You can hear the bull gators roaring at night during mating season," Jack said.

"Do you hunt 'gator?" Carlo asked.

"Pretty dangerous," Jack said. "Landing a big 'un is not a one-man job. If we could do that and render the oil, the money might make it worthwhile. I'm not fond of 'gators. They raid the trotline, and we lost a couple of good dogs to them." He nodded toward Nip, sprawled out next to Carlo. "They like dog meat."

Carlo squatted down to pat Nip.

"I always lived in town." Martina shivered. "This is a wild place."

"Don't you like it, though? I used to sit out here after the work was done. There was a hawk's nest up in that pine across the cove. Gone now. Margaret, my stepmother, didn't seem too happy in the woods. The critters made her nervous. While the Seminoles were making trouble, she went into town and stayed there until things got quiet. She's done the same thing again. Can't say I blame her."

"I'm surprised she didn't come with your father to see you," Martina said.

Jack shrugged. "I guess she's seen enough of me."

"Don't do that."

"What?"

"Talk yourself down."

He fell silent, watching the reptile ripple past.

"I'll miss going to Mass," Martina said.

"The priest used to ride over from St. Augustine and hold Mass at the Colee place every so often. Maybe he still does."

"You are Catholic?"

"Fancy that." He did not mention how much time had lapsed since he had darkened the door of a church.

Carlo pointed down the bank. "There's a coon!" he whispered. The creature waded into the shallows, hunting along the river bottom for its supper. Carlo left the dock and stalked after it among the cypress knees. The animal immediately spooked and lumbered away. Carlo didn't give up but followed along the bank.

"Pop said he wouldn't tell the Yankees you're staying here," Jack said. "I guess he doesn't want to mix up the situation any worse than it is."

"What happened between you and your father?" Martina shook her head sadly. "So much anger."

"I lived, and my mother died." Jack rubbed his jaw. "Anyway, we kind of got a bad start, and I never could please him so I quit trying. I left home as soon as I could find somebody willing to hire me. I did pretty well, working for Mr. Samuel Morse's company, stringing telegraph wire along the rail line from Jacksonville over to Cedar Keys. Worked myself out of a job, so I to came back to St. Johns County and found other things to do."

"And plenty of girlfriends?"

He snickered. "Had to beat 'em off with a stick."

She popped his ear before he could dodge her blow. "Jack Farrell, you're the most conceited man I ever met." Her voice rippled with laughter.

He captured her hand, and she surrendered it.

"What do you intend to do? Keep on farming?" she asked.

"Here, I'm nothing but a tenant. It's just a convenient place to live until I sort things out. My father needs somebody to manage the place now that Isaac is gone. I'm not his first choice, but he doesn't have any others."

"It's strange how you ended up on different sides."

"My brother Dan joined the army to fight the Seminoles back in '55 and stayed with it. His sentiments were with the Union, like my father. I never agreed with either of them about much. I joined the St. Johns Grays. Francisco and I were in the same company until I got pulled out for the extra duty. We got along all right as long as I wasn't dancing with his sister."

"Francisco wouldn't be very happy with me right now," she said softly.

He let that slide. "The captain selected some of us, who were good with a rifle, for a sharpshooter unit. We got special training and equipment. I can judge distance and have a steady hand. It was dangerous duty, but I had more freedom than the usual foot soldier."

She seemed interested, so he continued telling her things he had always kept inside. "You can't make out faces at hundreds of yards. Never know who you're shooting at, nothing personal about potting some fellow at a distance. I knew Dan was in the eastern army and worried about him ending up in my telescope. I usually went for the officers…" He shrugged. "Anyways, Dan is safe from me now."

"Then you won't reenlist after you're well. I'm glad to hear that."

"Dickison asked me to join his troop."

"Why should you? You've done your share. The army said you were disabled. You can stay here and wait out the war."

"You think either side will let me do that? Once I'm fit enough to go back to the fighting, I'll be a wanted man."

"That doesn't seem right," Martina said.

"I've thought about my choices. I could take the loyalty oath and be subject to draft into the Union Army. I can let the Confederates draft me and send me God knows where. I can volunteer with the local partisans." He paused. "Or I can hide in the swamp and tell them all to go to – well, you know what I mean."

The silence between them grew troubled. Then he said, "If I go with Dickison, I probably won't have to leave the state and maybe I can do some good. He covers the ground between Jacksonville and Palatka. I can help him protect folks from the Yanks. Folks like you and Carlo."

"I don't know what you should do. I'm just grateful you took us in."

"Everything is better with you here." He made bold to bring

her unresisting hand to his lips.

"We try not to be a burden." There was a smile in her voice.

He kissed the back of her hand, and she leaned closer. He turned his head and found her accepting lips. He slipped his arm around her back and pulled her to him. Their kiss deepened, and he breathed in the clean scent of her, savored her light salty taste and sensed her responding to him.

She broke free, sidelining his urgent reaction and thwarting his intentions. "My goodness, Jack."

"Just my luck to lust after a good Catholic girl," he murmured.

She laughed and stood up. "Let's go to our own rooms before you break down my resistance."

He grinned up at her, thinking he wasn't far from doing just that. "You won't let me storm your breastworks?"

She cuffed his ear again, laughing harder. "You are a very bad man."

"I have a reputation to uphold, you know."

"And tonight I'd better say ten extra Hail Marys."

CHAPTER SEVENTEEN

A few days later, after Carlo finished his morning round of feeding the livestock and baiting the lines, he took advantage of free time. He knocked about the farm with Nip, exploring places he had not yet investigated. At the sugar cane field he hacked off a long stalk with his pocketknife then disjointed it into short lengths. He stuck all but one in his jacket pocket. With his knife he skinned back the rind on the piece he kept out to get at the sweet, stringy pulp.

Martina was busy as usual with household concerns, and Jack had disappeared without telling him where he had gone. Now it seemed Nip had deserted him as well. He looked around and spotted the dog slipping off into the woods.

Carlo rushed to the place he had last seen Nip and located an opening hidden by dense underbrush. "Nip! What are you chasing?" He heard the dog shuffle through the leaves and followed a foot-trail that led along the spring run. A good ways through the woods the path opened into a clearing. He stopped at the edge, startled to find a complicated-looking arrangement of barrels, tubes, jars and a metal cooker over a fire.

"Hey, Carlo," Jack said, looking up from where he squatted stoking the fire. "You found our little enterprise."

"Nip led me here, sir."

"Bad dog." Grinning, Jack stood up and wagged his finger at Nip, who panted and waved his long tail.

Carlo looked into one of the barrels and sniffed the sweet, alcohol-smelling liquid gruel inside. "What are you doing, Mr. Jack?"

"Making a cash crop."

"So you made what you were drinking the other morning."

"Isaac made that batch. Most likely it didn't mix with the laudanum I took. I won't be doing that again."

"No, sir, I hope you don't. I was afraid you weren't going to wake up."

"Isaac showed me how the liquor is made. I hope I didn't forget anything." Jack went on to explain how the corn mash fermented for a few days in barrels, then he added cane syrup. "The sugar makes it boil up. After the whole mess settles down, I dip out the liquid and cook it here." He pointed to the hot closed kettle, which rumbled at a boil. "The good part steams off and goes through this tube. I have to keep water running into the barrel to cool the liquor, which drips out where I collect it in this jar."

Fascinated, Carlo studied the setup. "You need any help?"

"Could always use help." Jack rubbed his chin. "I could teach you how it's done."

"What does it taste like? Is it anything like wine?"

Jack shook his head. "It comes out stronger, and it isn't sweet. You have to dilute the stuff before you can drink it."

"Can I try it?"

Jack raised an eyebrow. "Martina will kill us both."

"I won't tell her."

Jack picked up an empty jar and held it under the dripping tube. The clear liquid dribbling into the jar reminded Carlo how bad Jack looked the morning he found him on the dock. "I don't know. Maybe I'd better not."

"Suit yourself. I don't drink it straight. Add water at least."

"I want to see what all the fuss is about."

Jack dipped water from the spring, added a few drops to the jar and handed it to him. "Don't say I didn't warn you."

Carlo took in a whole mouthful, but when the stuff blasted into his mouth the burn and the astringent taste made him gag. He spat out what didn't trickle down his protesting throat.

"Don't like it?" Jack seemed amused.

"How does anybody drink that stuff?" Carlo croaked. "Uh, why would you?"

"Think of it as medicine. A soldier gets shot; it eases the pain. But you'd better stay away from it until you're old enough to shave. Or get shot."

"I think I'll stick to wine."

"Yeah, good idea."

Carlo sat on a fallen log and watched Jack add dry sticks to the nearly smokeless fire. "Tina said you're going to join Dickison's troop."

"Seems so."

"I want to go with you," Carlo said.

"Give it a year or two. Maybe when you turn sixteen."

"When are you going?"

"Won't be long. A few weeks. After I enlist, I ought to be able to visit now and then, make sure y'all are all right." Jack sat down next to him. "You can support yourselves here, and my father doesn't seem to mind you staying. He wants somebody taking care of the place anyhow."

Carlo reached into his pocket. "Want a piece of sugar cane?"

Jack nodded. Carlo handed him a segment then took out his knife to peel his second piece, thinking how much he missed Francisco. He and Martina were a good team, but because she was a girl she wasn't always interested in the same things he wanted to do. He enjoyed the time he spent in Jack's company.

Carlo took a long breath before speaking. "Can I ask you something?"

Jack started to husk the stalk Carlo gave him. "Yeah."

"Are you going to marry my sister?"

Jack let out a startled laugh. "You got a shotgun?"

Carlo shifted on the log, not liking the joke.

"Why are you asking?" Jack turned serious. "You know where she's been sleeping."

"It isn't that." Carlo's face burned. "I – I'd like to have you for a brother-in-law."

Jack continued to peel his sugar cane. "That's nice, Carlo. That's a real nice thing to say. You know, it's the first time a fellow has ever proposed to me."

Carlo barked out his own startled laugh, breaking some of the tension in his chest.

"Martina would make some man a good wife," Jack said.

"She can cook, and she works hard." Carlo said. "Don't you think she's pretty?"

"Real pretty. Once I told her she was the most beautiful girl in the state. I meant it, too."

Carlo gathered his courage to ask the next question. "You love her, don't you?"

Jack gave him a long look. "Who wouldn't? She is just about perfect."

"We're almost a family anyhow."

"That's so. Has she talked to you about it?"

"No, sir."

"I'm not so sure she would like the idea. If she doesn't... she hits, you know."

Carlo made a face. "That's the truth."

Jack cut off a piece of cane pulp to chew, then stood up and peered into the jar collecting the liquor. "It's coming along, but slow. I'd better stay with it 'til dark, probably finish the whole batch tomorrow."

"Teach me how it's done. After you leave I can keep making it."

"That's up to Martina. You are her responsibility."

"She's my sister, not my mother."

"I'll talk to her." Jack chuckled. "And I'll be sure to keep my distance."

*

"You want him to help you do what?" Martina planted her hands on her hips and glared at Jack. "You want him to help you make whiskey?"

"I can trade it for stuff we need." Jack lounged against the porch support looking innocent, as though he hadn't just suggested an outrage.

"So that's where you got the liquor. You made it."

"Isaac made that batch. I'm new at it. Like I told Carlo, I'll be selling it or using it for trade. He can do the same after I'm gone."

"Jack Farrell, you can do whatever you please. It's your business, it's your home, and you are a grown man, though sometimes I wonder." She chopped her hand toward Carlo. "My brother is only fourteen. He doesn't need to learn such a trade or acquire a taste for corn liquor."

"It tastes like medicine," Carlo said. "I won't be drinking it."

She whipped around to face Carlo. "Chico, leave us now. I need to talk to Mr. Farrell privately."

Carlo slunk down the porch steps and stalked off.

Martina whirled on Jack. "How does he know what it tastes like?"

"I played a dirty trick, gave him a good dose. We agreed it was nasty."

"What are you doing to my little brother?"

"He's got to learn stuff, Martina."

"How to be a drunk?"

Jack's jaw tightened. "How to handle himself. How to support himself and you, with more ways besides fishing. Do you want him to turn into a mama's boy?"

"We do fine without him making corn liquor."

"What he really wants to do is shoot at Yankees. Working the still would give him a job that keeps him home and out of trouble."

"I forbid it," she snapped.

"As you wish. I'll tell him to stay away from the still."

"What about you? Are you going to be sampling your own cooking?"

His eyes turned to stone. "I'll be keeping some of it."

"Promise me... promise me you won't let Carlo find you in that condition again."

"We've already discussed that." Jack turned on his heel and left.

Martina fought back tears. She depended on this contradictory man whose faults were as glaring as his strengths. Yet, she feared her lack of faith in his judgment had rubbed salt in his raw places. Wiping her eyes, she groped for the rosary she kept around her neck and stroked the beads, craving serenity.

*

Next morning Jack rekindled the banked fire with fat wood and dipped more buck, the fermented liquid, into the cooker. Yesterday's labor filled a few jars, but he had plenty left to distill. Because of the shortage of glass jars, he had to clean out a barrel to contain the hard-won fluid.

He fought the urge to down a good-sized sample, what Martina obviously expected him to do. "I promised her I wouldn't get sotted," he said to Nip, who hiked his leg on a clump of moss at the edge of the clearing. "What was I thinking?"

Yesterday's chat with Carlo had encouraged him to consider approaching Martina and asking whether she had the slightest interest in signing up with him for the long haul. It seemed unlikely. He wanted Martina desperately, but every time she warmed to him, he found a way to infuriate her.

He picked up his axe from the wheelbarrow, chopped a length of oak in two with satisfying violence and added the halves to the fire. During their discussion, she had made it plain what she thought of him. He should have expected it, considering she had seen him at his worst. Nonetheless, her quick assumption that he was up to no good rankled. He didn't need to put up with a woman telling him how to live. Martina was too damn perfect.

He demolished the next chunk of oak with enough force to send pieces flying into the underbrush.

Martina wasn't the only pretty girl he had known, but she was the only one who had lit such a fire of longing in his heart. And brought him to heel.

Maybe if he tried harder….

Carlo called out from down the trail, letting Jack know he was coming before he burst into the clearing. Nip trotted over to greet the boy.

"You aren't supposed to be here." Jack picked up another log from the supply in the wheelbarrow.

"Yes, sir. That's what Martina said."

"Then skedaddle. Your sister is mad enough."

"Did you ask her?"

"You heard her."

"I mean about marrying you."

Jack split the log and added it to the growing fire. "Carlo, Martina and I, we're none too happy with each other right now."

The boy's shoulders slumped in disappointment. *All the poor kid wants is a daddy.*

"She just got mad, like she does with me sometimes." Carlo stood straighter. "She still likes you."

Jack had his doubts. "Anyway, you'd better not let her catch you here. Martina packs a punch, and we're not allowed to hit her back."

*

"Have you seen a young St. Augustine woman named Martina Sanchez?" Prescott looked down from atop his horse at the Cracker woman.

Surrounded by her ragged, towheaded brood, the smallest thumb-sucker crooked in one arm, Mrs. Tanner narrowed her eyes, showing hostility. "Even if I did, why should I tell a Yankee officer?"

"I might be grateful enough to show you a little consideration." Prescott leaned forward in the saddle. "Tell the boys to go easy on you."

She shaded her eyes with her hand and looked toward her smokehouse, where Prescott's men were busy loading its contents into a wagon. She turned back to him and shook her head. "Ain't seen nobody like that. And I'll thank you to tell your thieving darkies to put my meat back."

"Tell your husband to quit the rebel army and take the oath. Then we'll leave you alone."

"He didn't have no choice. He was conscripted."

"That's what they all say, but it matters not a whit." If she were better looking, he might have been tempted to make her a different deal. As it was, he felt no such interest in the rawboned, sun-browned woman. She might have been pretty in her day, but the four brats, only a year or two apart, had worn any trace of allure from her. He wouldn't be surprised if a fifth whelp was cooking under her apron. Her hardscrabble husband was welcome to her.

"We call this a traitor tax. You ought to get him to desert and take the loyalty oath so you won't have to endure this privation."

"The army took him up north."

"Down here, everywhere is north," Prescott mused.

The woman shooed her three eldest into the house. After they scurried off, she marched to the smokehouse, the baby on her hip. Prescott nudged his horse closer, curious to monitor her actions.

She said to one of the colored soldiers. "Zeke, put that ham back. It ain't yours."

"Army property now." Zeke tossed the ham to Isaac, who set it carefully in the wagon bed.

"Mr. Miller could a known about this, he'd a whipped you good."

"He dead." Zeke stuck his hand inside his jacket, affecting a pose. "And I am in the Union Army now."

Prescott had been learning about the Negroes. They seemed to enjoy taking from their former masters. He hoped they enjoyed standing up to gunfire as much.

Next she appealed to Isaac, who shook his head. "Ma'am,

Captain tell us what to do. I got to follow orders."

Another of the colored recruits, whom Prescott's party had just picked up, tied Mrs. Tanner's mule to the wagon alongside a skinny cow.

"How am I to plow with no mule?" The woman's voice raised to a bothersome pitch. "That cow was supposed to help us get through the winter."

Prescott said, "Boys, after you clean out the smokehouse, get those chickens. Truss them up, don't kill them yet, so they'll be nice and fresh when we cook them for supper."

Mrs. Tanner just stared at him. It was good she had gone speechless, making it easier on the ears.

She recovered enough to ask, "What are we supposed to eat? I have four little ones to feed."

"I suppose that's your problem, ma'am." Prescott said blandly. "Perhaps you should get your husband to come home and take care of you. Or consider removing yourself from here. We're reserving this side of the river for good Union folks."

The woman watched, defeat on her face, as the men rounded up her chickens and added them to the bounty.

"People who declare war on the United States better get used to the consequences, Prescott opined.

Sergeant Owen rode up from where he had been supervising confiscation of the rest of the livestock. "I think we're about done here, sir." He seemed subdued, as though he was not as enthusiastic about the work as the other troops.

"Shouldn't we fire the house, too?" Prescott thought out loud.

At overhearing this, Mrs. Tanner edged toward her shack, panic in her eyes. Prescott laughed, enjoying his joke.

Owen didn't reply but seemed to be waiting, stony-faced, for confirmation that his commanding officer really meant to burn the place.

"We'll save it for another time," Prescott said, feeling magnanimous.

"Yes, sir," drawled Owen. "When we come back, we can pretend they're Indians and shoot the woman and her kids too."

Prescott gave him a suspicious look. "Are you being sarcastic, Sergeant?"

"No, sir. I really meant it." The noncom yanked his horse's

head around and bawled at the men to get a move on.

Prescott tipped his cap to Mrs. Tanner and headed out with his little band. "The Farrell place is next to the north," he told the sergeant. "I'd sure like to find an excuse to arrest that fellow."

"Maybe he'll show some fight," Owen said. "But I don't take him for that big a fool."

"If we can prove he's been aiding the guerillas, that would give us cause to bring him in." Prescott had not told Owen about the upbraiding Colonel Putnam gave him for taking Farrell's chickens and pig. When Prescott had pointed out an unrepentant rebel lived there, the colonel said it didn't matter because the younger Farrell had connections and was out of action anyway.

"If he points a weapon at us, we have every right to put him down," Prescott said. "Give the boys a taste of blood. This patrol is their only chance before we ship the coloreds up to Beaufort for training."

Between recruiting efforts around the countryside and the Negroes who had drifted into St. Augustine, Prescott had gathered enough Negroes to fill a company. He had left most of them on work crews at the garrison. Sergeant Owen had suggested he bring a couple of darkies on this patrol as guides, as they seemed to know their way around. He had found Owen' counsel correct, as he often did. It annoyed him that he had to lean on an enlisted man for advice.

Prescott's thoughts wandered to Martina Sanchez, as they often did. Fortunately, he had convinced the colonel his accusations against her were valid. He regretted making good on his threats to get her banished. Now he had no idea where to find her.

Nobody, whether in town or the countryside, would tell him where she had gone. He hoped he might find her hiding place before he had to leave for South Carolina, and entertained himself imagining what he might do about her when he did.

CHAPTER EIGHTEEN

Jack scraped dirt off his boots before stepping onto the porch. He and Carlo had spent the day hiding provisions near the still, out of sight of Yankee foragers or other thieves. Next, he planned to build holding pens deep in the woods for the livestock.

Nip's carrying on made Jack turn around. When he spotted the dark blue coats, he caught his breath in alarm. He ran out back, where he found Carlo bringing a load of firewood to the kitchen, and Martina preparing to fix supper.

"Yanks coming." He unbuckled his gun belt and handed it to Martina. "Don't use this unless you have to. Both of you hole up inside where nobody can look through a window and see you."

"What about you?" Martina asked. "What are you going to do?"

"See what they want."

"Be careful, Jack." She looked frightened, but he did not know how to reassure her. "Don't give them an excuse to hurt you."

Carlo stepped forward. "I want to help you stand up to them!"

"No. Keep out of sight." Jack gripped Carlo's shoulder for emphasis. "That's an order. Don't give yourself and Martina away."

He watched Martina and Carlo rush in through the back door, confident the oncoming Yankees couldn't have spotted them. Then he walked around to the porch, trying to calm himself. Facing his enemies unarmed was hard to do, but wearing the service revolver would only provoke them.

As far as they know, I'm still a cripple. He nestled his right arm close to his body, let his hand dangle as though useless, and rehearsed a hacking cough.

The Yankees had gained the front yard. He recognized Prescott and the sergeant leading the pack, mostly consisting of white soldiers. Isaac drove a wagon, loaded with goods, trussed fowl, and a cow tied behind it. Nip had jumped onto the wagon and stood perched on the shotgun seat next to Isaac, hanging on with his toenails as the wagon swayed and bumped to a halt.

Jack recognized Zeke, who used to live at Miller's place. Zeke rode a little marsh tackie, his feet dangling below the pony's barrel, as did a couple of other Negroes in civilian clothes. The sergeant looked the house over, turned his head and spat tobacco juice.

Jack whistled for Nip. The dog bounded off the wagon and ran to the porch. Jack told him to lie down, and Nip flopped at his feet.

"Another social call, boys? Captain Prescott, Sergeant Owen. If I'd known you were coming I would've put on a clean shirt." Jack coughed into his free hand.

Prescott said, "You been behaving yourself, Farrell?"

Jack faked an easy-going grin. "Now Captain Prescott, do you really think I'd risk offending you fine Union boys by misbehaving?"

"Better not," Prescott said.

Jack met Isaac's eyes. "Got to say you look good in blue, Isaac."

Isaac nodded. "I told 'em not to shoot my dog."

"Good thing." Jack glanced down at the hound, which for once was minding him by lying at his feet. He hoped Carlo was as obedient about staying inside the house.

"Well, now, Farrell." Prescott regarded him from astride his horse. "It appears you're almost back to fighting weight."

"Who's fighting? I don't have a quarrel with anybody these days." Jack hawked and cleared his throat. He spat and noted Prescott's look of distaste.

"The woods are full of rebel guerrillas," Prescott glanced toward the road. "Surely you've had contact with them—so, where are they? What's their strength? What are they up to?"

"You think I know all that stuff?" Jack snorted. "I should be flattered." He coughed again.

"I catch you getting mixed up with those rebs, and you'll pay dearly. Take the loyalty oath and keep us informed… maybe – we'll leave you alone," Prescott said.

"Sure you will. Did you get the bill from my father yet? For taking those chickens and the pig that belonged to him?"

Prescott's face darkened, and Jack knew he had hit a sore

spot. The Yankee officer turned to his sergeant. "Have Isaac give you and the men a tour while I finish my conversation with this self-professed ignoramus."

*

Martina and Carlo sat on the floor, backs to the wall, so the Yankees could not see them through the window. She held Jack's revolver in her lap, a puny defense against twenty armed men.

She had recognized Prescott's voice. Her mouth dried up, and her temples pounded. Her own safety seemed less at risk than Jack's. She did not believe Prescott knew she had taken refuge here. "Pray," she told Carlo under her breath. Both of them crossed themselves. Clutching her rosary, she mouthed a plea for their safety.

After Prescott sent his men off, he continued to badger Jack for information. Then she heard the Yankee captain say, "I'm looking for a St. Augustine girl, a Martina Sanchez. Know where she went?"

"Miss Sanchez." Martina imagined Jack looking off, pretending to gather his thoughts. "I think I remember her. Good looking Minorcan girl?"

"She told me she knows you. I thought she might have come here."

"Don't I wish!" Jack launched into another coughing fit. After he recovered, he panted, "Is she one of those guerillas you're going on about? What do you want with her?"

"That's my business," Prescott said. "I ought to take a look inside the house."

Martina exchanged a panicked look with Carlo. He started for the revolver, but she slapped his hand away and drew the heavy weapon closer. "No! Let Jack talk him out of it," she whispered.

She prayed he found the right words.

"I've got nothing to hide," she heard Jack say. He coughed again. "You're welcome to come on in, if you're not afraid to catch what I've got."

Martina could not stand to let Jack face the monster alone on her account. She stood and held the revolver muzzle down, hidden in the deep folds of her skirt, ready to step outside and confront Prescott if it came to that.

*

153

After what happened at Mrs. Tanner's place, Isaac was surprised when the captain ordered the men not to take anything from the Farrell homestead without his say so. He guessed it had something to do with Mr. Leon and Mr. Dan being Unionists.

Isaac drove the mule to his old cabin, and Sergeant Owen gave him permission to enter. The sergeant had taken to him, said he was smart for a colored man. Not many could read a little and do sums. Maybe he could get a promotion.

He climbed down, opened the door and stepped inside. Everything was as he had left it, but the sacks of corn meal were gone. He figured Jack had put them to good use souring mash. His good humor left when his gaze fell on the bed he had made for Simon and Micah.

Isaac had been hopeful about this ride in the country, thinking maybe he could find out something about Lacey and the boys, but nobody he had met on this side of the river claimed to know a thing. He still had that wad of money he had earned and kept it secret so nobody got any ideas to steal it. But it couldn't buy him what he wanted, so what good was it?

He turned away from the unused bed and gathered up personal items he had left behind, knives, a blanket and his extra underwear, then climbed back onto the wagon.

He didn't know what the captain and the sergeant expected to see. The garden appeared to be in good order, planted in winter vegetables. Everything was mostly as he recalled. He didn't want the other soldiers to find his still and bust it up because some day he might come back and need to make a living.

The sergeant said, "Well, boys, I don't see no sign of rebs. What about it, Isaac?"

"No, Sergeant. Don't see nothing out a place." Isaac could have told them about Dickision's scouts coming around to see Jack. Probably he ought to tell now that he was in the Union Army. If he did they might burn Mr. Farrell's place and make a prisoner of Jack, especially if they figured he still had fight in him.

The captain already knew Jack used to be a reb, so maybe he knew enough.

The sergeant grumbled something about wasting their time if they weren't allowed to forage or arrest the Farrell boy. Isaac didn't think Sergeant Owen had much use for the captain.

They looped around by the river and back to the house, where

Jack remained on the porch, hanging onto the support like he needed it to hold him up. Isaac knew him well enough to see that underneath he was kind of coiled-like. The captain sat on his horse watching Jack like he might look at a varmint.

The sergeant had mentioned they had taken Jack's revolver last visit and his smart mouth almost got him arrested. Isaac believed it. He had a bad feeling the Yanks were going to push Jack too hard and his temper would blow. Jack didn't start fights, but he sure had a way of finishing them.

Sergeant Owen said, "I don't see no sign of a reb campsite."

The captain said to Jack, "We're going to keep checking up on you."

Jack glanced up at Isaac. "You ever find Lacey?"

Isaac shook his head.

"I hear anything, I'll see what I can do."

"'Preciate that, Mr. Jack."

"See here, what's all that about?" Captain Prescott broke in.

"My wife, sir," Isaac said. "She got sold, and we don't know where she went to."

Prescott glared at Jack. "You sold his wife?"

"I never owned anybody, never sold anybody." Jack cleared his throat. "Isaac was a free man until y'all got hold of him."

"That's so, sir. It was Mr. Miller sold Lacey." Isaac caught Jack's quick sidewise look and wondered how much he had guessed about how Miller got dead.

Prescott turned to Isaac. "You try to desert, we'll have you hanged."

"No, sir. I ain't deserting."

"Let's get out of here," the captain ordered. "Sergeant Owen, form the men up."

"Isaac," Jack said, "take care of yourself, hear?"

"I will, Mr. Jack. You, too."

*

Weak with relief when she finally heard the horses leaving, Martina sagged against the wall. Jack finally opened the door and came inside, the dog padding close behind. She handed over the revolver.

"They're gone." Jack looked drained after dealing with the Yankees.

"Thank the Blessed Mother," she said. "I was afraid for you."

"I guess my father still has some influence, too. They didn't steal any chickens this time. Did you hear Prescott ask about you?"

"I never heard you cough so much. That was a clever idea." She smiled weakly. "I'm grateful you kept him from finding us."

"He wouldn't have gotten past me."

She pressed her knuckles to her throbbing temple. "I was going to shoot him if he tried to harm you."

Carlo added, "She had the revolver ready."

Jack gave her one of his penetrating stares. "Good thing you didn't have to."

"We prayed hard."

"Maybe that's why." Jack slipped the revolver into the holster and fastened the gun belt around his waist. "They didn't take me prisoner either." His expression relaxed.

Carlo said, "Were you talking to Isaac?"

"Yeah," Jack said. "He's a regular soldier boy."

"I'd better start the fire so Martina can fix supper," Carlo said.

"Ought to be safe to go out now. I doubt the Yanks have any reason to come back, for the time being. Take Nip with you."

Carlo opened the door a crack, then slipped outside.

Martina wanted to go to Jack, craving yet fearing his embrace. The thought of him standing weaponless, the only barrier between her and Prescott, shamed her.

Last night Jack had come in for supper after dark, smelling of wood smoke, tired and unsmiling, saying he had finished distilling the batch. Martina had detected no sign of drunkenness and felt guilty for wondering.

He had wolfed the fish chowder then told her, as he always did after a meal, how much he liked it, but remained distant and quiet. She had apologized for her sharp tongue when Carlo went to fetch wood for the fireplace. Jack had accepted the apology, but his coolness remained. Had she wounded his pride beyond repair?

She stepped forward and laid her hand on Jack's arm. His eyes met hers. She studied his face, the sharp, hungry features. The hope and self-doubt she read ran counter to his typical cocksure attitude, and she understood he needed for her to trust him.

Jack's nonchalant roguishness and the dark places in his soul challenged her, but she recognized the folly of accepting only his best qualities while trying to change the rest. He deserved better.

She slipped her arms around him, pressing her cheek against his bony shoulder in wordless thanksgiving. He gathered her to him and held her for a long moment. She drew away, fearing she would enjoy his embrace too much.

"Martina," he said huskily. He pulled her close again and kissed her with an intensity that caught her off guard. She forgot to resist, yielding to a rush of joyous acceptance.

The barking dog and a shout from Carlo seized their attention. Martina broke from Jack and rushed to the front door in a panic. He gripped her arm, restraining her. "Wait until I find out what's going on." He went outside, closing the door behind him.

She heard Carlo run up the porch steps calling out, "Tina! It's Cousin Ramon!"

"You can come out," Jack said from the other side of the door.

She stepped onto the porch and peered at the two horsemen riding to the house, both wearing gray cavalry jackets. Jack lifted a hand in greeting as the pair reined in. When he spotted her, Ramon Andreu removed his hat, his confusion evident. Both men dismounted. Carlo ran up to Ramon, and the two engaged in a bear hug.

Martina rushed forward to meet her favorite cousin, her closest living male relative besides her younger brother.

"Tina, what are you and Carlo doing here?" Ramon asked, glancing from her to Carlo, then to Jack.

She embraced him and kissed him on his rough, darkly stubbled cheek. "We were banished, Carlo and I," she said.

"Yanks paid us a visit, then went that way." Jack pointed south. "About twenty mounted infantry, mostly white, handful of colored."

"We've been keeping an eye on 'em," Cates said. "Good lord, what is this, a family reunion?"

"Cousins," Jack said.

"I believe I must be cousins, too." Cates grinned broadly. "Ain't you going to introduce me to the little gal – "

Martina was aware of Jack subtly closing in, cutting off the trooper's approach. In a friendly voice he said, "Russell Cates, these are my guests, Martina Sanchez and her brother, Carlo."

Martina took in the rapidly drawn conclusions on Ramon's face, the delight on Carlo's, and the thin, possessive smile on Jack's. She was most aware of Jack's hand around her waist, holding her firmly. She said, "Ramon, I'll explain everything."

Cates drawled, "I hate to bust up the party, but what about the Yanks – "

"We won't lose 'em." Ramon said to Cates, "Why don't you water our horses and keep a lookout?" He glanced at Jack, then at Martina. "Don't we have some catching up to do, Cousin?" He tossed the reins to Carlo. "Here, Chico. Give Cates a hand with the critters while I talk to your sister." He shot a warning look at Jack. "In private."

Martina led Ramon to the kitchen area behind the house, telling him how she ended up at Jack Farrell's home. "He told Carlo we could stay here. We didn't have anywhere else to go." She shrugged. "Here we are."

"You could go to Lake City, stay with Teresa. She and Ana are living in a boarding house up there."

"We have plenty to eat here. How would we support ourselves in a strange town? Poor Francisco is gone, and Carlo is just a boy. We can't live on your charity, Ramon."

He frowned. "You're living on Farrell's charity now."

"We're earning our keep. He needs our help, at least until he's well."

"He's well enough. Anyway, it's safer in Lake City. Here you've got Yankee patrols like the one we're following, gunboats destroying people's houses up and down the river, killing their livestock, destroying their crops. Martina, this is a disputed area, and you could be harmed here."

"Ramon, is it really safe anywhere?"

He cleared his throat. "That's not the only thing, Cousin."

She glared at him, knowing what was coming from her very proper kinsman.

"I was watching Jack, how he acted with you. He didn't like it when you kissed me, and he wasn't going to let Cates near you."

She had noticed Jack's attitude, too, and found it reassuring. "He just wanted to protect me. We're friends."

"Jack has had his troubles. I fear he isn't suitable –"

"Don't. I won't listen to you speak ill of him."

"There is something between the two of you, Martina." Ramon's expression softened. "It's plain to see. The priest used to come out here from St. Augustine every month. Only if you believe Jack will be good to you."

"He hasn't asked me to marry him, and I'm not...."

"Shouldn't I talk to him?"

She stamped her foot. "We are not living in sin." Martina was tired of arguing that occupying the same property as Jack did not make her immoral. If Ramon had seen them locked in that embrace, her denials would have rung hollow anyhow. "We're just good friends." She touched her fingers to her lips, recalling the thorough kiss, knowing her protests did not succeed in hiding her truth. Jack was more than a friend.

"I can arrange transportation for you and Carlo to Lake City. You can stay in the same boarding house as Teresa."

"I don't want to leave. I like it here."

"With him."

"Yes." She smiled at her cousin, through with the denial, feeling lighter, liberated. "I like him. Maybe I love him. Carlo looks up to him. We're taking care of each other, we three. Yes, he has been good to us, but he isn't perfect, and neither am I."

"Martina, I just want you safe and happy."

She kissed her fingers and pressed them to Ramon's lips. "Thank you for wanting to help. Will you be able to come by and see us from time to time?"

"Captain Dickison keeps some of us local men on this side of the river watching the St. Augustine garrison on account of we know all the trails. Jack was telling us whatever he found out from Carlo, but that's over with. Jack is going to join Company H soon. Real soon."

Martina folded her arms over her chest, aware of the cold wind. "He's already been wounded. Wasn't that enough?"

"We need fighting men like Jack." He looked off toward the watering hole. "We'd better get going, see where that Yankee patrol is off to."

"You aren't going to fight them, are you?"

"Jack said there were about twenty of them. We wouldn't take on that many, not by ourselves."

"Good," she breathed. "That's good. Be careful, Ramon."

Martina and her cousin walked back to the front of the house, where she found Jack tightening the cinch on Ladybug's saddle, Carlo holding the bridle. Jack was wearing his gray jacket.

"Farrell's going with us," Cates told Ramon.

"Jack, why?" Martina threw up her hands. "You don't have to –"

"Sure would like to have one of those Enfields." Jack nodded to the rifle boot on Cates' saddle. "Used one like that when I was in the ANV, except mine had a telescope."

"We only have our two rifles," Cates said. "Captain'll get you outfitted once you're sworn in."

Martina said, "Jack –"

"I am sick and tired of letting those bluebellies push me around." He kneed Ladybug in the side and gave the cinch strap a final jerk. "I'm ready to take it to them."

Carlo stroked Ladybug's neck. "I'm going with you."

"Nope," Jack said. "You'll stay with your sister.'

Ramon said, "He's right, Chico. Don't leave her alone."

"Don't have another horse anyhow," Cates added.

Coming from behind, Martina wrapped her arms around Carlo and drew the boy close, sensing the tension in his body. "Jack, you don't have to do this."

"I'd like to capture a good horse." Jack's smile was hard. "Prescott's riding one that would do, except for the U. S. brand. Wouldn't you like to see us give that son-of-a-gun a hard time?" He appeared much too cheerful at the prospect of taking on the Yankees.

Martina shifted her attention from Jack to Ramon. "You said you weren't going to fight them."

Ramon shrugged. "Don't plan to."

"Might catch a straggler. No telling what we can do," Cates said with a wicked grin. "Three to twenty is better odds then two to twenty any day. Jack's welcome to join up."

"We ought to be back in time for supper." Jack swung into the saddle, and Martina noticed his movements had become freer, less cautious. Soon he would be declared fit and the army would snatch him. She now realized going after the Yankees was more than an obligation. It was his preference.

She fingered her rosary, praying to Jesus, Mary, Joseph and all the saints she could think of as she watched the men ride away.

CHAPTER NINETEEN

Isaac stepped into Lacey's vacant cabin and felt the emptiness settle into his soul. Part of him had cherished the illogical hope that she was home and waiting for him. Instead, he faced a home stripped of inhabitants and their possessions.

He sat down on the cot where he had spent his weekly visits with her. He inhaled, trying to catch the lingering scent of his wife and little boys. All he smelled was smoke from campfires the soldiers had built and the persistent wood and earthen odor of the cabin.

A bit of faded green on the floor next to the cot caught his eye. He spotted the toy horse he had fashioned of palmetto fronds for Simon. He picked up the thatch of dry, brittle leaves and fingered it, tears welling into his eyes.

The patrol had reached the Miller farm late in the day, and Captain Prescott deemed it a good place to spend the night. The captain right away claimed the house for himself and the sergeant. He said the others could sleep outside or in the slave quarters. That was all right; Isaac would be content to sleep in Lacey's cabin. He had hurried through his tasks; unhitching the animals and taking care of them before Sergeant Owen allowed him free time in between duties.

He had rushed here, hoping to find some trace of his family or a clue as to their whereabouts. All he had found was this sad reminder of the last time he had seen them.

Finding nothing but heartache, Isaac left the cabin and walked past the main house onto the dock, recalling how easily he had cut Mr. Miller's throat. A savage thought that he wouldn't mind doing it again surfaced in his mind.

Zeke, coming up behind him, said in a singsong voice, "Old man Miller's dead and gone, and I ain't grievin', no sir."

News of Miller's death had followed Isaac to St. Augustine but no details of what people guessed happened to him. "Anybody know who killed him?" Isaac asked, playing dumb, thankful he was the only person who did know.

"You got any ideas?"

Isaac shook his head. "Maybe nobody did. Maybe he got drunk, fell off and drowned."

"Old man Miller? Most likely somebody pushed him in after they beat his brains out. Good thing I run away before he sold everybody off. I'd likely be in Georgia by now. Wasn't his people done it. They was already gone, from what I heard."

"People standing in line wantin' to do him in." Isaac had often gone over this ground with Zeke, who didn't know any more than he did about Lacey's whereabouts.

*

Jack and the scouts followed the wagon wheel tracks and hoof prints the Yankee patrol had left. The tracks, still visible in the deep sand at dusk, clearly took them to the Miller homestead. The three of them rode slowly, wary of meeting the enemy.

Jack considered the risk. If the Yanks spotted him he could bring disaster down on himself, as well as Martina and Carlo. Yet he felt the need to take action, even if it seemed unwise. He felt fit for the task despite his sickly act in front of Prescott, stronger and more confident than even a week ago.

"They must be headed to the Miller place. It would make a fine camp," Jack said in a low voice.

"They get to sleep under a roof tonight," Cates said. "What do you know about this set of Yanks, Farrell?"

"Captain Prescott is a nasty piece of work, a bullying bastard. The sergeant is a tough old soldier and seems to know his business. The Yanks have been recruiting coloreds, but I don't think they've trained them yet. I believe the New Hampshire boys haven't seen much fighting. Mostly they seem to be good at plundering."

"Appears the Yanks didn't do your place much damage, Farrell," Cates said, "You got off luckier than most folks. They cleaned out Mrs. Tanner, down the road. Stole her stock and provisions."

"Sorry to hear that. What is she going to do?"

"Live on swamp cabbage, gopher stew and poke salad, I guess." Cates shrugged.

"They'd like to do the same for me," Jack said. "But it's my father's property, and he seems to have some influence."

"Influence? With the Yanks?" Cates raised an eyebrow.

"I guess you don't know much about my family. They aren't good Confederates."

"I knew that." Cates said, "What about you, Farrell?"

"I'm the black sheep of the family."

Cates gave him an odd look, as though uncertain of his loyalties. Jack glared back at him, not deigning to explain himself, daring Cates to voice any doubt.

"I don't guess you have anything to prove," Cates admitted. "You've bled for your country, and you're borrowing trouble coming along with us."

"Word is your brother's a Union officer," Ramon said. "Got to be hard on you."

"He left home about the same time I did. Haven't seen him in years." Jack looked straight ahead, letting them know the subject was closed.

They rode in silence for a short ways before Ramon said. "Jack, I told Martina I can move her and Carlo up to Lake City, where they can stay with my wife."

Jack tried not to show his disappointment, but Martina had sought his help as a last resort. Given a better choice, of course she would leave. "When are you taking them?"

"She doesn't want to go."

Jack suppressed a smile, hiding his rush of elation. "It *is* up to her."

"Her situation is awkward, living at your place. Compromising. Besides, the two of you act mighty familiar."

Not as familiar as I'd like. "She and Carlo are my guests, and they're staying in separate quarters. Whatever you think of me, you ought to have more faith in your cousin's virtue."

"Don't get me wrong. I'm grateful you're helping my kinfolk when they need it. With the war going on, things are different, and we have to make allowances. But I still don't approve of Martina staying at your house. She needs to let me take her to Lake City. You ought to tell her so."

"It's up to her."

"Then I have to ask you. What are your intentions regarding Martina?"

"Intentions? Can't anybody in this whole damn state mind his own business, Andreu?"

"As her cousin, It's my –"

"If Farrell don't want her, I'll take her," Cates interrupted.

Ramon snapped, "Nobody asked you. Ride ahead and keep an eye out."

Cates snickered and nudged his horse forward.

Jack slowed Ladybug to give Cates distance. "Has anyone bothered to ask Martina's opinion?"

"Don't you think *you* should?" Ramon turned his horse's head around and faced him.

Jack and Martina functioned as a couple, doing everything but sleep together, to his continual frustration. He wanted her, wanted her for keeps, and knew only one way he could persuade her to let him love her as completely as he desired.

"I intend to. If she'll have me, I'll be honored to make her my wife." He shot Ramon a sarcastic grin. "Then you and I will be relatives. Fancy that."

"Oh, lord." Ramon chuckled. "I ought to be more careful what I ask for."

"We'd better move on quiet," Jack said. "We're getting close. Full moon, not sure I like that."

They caught up with Cates, who said, "It's dark enough to give us cover as long as we stick to the brush."

They tied their horses in the woods and stalked closer to the Miller house on foot, calculating the darkness and scrub would conceal them despite the moonlit clarity of an early night. Jack picked his way stealthily, placing his feet to make the least possible noise. The clutter of dead wood, vines, roots and underbrush, unseen in the deep shadows, threatened to trip him with every step.

Typical of Florida homesteads, a jungle of pine, blackjack oak and palmetto surrounded the cleared fields. The scouts halted at the edge of the brush.

Undulating candlelight dimly illuminated the windows of the house, probably where Prescott had holed up. A sentry, silhouetted by the light of a campfire, walked his section of the perimeter between where the scouts watched and the Miller compound. As he completed a pass he met another sentry, turned, and walked back.

Jack counted a half dozen soldiers lounging around a fire, most likely cooking supper. Apart from them the horses stood, spaced along a tether line. He could not see much past the campfire.

"Probably three or four sentries around the perimeter," Jack whispered. "Anybody see the captain? I really want to burn his bacon."

"You think an officer would be outside in the cold when there's a house to sleep in?" Cates said.

"Wagon and horses are in the center," Ramon pointed out, cradling his Enfield. "We can't get to them without stirring up the whole camp."

"It's a good hundred-yard run with no cover," Jack agreed. "Even in the dark they'd spot us."

"I wanted to capture a picket," Ramon said, "but there's no sneaking up on that boy."

"Take a prisoner and have to guard him all the way back to Jacksonville?" Cates growled. "I don't crave taking care of no pet Yankee."

"We only have two rifle shots at this range," Jack said. "Only one I could hit with a revolver is the sentry. Maybe. I could take him, y'all could pot a couple of the ones around the campfire, then we run like hell. I doubt they'll chase us into the woods. They'll be afraid of ambush."

"That would sure spoil their evening," Cates said.

"Mine, too," Ramon said. "Seems too much like murder."

"They'd do it to you," Cates grunted.

"Yeah, war is nothing but murder." Jack shrugged. "What would you like to accomplish besides raising a little hell?" he asked Ramon.

"The standing order is to bother the Yanks any way we can. We came across them this afternoon, and we've just been watching them, haven't been able to do anything more."

"Don't like the odds," Jack mused. "Anybody else around to even them up?"

"If one of us rode all night and crossed the river, we could let the captain know about what the Yanks are doing. He's way up at Camp Finnegan, clear on the other side of Jacksonville."

"The Yanks will finish their sweep and be back in St. Augustine by the time he could get his troop here," Jack said. "If he thought it was worth the bother."

"Sure would like to put a scare into them," Cates said.

"Then why don't I slip around and see what's on the other

side?" Ramon handed Jack his Enfield. "Y'all can cover me. I'll rely on my pistol."

Jack accepted the rifle and checked the cap to make sure it was in place. "Loaded and ready to fire?"

"Ready," Ramon gave him his cartridge pouch.

Jack hefted the full pouch and attached it to his belt. He lifted the Enfield to his shoulder and aimed toward the sentry, the rifle secure and familiar in his hands. He followed the soldier's slow march with the muzzle of the weapon. "I have the guard in my sights," he said to Cates. "Why don't you watch the fellows around the campfire in case they spot Ramon?"

Cates grunted assent and brought up his Enfield.

Ramon moved off to the right and disappeared within the screen of thicket. "Might be tricky," Jack whispered to Cates. "Hard not to make noise in the dark."

Just then the snap of a breaking stick cracked like a pistol shot in the still night air. Cates swore under his breath. Jack kept Ramon's rifle aimed at the center of the guard's body and curled his finger around the trigger. He did not want to shoot and rouse the whole camp unless he had to.

The guard halted in place, rigid, poised like a pointer, homing in on the sound, his rifle barrel shining in the moonlight. "Who's there?" he called out.

Alerted, the soldiers around the campfire grabbed their weapons. At a distance Jack could not make out their low conversation, only voices sharp with suspicion.

The guard must have sighted Ramon or thought he did. He swung the rifle to his shoulder, aiming in the direction the scout had taken. Jack thumbed back the hammer and squeezed the Enfield's trigger. The blast flared brightly, his shoulder absorbing the recoil. The sentry dropped his rifle without firing, groaned and folded to the ground.

Cates fired next. Shouts and a couple of wild shots erupted from the camp.

"Drop!" Jack shoved Cates sideways and hit the ground. He expected the Yankees to aim toward the muzzle flashes. He judged right. A ragged volley sent bullets buzzing overhead, zipping through the brush.

Jack crawled, holding onto the rifle, then gathered himself and scrambled away from the blown cover. No time to reload the

Enfield. He dragged out his revolver and looked over his shoulder. He could not see Ramon, but he didn't think the Yankees had gotten a chance to shoot at him. He and Cates had drawn all their fire. He was aware of Cates stumbling alongside, apparently unhurt.

Firing paused while the Yankees reloaded. The door to the house banged open. "Fire and move. Keep them off Ramon." Jack raised his revolver and squeezed off a shot at a figure that ran out of the house. Then he moved again. Cates did the same. As before, the Yankees fired at the muzzle flashes, but their marks had already left.

"How goddamn many are there?" A voice shouted.

A figure burst out of the woods and sprinted toward them.

"He's running! Over there! Get him!" someone called out.

"It's Ramon," Cates said. Jack continued to make a diversion, firing and shifting position.

Ramon dived back into the woods, breathing hard. "Let's get out of here," he panted.

The three of them crashed through the dark woods making too much noise, but it did not matter any more. They found their horses, mounted, and dug in their heels to spin away from the aroused camp.

A short distance down the road they reined in to reload their weapons. Jack handed the Enfield and the ammunition back to Ramon.

Cates started laughing, blowing off steam. "Ramon, buddy, you sure can run. I'd sure be proud to bet money on you in a foot race."

"Dry up," Ramon bit open a cartridge and poured powder into the muzzle of his Enfield.

"You wanted to put a scare into them," Jack said. "I believe we accomplished that."

"Who got scared more, them or us?" Cates cackled.

"Think they're likely to give chase?" Jack drew his revolver and opened the cylinder.

"Not likely. Probably won't want to do that in the dark," Ramon said. "I sure wouldn't. Anyway, their horses weren't saddled, so it would take them a while to mount up and follow."

"They'll try to guess how many of us were there," Jack said. "We made a lot of noise. Could be they overestimated."

Cates said, "Want to set up an ambush, just in case they come down the road like a bunch of arrogant bastards?"

Ramon turned on him. "Haven't you had enough for one night?"

"Didn't you have a good time?" Cates' laughter seemed a little too wild.

"Your blood is up," Jack said. "Just because the Yanks might overestimate us doesn't mean you ought to."

"You're no fun," Cates snorted.

"Skulking behind sticker vines in the dark, just in case they decide to chase us is your idea of fun?" Ramon thrust his rifle back into its boot.

"We're only alive because God protects drunks and fools," Jack said. "Ramon has a wife and daughter to think about."

"I got to admit, Farrell, you're a good man to have at my back," Cates said.

Jack touched his revolver barrel to his hat brim in salute. "Come back to the house. Y'all get to sleep inside tonight."

Ramon said, "Think they'll track us back there?"

"Even in daylight the road is too cut up for them to make out which track is which. For sure not until morning. Though we'd better take turns keeping watch all night."

"We'll leave before daylight," Ramon said. "You took a big chance coming with us, Farrell. I hope they don't connect you with our little raid."

"Prescott knew the woods were full of rebs, told me so himself." Jack let out a long breath. "He should have expected trouble."

*

Prescott waited until after the gunfire died down before leaving the house. Sergeant Owen had run outside the moment the shooting started, and Prescott was willing to let him investigate the situation. It would have been unwise to expose the commanding officer to fire. His men needed him too much.

Prescott stepped outside, not wanting to believe the chaos that had struck his secure, well-guarded camp. The sergeant was busy organizing the excited, rifle-brandishing troops who had scattered about the yard, one or two emerging from behind the cover of outbuildings. One of the sentries lay groaning in Prescott's path, clutching his chest, blood oozing between his fingers. Prescott stepped around him and spotted another man lying by the campfire. He strongly suspected the man was not merely asleep.

Sergeant Owen rushed over. "Did we get any of them?" Prescott asked him.

"Don't know yet, sir." Owen sounded out of breath. "Have to check the bushes. We could see where they were shooting from."

"How many were there?"

"My guess is at least a half dozen, sir. We ran them off." Owen paused, then said, "Our men fought bravely."

Prescott blinked, thinking Owen had just handed him a sly rebuke, one he could not counter without laying it open. He looked toward the woods, where a couple of soldiers skittishly probed in the dark. He began to reconsider his first impulse, to order Owen to have the men saddle their horses and give chase.

Owen shifted on his feet. "Tell us what to do, *sir*. If we go after them, we don't know which way they went and we'd never see them before they see us."

Prescott did not relish the idea of leading his men on such a hazardous adventure. Nor did he like the tone of Owen's voice.

"If they're layin' for us, you could lose your whole command," Owen added. "I suggest we increase our guard and wait until daylight to move out."

"Give me a full report," Prescott said. "How many casualties?"

"I know of two, sir. Both New Hampshire boys shot bad."

"None of the Negroes?"

"No, sir. Most of them haven't been issued weapons yet. I guess they stayed low."

Prescott shoved his hands into his pockets and rocked on his heels, thinking of how his little command just got smaller. "Well, then. Carry on, Sergeant. See that the wounded are cared for." He glanced at the stricken man he had first noticed. "We have to get busy and recruit more Negroes, don't we? Best teach all of them how to shoot."

One of the soldiers who had been searching the woods returned. "Didn't find any dead rebels, sir. We must have missed them."

Prescott knew he ought to do what he could to show concern for the wounded. He walked to the campfire and regarded the fellow who was lying down, The Negro, Isaac, bent over him. He recognized Williams, who lay bleeding from underneath his eye. The injured man stared up at Isaac, his eyes glassy in the firelight.

Prescott said to the strapping Negro, "Get the colored boys together and carry the wounded men into the house. Take care of them." He noticed Isaac carried a rifle in the crook of his arm. "You know how to shoot that thing?"

"Yessir. I picked it up when Private Williams dropped it, and I shot at them rebels."

"Well then. Commendable. But not advisable because you lack training."

"Sir, I knows how to shoot a rifle. I fought Indians."

"Is that the truth?" Prescott stared at him, digesting what the colored man just said and picturing the unlikely scene. "I'll be sure to tell the sergeant."

Williams made a gagging sound, coughed and whimpered. "Get that man indoors and patch him up." It occurred to Prescott that by bringing the wounded into the house he would have to listen to that sort of carrying on and worse all night.

Not if he closed the door to his room and shut out the noise of suffering.

*

Martina had heard the sound of distant gunfire in the still night air, and it sickened her with fear. With Jack and Ramon in danger, she had a great deal to worry about. Finally the men returned, not in time for supper as Jack had promised, but they did return. For that she murmured a prayer of thanks. Candlelight showed the gunpowder stains on their faces and hands before they took care of their horses and washed the smudges away.

She served them the chicken she had fried, along with roasted sweet potatoes and string beans. The men did not seem to care that the food had gone cold. Jack moved his chair next to the window, where he had a view of the outside yard while he ate. He had mentioned he would take the first watch in case they had company.

Carlo asked them what the gunfire was about. Russell Cates gleefully recounted their scrape with the enemy while the boy listened wide-eyed. "Jack saved Ramon's life," Cates said. "He shot that Yankee that was pulling down on your cousin."

Ramon gave Jack an odd look. "I didn't know which one of you did that. I had my revolver out but didn't want to move and give myself away. You were quicker."

"He was already in my sights." Jack set his empty plate on the floor.

"I owe you one," Ramon said.

Martina frowned at Ramon. "You said you weren't going to fight them."

"Didn't plan to. We just sort of got into it."

Cates snickered. "Ramon blundered around and let them know he was there. That opened the ball."

"Couldn't see that stick in the dark," Ramon grumbled. "Could have happened to you, too."

Carlo turned to Jack, eyes wide. "You killed a Yankee?"

"I shot at one a couple. Don't know their condition." He continued to stare out the window. "Martina, Cates is making more of it than it was. Ramon and I don't want to worry you."

"You were going to pretend nothing happened?" she said. "Did you think you could get away with that?"

"Came out all right." Jack shrugged. "Your cousin is fine."

Martina wanted to tell him Ramon was not her only concern. "You like the fighting. You really like it."

"He's good at it," Cates said. "So are we."

Ramon looked at her. "We need men like him to join the cavalry and help defend our state."

"So, Jack, when are you going to swear in?" Cates said.

"When I'm good and ready."

Martina glanced at Carlo, who looked from Jack to Ramon to Cates, fascination enlivening his face. How long would she be able to keep her little brother out of the killing, too?

"I was satisfied to leave the war behind, but it has followed me home." Jack mused. He turned from the window and fixed his gaze on her face. "You know that."

"I don't have to like it." Didn't she sound like a clingy woman? Yet she had no claim on him. "I was terrified for you. For all three of you. Yet you make it into a joke."

Jack stood up. "Excuse me, gentlemen. Martina, let's go outside."

She walked out onto the porch with him. He took her hand and led her away from the house, into the yard. A full moon brightened the landscape and deepened shadows from the trees. "You don't want anyone to overhear what you have to say?" she asked him.

"This is a private conversation, between you and me." She made out his serious expression plainly in the silver light. "I didn't want you to worry, but it's nice to know you gave my safety a thought."

Her eyes stung, making her blink. "Of course I care about you, Jack. I want you safe. How could you ever think I wouldn't?"

"Darlin', we've had our squabbles." Jack caught both her hands in his, and mischief danced in his eyes. "I have to ask you something, and I don't want you to hit me."

Martina looked down at her hands, imprisoned by his firm, warm grip, but did not struggle to free herself. She turned her gaze back to him, smiling through burning eyes. "Do you intend to make me angry?"

"I intend to make you my wife. Does that make you angry?"

She shook her head. "Is that what you really want? Or did Ramon fuss at you because I live here? Is that the real reason you are bringing it up?"

"Ramon can't make me do what I don't want to do."

She laughed softly. "Jack, nobody can make you do anything, can they? Unless it's at gunpoint."

"You could."

She studied his face while his words sank in. In his eyes she read fear that she would reject him, just as she had that night at the Posey Dance.

"Carlo wants us married, said so the other day. Seems everybody is all for it, especially me. If you agree, we're unanimous." He flashed a grin. "Timing couldn't be better. The Yanks keep bothering us, and I'll be joining Dickison's cavalry soon."

"Jack, Jack." She shook her head again. "Isn't there anything you won't turn into a joke?"

He nodded, his expression intense. "You and me, Martina. I love you to distraction. It won't be easy, because I'll have to go away soon, though I hope I can remain close by. You and Carlo are my family now. I want to make that permanent."

His earnestness touched her deeply, and she spoke from her

172

truth. "I fear for you. Sometimes I get furious with you, then I hurt for you. I feel safe with you, and I want to be with you." She tilted her head, studying his face. "Doesn't that mean I love you?"

"Why wait for a priest?" He let go of her hands, drew her close and kissed her deeply.

Why indeed? Caught up in an overwhelming response, certain aspects of her agreed. But she pulled away, laughing, and slapped his ear lightly. "You are a wicked, wicked man."

He grinned. "I believe you enjoy torturing me."

Martina rested her cheek on his shoulder and shut her eyes, liking the feel of his arms sheltering her.

Yet... she had seen him drunk enough to get into trouble. Twice. Would there be a third, a fourth, and a fifth time? Or could she help heal his hurts so he wouldn't need to dose himself with opium and alcohol?

"I haven't said I would marry you." She considered his raw courage in facing their enemies. He could make her laugh when she had cause to weep. He had given her a place of refuge then acted as though she were doing him a favor. He naturally filled the role of elder brother to Carlo. She imagined what it would be like to share his bed and bear his children.

She lifted her face from his shoulder. "But I will."

Tension left his face, and he let out his breath. "For you, Martina, I will do my best."

"And I promise to love you for who you are."

He said softly, "I don't recall anybody ever saying that to me before."

"Maybe that's because nobody ever saw you clearly before. You need someone to believe in you."

"I will do my best," he repeated, his voice husky.

"And so will I." She prayed her heart's inclinations were not overriding her good sense.

CHAPTER TWENTY

Jack settled on the porch, his revolver in his belt, Ramon's Enfield secure in his arms, Nip curled up at his feet.

After a while Carlo crept out of his side of the house and sat Indian style next to him.

"Couldn't sleep?" Jack asked.

"No, sir. Too much to think about, so I figured I'd keep you company."

"It'll be good to have somebody to talk to. The dog isn't much of a conversationalist."

"Do you think the Yankees are going to come back?"

"If they do, it probably won't be in the dark. This is just a precaution. We'll ride out first thing in the morning and see what they're up to."

"What if they do come?"

"They're going to be mad. Let's hope they don't connect me with tonight's little skirmish. It got out of hand." Jack did not mention his worst concern: that they would rightly blame him for the attack and come looking for revenge.

"I can help you fight them off."

Jack decided not to mention he was only a year older than Carlo when he experienced his first gunfight. "If they show up, you and Martina better hide in the woods. Take her to the still. Only way they'd find her there is if Isaac tells them where it is. He didn't let on earlier, probably won't now." Jack paused. "Unless he's mad at me, too."

"I'd rather fight."

"There's a time to fight and a time to run like hell." Jack changed the subject. "We're going to be brothers-in-law. What do you think about that?"

"I'm glad."

"Yeah, me, too."

When they had made their announcement earlier that night, Cates had slapped him on the back and Carlo had let out a whoop. Ramon looked relieved at the easy resolution of his cousin's awkward situation. He allowed that although Jack was not a Minorcan, at least he was Catholic.

"Father Aulance used to come by the Colee place once a month," Jack told Carlo. "I need to see them and find out if he's still making his rounds. Maybe you and Martina will want to do a social call, too."

"Martina wants me to give her away," Carlo said.

"Nothing much will change, except your sister will be sleeping with me." Jack sure liked the way that sounded. "Maybe someday you'll get a niece or a nephew out of the deal."

*

Isaac spent most of the night trying to help the wounded soldiers. He knew little of medicine but figured he had enough common sense to tie bandages made from underwear around the bullet holes and give the poor fellows water and tobacco when they asked for it. He thought about getting some popskull from Jack but didn't know how he would do it without letting the captain know about his still.

Williams was hit in the upper chest and had been spitting blood. Payne had lost a few teeth, and his cheek had swelled something awful.

At daybreak the captain stuck his head out the door of the room where he had spent the night. "What are you doing in the house?" he asked Isaac.

"You told me to take care of the wounded, sir," Isaac said.

"Oh, so I did. How are they?" Captain Prescott stepped into the front room in his stocking feet and peered at his men. He appeared sleep-wrinkled, and his oiled hair stuck out. He smoothed his moustache and hitched a suspender over his shoulder.

"Mornin', Captain." Williams gave him a faint smile. The white boy was paler than ever from the effects of getting shot. The cloth-covered hole in Payne's face and the swelling kept him from speaking.

"We'll get you boys to a doctor." Prescott strode to the front door and bawled for Sergeant Owen. Isaac could have told him the sergeant had spent the night outside making sure the men were ready for another possible attack.

The sergeant ambled in, bloodshot of eye, his expression ill-humored. "Sir?"

"Have you sent any scouts to look for our attackers?"

"Of course, sir. They reported back. Those guerrillas are nowhere to be found, and the road is too cut up to give us a clean track. They could have taken any old trail."

The captain scratched his head. "I need coffee. Anybody make coffee?"

Sergeant Owen said, "I can see you get coffee, Captain. Shouldn't I prepare the men to pull out? We ought to be getting these wounded boys back to St. Augustine."

"Of course. We'll have to cut our patrol short. Have them loaded onto that wagon. Throw off some of the stuff if you have to make room."

"Yes, sir." Sergeant Owen saluted and backed out the door.

"You, boy." The captain pointed to Isaac. "What is your name?"

"Isaac, sir."

"You got a last name?"

"Farrell. My name is Isaac Farrell, sir."

"Huh. Another Farrell. I presume you took the name of your master."

"Not my master, sir. I been free since I was a child. I took the name because they my onliest family. Until I married Lacey."

"Well, then, Private Farrell." The captain scratched his head. "You know that rascal Jack Farrell pretty well, don't you?"

"Yes, sir."

"Think he had anything to do with what went on last night?"

That idea had occurred to Isaac. Although he was ready to fight rebels, old ties were still strong, and he hated to condemn a man he had always considered almost as close as blood. "Sir, I seen plenty regulators and rebel cavalry around these parts. Could a been most any of 'em. Anyways, don't you think Mr. Jack looked too poorly to be fighting, all that coughing and hacking?"

When the sergeant returned with coffee, Captain Prescott said, "We ought to go back and arrest Farrell."

"Whatever you think, sir. We have two severely wounded men—"

"Then send some of our men to fetch him." Prescott took a sip of coffee. "We'll head back to town straightaway and let them catch up."

Sergeant Owen didn't move, just stood there looking at him,

frowning. "Permission to speak freely, sir?"

"Well, Sergeant?"

"Are you sure you want to split the command? The rebs will be out there watching the roads. Wherever we go, we need to go in force. Besides, you said Farrell was sick, and it might be catching."

"Hrumph." Prescott slugged down more coffee, then turned to Isaac. "Private *Farrell!*" He spat out the name then waved toward the two wounded men. "Get the other Negroes to help you make room for these men in that wagon. Make Williams and Payne as comfortable as you can, understand?"

"Yes, sir." Isaac saluted and left to carry out the order.

*

Leon Farrell fished a jackknife out of his pocket and opened it to peel a ripe orange he pulled from a low-hanging branch. "The rebels attacked a Union patrol the other night over at the Miller place. Couple of them were shot bad, and one of them may yet die." He started cutting away the peel and letting it drop to the ground. "Jack, you're under considerable suspicion."

"Thought I heard gunfire off in that direction." Jack set a double handful of citrus into a bushel basket.

"You didn't have anything to do with it?"

Jack quirked a smile. "Do you think I'd be so foolish as to go after a Yankee patrol all by myself?"

"You've never impressed me with your judgment. You're lucky Prescott was spooked about another attack. He was in a hurry to get his wounded back to town. He wanted to bring you in. It's getting harder to talk the authorities out of arresting you. I may have to give up on the effort."

"Prescott is a pestilence." Jack snarled despite his efforts to keep his temper. "His bully boys stole Mrs. Tanner's stored food and her livestock. She's done nothing to deserve that kind of treatment, her husband gone with the army and all those kids to feed." Jack tossed a rotten orange to the ground. "Then they threw away some of her stuff. After they cleared out, I salvaged what I could and took it back to her. She cried all over me."

"I don't always approve of their tactics toward civilians." Pop pried off a section and sampled it. His lips pursed to spit out a seed that barely missed Jack's foot. "The fruit is excellent this year. Sweet oranges are selling for a nickel apiece in town."

Jack moved the ladder over a few feet so he could reach a well-laden branch. "Did Prescott get hurt in the fight, by any chance?" He risked asking a question that had been on his mind since the fight.

Pop shook his head. "He's leaving for Beaufort with the company he raised. That's where the Union Army trains the colored troops."

"I'm going to miss that son of a bitch." Jack laughed out loud. "Martina will sure be grieved to hear it. Is he gone for good?"

"It's rumored the colored regiments raised in Florida will be brought back to fight after they're organized." Pop wiped the blade clean on a handkerchief, closed the knife and pocketed it.

"With any luck the rumor is wrong." Jack climbed up a couple of rungs to get at the high-hanging fruit. He looked over to where Martina and Carlo were helping to gather oranges a few trees over. "Did you know Prescott was looking for Martina? We made sure he didn't find her."

"Jack, I'm telling you, if you don't declare yourself for the Union, you're going to find yourself in serious trouble."

"Damned if I do, and damned if I don't." Jack pulled off oranges and handed them down to his father, who set them into the basket. "No matter what I do, somebody is going to want to skin my hide. I refuse to take up arms against friends and neighbors."

"I'm sure you've been cooperating with the guerillas."

"Is that what you're telling the Yanks?"

"You're getting your health back, and the rebs will be pressuring you to join."

Does he know how right he is? "And if I do?"

"I'd sooner see you in prison than back in the Confederate army."

"Good to know where I stand." Jack felt his jaw muscle tighten. "Why do you even bother to plead my case?"

"I told you I'm about done with it." His father shook his head. "I've been warned, and I'm passing it on. You'd better not be playing games. Next time the rebels go after a Union patrol around here, you will be arrested. Seems to me they've given you a lot of rope."

"They presume I have any control over what the Confederates do?"

"They don't care. I'm telling you, they'll be watching you

closely."

Whatever happens to me, what will become of Martina? I should just clear out and take her with me, somewhere far away from the Yankees. And my father.

Neither of them spoke for a time as they worked.

At length Pop said, "Miss Sanchez's house will be vacant now that Captain Prescott is leaving, and I wanted to know if she would let Margaret and me move into it. We can trade tenancy, so I can quit paying rent where Margaret and I are living now."

"I can see her going for that." Jack stepped off the ladder. "You should ask her."

"Does Miss Sanchez plan to stay here much longer?"

Jack braced himself for another tirade. "We're engaged. She's going to be my wife."

"Finally, you're showing a shred of good sense." Leon nodded his approval. "She's a fine young lady."

Jack stared at his father. "We agree on something. I believe lightning may strike."

"Perhaps the responsibility of supporting a wife will keep you from doing something foolish. When do you plan to get married?"

"As soon as we can locate a priest."

"I see. Of course she can't come to St. Augustine."

"None of us can. There's a Catholic church in Jacksonville, but there's a big old river in between and nobody would be here to feed the stock for a few days. We went over to see Mr. Colee. He doesn't know when, or if, Father Aulance will come out here for a mission visit."

"I'll tell the priest about your plans." Leon cracked a smile. "Maybe he can get a pass, and I can bring him. Margaret may want to come as well, if she feels safe enough."

It took a moment for Jack to recover from his astonishment. "I – we would be honored."

Jack called Martina over and climbed down from the ladder. He circled his arm around her waist. "I told my father about our plans. He's going to see about bringing Father Aulance."

She brightened. "Oh, would you? Mr. Colee is a notary, but I want a priest to marry us."

"Miss Sanchez," Leon said, "you are a brave lady indeed. I hope you're adept at taming such wild creatures as my wayward son."

"I believe it's better to tame wild creatures with kindness than with the whip." Martina smiled sweetly, but Jack sensed her annoyance. "He needs someone to have faith in him, and I do."

Jack gave her a grateful squeeze. "You see," he said to his father, "we're both right about her."

His father cracked another smile, as though he enjoyed Martina's comeback. "Well, young lady, you're certainly welcome to him."

*

Isaac stood on the deck of the *Burnside* as it steamed up the shoreline, taking him farther away from Lacey by the hour. The rolling waves pitched it from side to side, so he held onto the railing to steady himself. He said to Zeke, "I never been to South Carolina. Never been out of Florida."

Zeke allowed he hadn't either. "Sergeant Owen going to teach us how to be proper soldiers when we gets up to Beaufort. How to parade, how to shoot a rifle, how to fight Rebs like the ones came after us at my old place."

"Don't know why they have to take us to Carolina. We can learn that stuff just as easy at Fort Marion." Isaac glanced at Captain Prescott, who was hanging onto the rail looking down at the water, a sickly expression on his face. "I don't think the captain is liking his boat ride much."

Isaac didn't like it much either, for different reasons. He consoled himself, dwelling on talk that the colored troops would be sent right back to Florida after they trained. He'd like to take a gunboat ride down the St. Johns. It was the only chance he saw to find Lacey and his sons.

*

True to his word, Leon Farrell returned a few days later, bringing both his wife and Father Aulance from St. Augustine. Jack had not seen his stepmother in over a year, and she greeted him with her usual politeness. Margaret and Martina went off together making their plans for the wedding, which they decreed would be held that evening. Jack sent Carlo on Ladybug to invite the Colee family and Mrs. Tanner. He did not know where to

180

locate Martina's cousin Ramon, which was just as well. Having his Confederate friends attend the wedding with his father present would not be politic.

"It was good of Mr. Farrell to bring me." Father Aulance, not long removed from France, spoke English with a heavy accent. "It has been difficult to visit our missions ever since the Union Army occupied St. Augustine. Bishop Verot sought to escort the Sisters of Mercy to Savannah when he evacuated them last summer. The Union authorities held them for ten days before permitting them to leave."

To his father Jack said, "Thank you for coming, and for bringing Father Aulance and Margaret." Although deeply touched at the show of support, he would not reveal any sentiment. It had never paid for him to let his father know his true feelings.

"It is my hope marriage will keep you out of trouble," Leon said. "And I approve your choice. The young lady has spirit."

"She stands up to you." Jack smiled wryly. "Not many people have the nerve. I'm astonished you tolerate it."

"I suspect she will stand up to you, as well."

"That she does. I try to stay on the right side of her."

"If only you would come onto the right side of the larger conflict."

"You know my feelings on that, sir."

The priest took Jack aside and asked him how recently he had taken Holy Communion.

"A long time, Father. Not since I left home seven years ago."

"So it has also been years since you made confession, my son? You must make confession before you take communion and your vows."

Jack sighed, recalling Sister Mary Joseph's dire predictions of his hell-bound fate. "Father 'Lance, I hope you have a lot of time, because it's going to take all afternoon."

"With God's forgiveness, you can make a new beginning." The priest added dryly, "And I am looking forward to an interesting account."

"Next time I see you, I'll have a few more tales to tell, I'm sure."

*

Martina decided to hold the simple ceremony in the front yard under the winter-bare pecan trees. She had shucked her mourning dress and packed it away, wanting to leave it in the trunk forever. Then she had put on her best Sunday dress.

Ever since agreeing to marry him, Martina had agonized over whether she and Jack were doing the right thing or merely the convenient thing by rushing into a hasty union. It grieved her to think of what Francisco would have said about it, if he were alive and if his opinion of Jack still held. She prayed for a sign she should go through with the commitment.

She caught sight of Jack walking from the house after conferring with the priest, a comradely arm resting on Carlo's shoulder. Her brother looked ecstatic. If the way he treated Carlo were any measure, he would be a fine father to her future children, should they be so blessed.

Jack's firm stride and confident bearing suggested he did not share her hesitation. When he spotted her, he caressed her with his gaze, and she took heart.

After she and Jack were pronounced man and wife, Martina served ham. Margaret, her new mother-in-law, brought out pastries and lemonade she had made for the occasion. Soon after dark, by common consent, Martina and Jack bid their visitors good night, and he led her to his bedroom.

He swept her up in his arms and carried her through the door. When he set her down on the bed, Martina said, "You are so much stronger now."

"You've been taking good care of me." He let himself down on the mattress and nuzzled her neck where it met her collarbone.

Strong enough and well enough to join Dickison's cavalry. They would come for him soon, and she could not stop him from leaving. She never would have imagined she would want someone she loved to heal more slowly than he should, or at all.

She put her arms around him as though that action could keep him home forever. She enjoyed his clean male scent and the warmth of his hard muscled body pressing against hers. This was the moment she had approached with fear and longing. Her awakening desire warred with her deeply ingrained modesty.

He kissed his way to her lips, brushing her jaw line, and she responded with an eagerness that swept over her with surprising power. His hands busied themselves, unbuttoning the front of her dress, loosening the stays. Freed from the tight corset, she took a deep breath as he caressed her from breast to thigh. The pleasant sensations rolled over her like a wave, but she felt unsure, exposed, and afraid.

"I don't know what I'm supposed to do," she whispered. "I've never been with a man this way before."

"I know, and that means you are all mine." He kissed her on the mouth again. "Don't you trust me?"

She nodded. "I love you. I want your children, and I want to make you happy."

"You do." He gently brushed a stray strand of hair from her eyebrow. "We'll take it slow and easy. I'll show you how a man makes love to his wife."

"Show me," she murmured. "I want you to show me."

*

Jack opened his eyes to morning sunlight slanting through the curtains and his woman beside him. Martina watched him sleepy-eyed, her dark hair framing her face against the pillow. She had insisted they wait until the priest gave his blessing. Although he had felt the delay would drive him mad, in the end he had taken her without guilt. She had overcome her shyness and responded with joy.

Never in his life had he felt so loved. How soon would everything go wrong and rob him of this rightness? He lifted his hand and cradled his wife's cheek in it.

She kissed his palm, then elbowed up and touched his scarred arm. "Let me see."

"It isn't pretty." He realized she had never seen the full extent of his scars, normally covered by shirt and trousers. He pulled the blanket away, exposing his injured side, bracing himself for her reaction. "I'm still carrying around metal and bits of tree."

She ran her fingers along the ravaged flesh, a grave look on her face, as she studied the puckers and bumps. "You don't have to hide it from me." She kissed his arm, which had healed slightly crooked. "I know you suffered."

"Could've been worse." He loved her all the more for accepting him, damaged as he was. "I could be dead. Or fighting Yankees and frostbite back in Virginia. Either way, I wouldn't be with you wondering how I could possibly deserve this piece of heaven."

"If only it could last," she murmured.

CHAPTER TWENTY-ONE

Martina peered between the orange trees, hiding from the approaching riders in case it was another Yankee patrol coming to harass them. When she made out the gray jackets, she sighed with relief. Over the past few weeks Cousin Ramon and Russell Cates had stopped by often, seeking a good meal and a warm, dry place to sleep. So far they had managed to show up at different times than the Yankees.

She wiped her hands on her apron, left the basket partly filled with oranges, and walked toward the house to meet her guests. She looked around for Jack and Carlo, who were busy with other chores.

With the scouts rode young Charlie Colee in civilian clothes and three soldiers she did not recognize. Her attention was drawn to a slim man, older than the others, distinguished by the officer's stripes on his collar. She looked at Ramon. His somber expression told her more than she wanted to know. She stood still in quiet distress.

Jack, drawn by the commotion, came up alongside and slipped his arm around her waist while Carlo ran to meet the soldiers and greet his cousin. "Here comes Captain Dickison in person," Jack said. "Last I heard he was operating on the other side of the river."

"They've come for you." Martina lifted her hand to her temple to rub out the familiar pounding sensation.

"I see they've got Charlie, too."

She slipped her hand over Jack's and held on tight as though that would keep him home.

Jack greeted the cavalrymen, introduced Martina to the captain, and invited them to water the horses at the spring and take refreshment at the house.

The captain did not waste time getting to the point of his visit. "Mr. Farrell, we have pressing need of volunteers for our troop. It appears you've recovered from your wounds and are now fit for service."

Jack smiled grimly. Martina noticed Ramon would not look her in the eye.

"Saddle your horse and come with us." Dickison's authoritative tone assumed instant obedience.

"I guess I'm your man." Jack's voice crackled with false cheer.

Martina shut her eyes, feeling ill, then looked at Jack, who seemed lost in thought. "I'll pack some things you'll be needing."

"Think you can fit yourself in my haversack?" He gave her an encouraging smile, then headed for the pasture to fetch Ladybug.

Martina bit her lip as she rolled his clean underwear into a blanket. She had married Jack knowing this moment would come. Despite their stormy beginnings, he had become her lover and her best friend. Now the war was going to snatch him away.

The three of them had prepared the best they could, storing supplies in secret places. Although Prescott had been transferred away from St. Augustine, Yankee patrols still came from there. Fortunately, with Jacksonville in Confederate hands, few Union gunboats cruised this far upriver, and those that did showed no intent to land at Picolata or nearby Tocoi.

Jack had taken the bulk of his liquor distillation to Palatka, where he had traded it for a shotgun, powder and shot, several yards of factory cloth, and a gold band to fit on her finger. The valuables he brought back dampened some of Martina's objections to his still. So far he had kept his promise not to consume too much of his own product.

Jack had continued his mentor's role with Carlo. Their hunting excursions added turkey, venison and quail to their supper table, with enough to spare for the impoverished Tanner family.

After a time Jack joined her in the house. He gathered her into his arms, and she nestled against him, trying to be brave, trying not to make things worse.

"I've spun it out as long as I can," he said. "They've got me now."

"I stuffed your haversack with food," she murmured into his shoulder. "But there wasn't any room for me in it."

"That's a pity." His voice turned husky. "Captain Dickison said we've been ordered to bust up Yankee communications in St.

Johns County."

She understood the best choice Jack could honorably make was to enlist in Dickison's first-class, Florida-based cavalry unit, among men he knew and trusted. "You'll be close by, at least."

"I ought to be able to slip home from time to time."

"I'll be here."

"Ramon said his offer is still open. You can go to Lake City and stay with his wife."

"If I did, I'd never get to see you."

"It would be safer for you and Carlo in a town."

She shook her head. "We have everything we need here and nothing in Lake City. Besides, your father – "

"We'll be stirring up a hornet's nest, and they will want my hide." He smiled without humor. "So will he."

"I'm not going to tell anybody where you've gone."

"You probably won't be seeing much of Pop. Ramon said we're supposed to cut off civilian traffic as well as military. We won't let anybody through. Remember you and Carlo have the shotgun."

He had taught her how to use it. The shotgun's noise and kick had startled her at first, but she had gotten used to it. With Jack's patient instruction, she had learned she could pepper the scarecrow he had set up for target practice.

"I will try to get hold of another horse so Carlo will have the use of Ladybug. Naturally your little brother is hot to go with us, but I ordered him to stay home. Ramon and I reminded him we know he's underage, and we won't let him enlist. Though the army wouldn't care how young he is."

"That boy... he was doing so well with you in charge. He listens to you. I'm afraid I won't be able to manage him."

"There's no help for it. I have to go now." He gave her a lingering kiss, then turned abruptly away, shrugged on his gray jacket and picked up the blanket she had rolled.

Carrying the haversack, she followed him outside where the other soldiers waited, sitting on their horses, ready to leave. Jack hugged Carlo, who had been talking to the scouts and Charlie. "Take care of your sister."

Martina watched Jack swing into the saddle in one fluid motion. It struck her how much he had recovered since he had returned from Virginia. He tied the blanket roll to the pommel of the saddle. She handed him the bulging haversack.

Ramon shifted in the saddle, looking unhappy. "Martina, for your sake, I'm sorry. It's hard on Teresa, too. But for our sake, I'm proud Jack is joining up."

"I told Captain Dickison I'll be satisfied to have him watching my back," Cates said.

Dickison touched his hat brim, "I understand you have only been married a short time, Mrs. Farrell. We do appreciate your sacrifice."

She nodded, acknowledging the officer was trying to show her courtesy, though the sacrifice was certainly not her choice.

Carlo's face showed that fascination it always did when the soldiers came around. Martina put her hands on her little brother's shoulders, noticing how muscular he had grown. He had taken on more and more manly responsibility.

"I pray the war will be over quickly and all the soldiers will be able to return to their homes," she told the captain.

"For the duration, we'll do our best to protect you. No Yankee foragers will be getting out of St. Augustine as long as we're on duty," Dickison said.

"Take care of yourselves." Martina looked at Ramon. "And each other." She let her gaze linger on Jack. He had gathered the reins in his hand. His bearing struck her; he appeared at home with the cavalrymen and prepared to make the best of whatever came his way. She felt a surge of pride in her husband. He truly was doing his best. Surely she could be as strong.

Dickison saluted her and turned his horse to leave, the small band of troopers falling in with him. Jack spun Ladybug about and followed Ramon. Carlo broke away to jog to the road with the soldiers, Nip running ahead of him.

Jack turned in the saddle for a backward glance, and Martina lifted her hand. Then it crept down to the rosary at her waist, and she whispered, "*Vaya con Dios, my love. Blessed Mother, protect him.*" She watched until he rode out of sight.

*

Jack could not continue to look at Martina and maintain his composure. Turning his back on his family was the most wrenching thing he ever had done; he had come to cherish Martina beyond reason. He wheeled Ladybug and pressed his heels into her sides, before he made a fool of himself in front of his commander.

He had no grounds for complaint; he was not the only man who had to leave his wife to fend for herself because of the war. He would deal with whatever the army handed him, just as before. Perhaps by adding his efforts to the cavalry's they would effectively protect all their loved ones.

His fellow recruit, Charlie Colee, did not appear to share his misgivings. At eighteen, no doubt he was looking forward to a big adventure away from his aging parents. Jack remembered his own excitement upon embarking for Virginia, back when he had a hankering to prove himself and had nothing important to leave behind.

The little group struck the main road. Captain Dickison said to Jack, "When we join our wagons, I'll see that you and Private Colee are each issued an Enfield rifle and a proper Florida uniform. How did you acquire that jacket?"

Jack glanced down his front at the Alabama buttons. "My clothes had to be cut off. They were shredded anyway. I guess some poor fellow was considerate enough to die and leave it to me."

"I'll have our surgeon examine you," Dickison said. "But you appear fit enough."

"Yes, sir. I've healed up some." Jack managed a smile. "The metal I'm carrying around only clanks when I run."

"Don't worry, Jack. You'll pass," Cates said, "You've got all your front teeth, so you can bite open a cartridge just fine."

"I heard this was an elite outfit. I reckon that proves it."

"We're setting up pickets on the roads leading out of St. Augustine to isolate the Yankee garrison. No one comes in or out of town," Dickison said. "Cates and Andreu requested that I assign you to patrol with them on this road."

"This road," Jack mused. "Sir, that might cause an awkward situation."

"How is that?" Dickison bristled.

"My father will be using this road. I'll have to stop him."

"I expect you to attend to your duty, Farrell."

Jack let out his breath through his adequate set of teeth. "I will, sir."

*

"Buggy coming up the road," Ramon said. Jack peered from where he stood behind a cover of palmetto fronds and instantly recognized the mule and the man driving the rig. *Damn. Right on time.* Having to arrest his father making his weekly visit was only the latest disagreeable but inevitable duty life had thrown him.

Yesterday, he and his comrades had captured a Confederate infantryman they suspected was a deserter. It appeared he was trying to make his way into St. Augustine where he could give himself up to the Yankees. Sitting on his horse in the cold rain, homesick and miserable, Jack had felt no sympathy for the wretch and suffered no regret in placing him under guard, to be returned to his unit.

Besides the would-be deserter, last night they had encountered a few Negroes on the loose and returned them to their homes. Jack considered it an odious job, but he understood the need to keep them from enlisting in the Union army as Isaac had done. They didn't need more Yankees to fight, of whatever complexion. He also recognized the need to keep laborers on their farms, or crops would go unplanted and unharvested. Everyone would go hungry – black and white alike.

Cates moved his horse into the road, showing his revolver to Leon Farrell. "Stop right there, sir," he said. Ramon rode up alongside the buggy and held the mule's halter. Jack walked to the buggy from the other side. He did not draw his weapon, and to his relief he noted his father's hands were in full sight, holding the lines.

Jack's father glared at Cates, then at Ramon, and finally his gaze rested on Jack. As meaning sank in, the older man's neck reddened and the flush extended to his face.

"Howdy, Pop," Jack said. "Sorry to say we can't let you pass through."

Cates shot Jack an amused look. "This is your daddy?"

Ramon said, "Good day, Mr. Farrell. I'm sorry we have to detain you."

"Well, Jack," Pop said. "I am disappointed. Again. I hoped having a wife would settle you down."

"I got volunteered, and I'm having the time of my life." Jack laced the obvious fib with a smile.

"How do you suppose your wife is getting along?"

"The best she can, I reckon, same as other soldiers' wives." Jack's smile faded. "We need to disarm you."

"Think I'd shoot you?" Pop harrumphed.

Jack set his jaw. He wouldn't put it past his father to plug him in the leg to disable him all over again and take him out of action. For his own good, of course. He reached into the buggy and dragged the revolver from his father's belt.

"I'm on my way to the farm to collect the last of my oranges. You know that," Leon barked. "Tell your rebel accomplices to let me through. And give me my pistol."

"I'll keep it safe for you. We have orders to put a stop to the traffic in and out of St. Augustine."

"The fruit will rot on the trees if I don't bring it to town to sell."

Jack shook his head. "The Confederate commissary department can buy them."

"For worthless Confederate money?"

"They won't rot. And our soldiers won't get scurvy."

Cates said, "We let him go back to town, he'll tell the Yanks about our picket post and what we're doing."

"Yeah, he would do that," Jack murmured. So far they had not stopped anyone coming out of St. Augustine, though they had prevented one of Jack's neighbors from taking produce to town. Their stealthy presence had not yet attracted the Yankees' notice, but letting Leon return to St. Augustine would change that.

"We have to detain him until the lieutenant decides what to do with him," Ramon said.

"Come on out of the buggy, Pop," Jack said.

"You're arresting me?" Leon scowled. "You're no better than the regulators that threatened to lynch me."

Cates snickered. "So much for your inheritance, Jackie boy."

Ramon said, "Mr. Farrell, you'd better do what he says. Nobody is going to harm you, but we can't let you go about your business."

Jack's father climbed out of the buggy. Ramon led the mule pulling the rig off the road where it wouldn't immediately be seen by travelers coming from either direction. Jack escorted his father to the fly tent that had kept most of the rain off him and his comrades last night. "Ramon is going to consult with the lieutenant," Jack said. "He isn't far away."

"This is a sad day," Leon said. "I had hopes you would refrain from taking up arms against your country again."

"Pop...." Jack shook his head, "it's a matter of honor."

"Your sense of honor is misguided."

"Protecting my family is misguided?"

"You should be home protecting them instead of harassing civilians."

"No Yankee patrols will get through to them, at least by land. We'll cut them off. I can't do that all by myself."

"Well, Jack." Leon folded his arms across his chest. "I have to admit one thing. You may be wrong-headed, but at least you're game. You've always been willing to stand up for yourself and damn the consequences. I have to give you that."

"You did give me that." Jack grinned. "It seems we have more in common than you'd like to own up to."

"Unfortunately, you've always had to live with the consequences. What will you rebels do with me?"

"We can't send you back to St. Augustine, but I'll suggest to the lieutenant that we let you go on to the farm, where you can stay." Jack figured that was a reasonable solution, considering his father was a civilian. One more prisoner to guard would strain the troop's limited personnel and supplies. Moreover, Leon would find it difficult to get past the cavalry watching the roads, and his buggy wouldn't pass through the more primitive trails.

Best of all, Martina would benefit from her father-in-law's presence. If nothing else, he could be counted on to protect her during Jack's absence.

Fortunately, Lieutenant Brantley agreed that it made more sense to allow Leon to continue on his way than to send him back to St. Augustine or to hold him any longer. Jack hurriedly wrote Martina a letter and asked Leon to give it to her, wishing he could go home in his father's place.

*

Martina welcomed Leon Farrell's arrival although she knew he would be irate over Jack's enlistment. When he told her about his detention she was relieved he had already learned where his son had gone and did not have to hear it from her. He handed her a letter from Jack and mentioned he seemed to be healthy, certainly healthy enough to cause his own father problems.

"Seems I'm on house arrest of a sort," Leon explained. "Until the rebels are cleared out, I can't return to St. Augustine."

"You want the Yankees to clear out my husband—your own son?" Martina was suddenly not so glad to see Leon. "You want the Yankees to kill him?"

"Of course not. I've done everything in my power to keep him from being harmed. But if he insists on fighting for the losing side, I don't have any control over his fate. I had hopes that if he wouldn't come over to the Union, at least he would not rejoin the rebel army." He paused. "I didn't think he would leave you to go back to the war."

"We always knew it would come to that."

"And you're all for it?"

"I want him home, but they didn't give him a choice. He's making the best of it. Jack is an honorable man. It was the only honorable thing for him to do."

"That so-called honor will not do you any good when he makes a widow of you."

Martina drew her wrap tighter. She had already learned her father-in-law was a harsh man. No wonder Jack had left home at a young age.

Leon shook his head. "I could be proud of him. I really could."

"You ought to tell him that."

"Too much has gone wrong between us."

CHAPTER TWENTY-TWO

"The Yanks haven't sent any foragers this way since we've been here. It's high time they sent a party across the bridge," Jack said. He and the other two scouts had ventured closer to St. Augustine before dawn, seeking a spot where they could intercept traffic headed toward Picolata and other points west. The three of them had found a post far enough from the bridge for the woods to screen them. Because this part of the road cut through dense forest, even a slight bend hid what lay ahead. The lack of visibility was a drawback, but any closer and they would give away their presence.

"So far we've just caught a few folks trying to run away from somewhere," Cates mused from the depths of his turned-up collar. His visible breath wafted away in the icy wind. "Or *to* somewhere, like Jack's daddy."

"Patrols usually come out close to daybreak," Ramon said. "They want to use all the daylight they can, whether they're foraging or hunting for us."

Jack settled in the saddle. Lacking gloves, he shoved his fingers under the saddle blanket next to Ladybug's warm hide. He had almost forgotten how quickly winters could turn mean in north Florida, from downright hot one day, to drenching rain followed by a hard freeze.

They remained mounted, ready to move quickly, prepared to wait all day for something, or nothing, to happen. He had learned long ago that military life consisted of boredom punctuated by moments of terror.

The Enfield musketoon Captain Dickison had issued him rested in its boot, reassuringly close to his leg, loaded and capped. His revolver, holstered tight against his hip, was also ready. He did not have spare cylinders to load but planned to acquire those as soon as possible. Nor did he have a saber, but if things went well he could capture one as well.

He did not have long to wait before Ramon stood up in the stirrups and whispered, "Do you hear that?"

Jack picked out sounds in the still, cold morning air. Metallic rattles, the rumble and squeak of wheels, a voice giving an indistinct order in a tone of command. "Here they come," he said under his breath. Now it wasn't just a matter of intercepting runaways and his own father. The Yankees were headed toward his home, toward his family.

"Have a look." Ramon nodded to Cates.

Cates urged his horse forward, hugging the wooded roadside, peering through brush in the direction of the bridge. He disappeared from sight, then after a short interval returned to where they waited. "Couple of vedettes is all I saw," he said in a low voice. "Can't tell what's behind them, but the rest can't be far, from the racket they're making."

"Did they spot you?" Ramon asked.

Cates shook his head and looked over his shoulder.

"Let's go back and tell the captain," Ramon said.

The scouts had stuffed rags around their hardware to muffle any rattling. The dull thud of hooves on soft dirt would not carry far. Jack hoped the enemy missed their presence as they backtracked ahead of the oncoming soldiers, toward the main body of Dickison's troopers.

After listening to Ramon's report, Dickison placed his dismounted troopers in the woods on both sides of the road with orders not to fire until he gave the order.

"An ambush might work," Jack said to Cates. "Wish we'd been able to tell how many Yanks we're up against."

"Don't matter. We'll whip 'em." Cates grinned.

Jack hid Ladybug deep in the thicket with the other horses and came back to the road. Aware of other troopers waiting in the woods, he crouched behind a pine tree, a man's length from Cates. He removed his hat and set it down behind him so the wide brim would not give him away.

The jingle of metal warned him of the Yankee's approach. He understood what Dickison wanted to achieve; let them pass through the gauntlet of armed Confederates, then pull down on them. He steadied his rifle and aimed it at about the height of a man on horseback. His cold fingers felt stiff.

Here they come, and they don't see us. Nobody better cough. Inhaling the fragrance of the pine needle-covered ground, he shivered with tension and chill.

He watched the vedettes ride by, apparently oblivious to the danger. Dickison allowed them through, giving no command to fire. The creak of wagon wheels grew louder. Long moments later, a lieutenant, surrounded by a half dozen other mounted bluecoats, hove into view. One of the Yankees reined in right in front of Jack. The soldier pointed toward where the horses were tethered and said in a low voice, "Look! Something moved. Over there."

They've spotted our horses. Still as death, Jack waited for a signal, aiming directly at the man's chest.

One of the concealed horses snorted, and the Yankee horse whinnied in reply. Before the Yankees could react, Dickison's voice rang out. "Halt and surrender! You are surrounded!"

The Confederates, hidden in the brush, echoed his demand with intimidating shouts and calls to surrender.

The Yankees looked around in confusion. Jack heard retreating hoof beats from the rear of the convoy and gunshots, followed by yells and more rapid hoof beats. The Yankee in front of him fumbled for his pistol. Jack yelled, "Don't do it! Hands up!" The man looked right at him and must have finally spotted him where he crouched, ready for a killing shot. The Yankee reluctantly lifted his hands. "Keep 'em up there and you get to live, Yank," Jack snapped.

He grabbed his hat, stood up and moved forward along with his comrades to disarm their prisoners. He ordered his captive to dismount, then realized he had caught one of the soldiers who had recently raided his homestead.

"I'll trade you a chicken for those gloves," Jack told him.

The New Hampshire man stared dazedly at him, recognition slowly swimming into his eyes. He frowned. "You. We had you figured for a guerilla. What chicken?"

"One you and your friends stole." Jack looked over the fine-looking chestnut gelding the Yankee had dismounted. Well-muscled, with good shoulder construction and in sleek condition, it stood equipped with a McClellan saddle and a full set of military accoutrements. The animal turned its large, mild eyes to him and pricked its ears. "And I'm trading your life for your horse."

"I've surrendered." The Yankee's eyes widened with fear. "You aren't going to shoot me."

"Already didn't," Jack drawled. "Never mind you asked for it, going for your weapon like an idiot. Take off those gloves."

195

He did not relax until the rest of the Yankees were dismounted, relieved of their weapons, and standing in a dejected, crestfallen bunch, surrounded by the Confederate troopers consolidating their easy victory. Along with the prisoners, the troop acquired valuable horses, wagons and equipment.

Dickison took aside the patrol's commander for questioning. The Yankee lieutenant seemed to be holding his composure with an effort. Jack's estimation of Dickison and his command leaped upward. He vastly preferred winning, especially when the victory entailed no loss.

Most important to him, this was one plunder party that would not threaten his wife.

"The vedettes and some of the rear guard got away," Ramon said. "Don't know if our boys can catch 'em."

Jack pulled on the yellow leather gauntlets the Yankee had given up, still warm from their previous owner. "Either way, they've heard about us now."

*

Martina threw her arms around Jack in delighted welcome. She kissed him thoroughly, letting him know she was thrilled to see him. He smelled of wood smoke and horse, but she didn't mind. Nor did she mind the week's length of beard he had grown. She laughed out loud, unable to contain her relief that he was home and unhurt.

He hugged her and lifted her feet off the floor of the porch in his exuberance. "Lord, how I've missed you, darlin'. Those nights are mighty cold out there, and I never did like sleeping with men."

"Is that the only reason?" She lifted her chin, loving the way he was looking at her, loving him.

"Want me to list them all?" He nuzzled her neck, and she wriggled at the bristly tickle. "Or just show you?"

"How long can you stay?" she murmured into his shoulder.

"Overnight."

"You can show me after I feed you a good supper." She ran her hands under his jacket, trying to take him all in. "You've fallen off. Have you been sick?"

"Homesick, maybe. Where's my father?"

"He's been replacing boards on the tool shed."

Jack looked off in that direction. "Have y'all been getting along all right?"

"He's nice enough to me."

"He was mighty put out when we stopped him." Jack's jaw hardened.

"He let me know about that." She shook her head. "He sure did."

"I felt all right about his coming here. I knew he wouldn't let anything happen to you."

"We've been fine," Martina said. "The Confederate commissary bought some oranges. Your father gave me the state money because he can't use it in St. Augustine. He hid most of the oranges. He would rather take them to town and sell them for U. S. money. The army didn't get any of our chickens or cows. Building pens in the woods was a good idea."

"Yeah, both armies will strip us of anything edible if they get the chance. Only difference is the Confederates pay."

Carlo ran up and bounded onto the porch. "You're home!" he shouted.

Jack threw his arm around the boy's shoulders. "Hey, brother-in-law. I brought Ladybug back for you."

"I can keep her?"

"She's all yours. I got myself another horse. Why don't you take the gear off her, give her a rubdown and put her out to graze."

"Can I take care of your horse, too?" Carlo stepped off the porch, looking over both animals. "He's a beauty. What's his name?"

"I call him Choctaw. I need to unpack him first," Jack said. "Then you can rub him down for me."

As Carlo led Ladybug away, Leon Farrell walked up and looked over the new horse. "Well, Jack. You seem to be prospering at the expense of the Union Army."

"Economy." Jack grinned. "I'm practicing what you always preached."

Martina noticed Jack always tensed in his father's presence. She had never seen them hug or even shake hands. She realized the frozen smile and the breezy attitude guarded Jack's defenses.

"Good-looking animal. I see he has a U. S. brand. Did you

steal him from one of our soldiers?"

"Call it what you will. I liberated him from a Yankee soldier without firing a shot."

"Our Union boys were cowards?"

Jack shook his head. "They weren't complete fools, that's all. We had the drop on them. Some of them got away anyhow."

"Then your guerilla band has had some success." Jack's father crossed his arms. "Perhaps I should congratulate you."

"We are not guerillas." Jack bristled. "We are regular cavalry."

"I need to get back to town. I'm sure Margaret is beside herself." Leon stepped up onto the porch. "I was due home days ago and have no way to contact her."

"The Yanks know we're in the vicinity now, so you can't do us any harm. They sent another party after the one we captured, and we did a little skirmishing with those boys."

Martina felt that familiar chill of fear and could not block out her father-in-law's brutal prediction about Jack making a widow of her.

"I have to leave in the morning, and you can go with me if you want. Most likely I can get you through our picket post." Jack glanced at Martina, then back to his father. "For Martina's sake I hope you aren't going to tell the Yankees I've gone back into the Confederate Army."

"I assured Colonel Putnam you would not take up arms again against the Union. You were disabled, and that was to be the end of it."

"I never made such a promise. And I got better, I'm glad to say."

"What will the Yankees do to us when they find out?" Martina asked.

"Jack should have thought of that before he did something so rash as to join Dickison's gang," her father-in-law said. "They don't want any rebel sympathizers to remain on this side of the river. I had Colonel Putnam convinced Jack was no threat, and now I find him back in rebellion. My son betrayed me."

"Damn it. What would you have me do? Skulk into the woods and hide when the conscription agents come around?"

"You had a chance to come in to town and reform yourself."

"Desert, you mean. I'm not a deserter, and I'm not a skulker."

Jack cocked his head, his eyes narrow. "You didn't raise me that way."

"That part took, at least, but it backfired on me." His father regarded him thoughtfully. "In any case, I will not put my daughter-in-law and my property at more risk."

"Thank you," Martina breathed.

"What I really want," Leon looked out over the orange grove, which had been picked clean of the golden harvest, "is to have something left after this war is over."

*

Jack handed his father the revolver he had confiscated from him a few days before. "I shot it out and cleaned it for you."

Leon checked the empty cylinders, grunted, and put it away. "Who'd you shoot?"

"I lost count." Jack rode in brooding silence for a while ahead of his father's mule and buggy. He had delayed leaving as long as he could but could not put off rejoining his troop any longer. He also planned to see his father through the Confederate lines.

How many such visits home he could expect to make he could not predict. Nor could he control what might happen to Martina in his absence. That worry made it almost unbearable to leave her. A few weeks of a normal life together had spoiled him. He had come to depend on Martina for his emotional comfort. He took heart in the certainty that she seemed to take the "for better or worse" part of their vows seriously. Things sure weren't better.

As though breaking into his thoughts, his father said, "Your wife is a good woman. She's a little bit like your mother."

Jack slowed Choctaw so he could ride alongside the buggy. "What do you mean? I never knew my mother."

"Martina isn't afraid to tell me what she thinks." The older man actually smiled. "She stands up for you."

"Is that really you talking, Pop?"

"Just saying you did something right. I hope it turns out the same way for her. Take care of her, boy, and don't keep letting her down."

Always the backhand. "I love her, and Carlo is my kid brother. It's new territory, having a family that gives a damn about me. I just about don't know how to act."

Jack remembered the note he had written and stashed in his saddlebag. "I discovered something that may interest you. I believe I found out where Isaac's wife ended up. One of the fellows in my troop is from the other side of the river and said a neighbor of his, Burton McCoy, has some of Miller's people."

"Raises cotton," Leon said. "Always looking for laborers, but not a bad sort, considering. His place is on the Bellamy Road, about ten miles inland."

"I believe she got to keep her kids."

"That is good news for Isaac," Leon said. "He's off training in South Carolina. Maybe I can get word to him."

"Fine. I promised I'd let him know if I heard anything." Jack reached into his saddlebag, found the note he had written and handed it to his father. "Maybe you can see that he gets the information."

CHAPTER TWENTY-THREE

March 1863
Jacksonville, Florida

Now a corporal in the 2nd South Carolina Colored Regiment, United States, Isaac reached into his pocket and touched the note Jack had sent him by way of Mr. Leon. Once Lacey and the boys had been taken across the river from his old home, they might as well have gone to the moon for all he could do about it. Until now.

He stood on the deck of the side-wheeler transport ship with his fellow infantrymen and watched woods outlined against the graying predawn sky slip past. At high tide, the gunships had escorted the convoy of troop carriers over the St. Johns sand bar, through the mouth of the river and toward the town of Jacksonville. He smiled in the darkness. Every stroke of the walking beam brought him that much closer to his family.

Isaac thought of all the effort he'd put in to his recent training as a soldier. As the boat rounded the bend, the rising sun lit the wharves and the low skyline of the town. He joined his fellow soldiers in triumphant shouts and backslapping.

He was going to liberate his family.

*

Carlo waded into the cold water to tend the trotlines next to the dock. The job would have been easier with Jack's help. His brother-in-law had continued educating him about handling weapons, raising livestock, hunting game and woods cattle, though Martina drew the line at the forbidden art of making whiskey. Dickison's troop had been picketing the roads between Palatka and Jacksonville, which at least allowed Jack to slip home from time to time for a visit.

Martina seemed happier when Jack was around but tense and

worried whenever he left. Lately he had noticed her appetite was off, and more than once she had given Nip her breakfast instead of eating it herself. When he asked her if she was sick, she just smiled and said nothing was wrong.

Carlo looked up from baiting a hook and saw smoke rising from the funnel of a boat moving upriver from the direction of Jacksonville. The only vessels that size on the river these days were Union gunships or transport ships, but none of them had landed nearby since he had lived here. Word had come that the Yankees' recent occupation of Jacksonville would likely increase hostile river traffic.

He continued working with the lines, removing a catfish from the hook. He finessed the wriggling, spiny creature into his bucket, which he set back on the dock. Then he baited the hook with a piece of cut fish. When he finished resetting the trotline he stood up for a better look at the approaching boat.

As the vessel steamed closer, he made out a U. S. flag flapping in the breeze and cannon ports along the deck. The deck was crowded with blue-coated soldiers. Mindful of Jack's warning that the artillerymen might shoot at him just for fun, Carlo carried his bucket off the dock, waded to the riverbank and hid behind the underbrush to watch the boat steam upriver. Eventually the boat maneuvered to the ferry landing on the other side of the river.

Carlo figured Dickison's men ought to be told a whole lot of Yankees were landing across the river, in case they didn't already know. He went to the house to tell Martina he was going to saddle Ladybug and find the nearest picket post.

*

Captain Prescott and the newly promoted Lieutenant Owen rode down the Bellamy road at the head of their infantry company, now filled out in force and officially mustered into the 2nd South Carolina. Prescott smirked at Corporal Isaac Farrell, who trotted to stay at the head of the column, a look of joyous anticipation brightening his dark features. "I believe Isaac is going to outrun us on foot."

"He's in a hurry to get his wife back," Owen said. "His kids, too."

"Colonel Montgomery liked the idea of putting a priority on

liberating his family," Prescott said. "He thought it would be good for morale and an object lesson. I don't want to be encumbered by a load of colored civilians, but those are the orders."

Owen nodded in agreement. "The colonel thinks it's a master stroke. Besides, don't you think Isaac ought to be rewarded for bringing us information about the McCoy place? We should find a good bit of contraband there, as well as recruits. I can't wait to see the look on peoples' faces when we bring all these colored troops – "

"Damned if I can figure out why he took the Farrell name." Prescott shook his head. He was still irritated he had not taken the chance to arrest that insolent rebel Jack Farrell before he left Florida.

"I guess Isaac doesn't have anything against the family. He was a free man, remember," Owen said. "Leon Farrell was his employer, not his owner. He seemed to be pretty friendly with the rebel son, too."

"We're not under Colonel Putnam's command now. I asked Colonel Montgomery about what to do about that rebel. He said go ahead and arrest him after we land at Picolata."

"What about the property? It belongs to his father. Remember the man is a sworn Unionist."

Prescott shrugged. Such hair splitting was of no interest to him, and he was no longer in Colonel Putnam's command. "We'll be needing provisions."

Under the protection of the gunboat, Prescott felt fairly safe, but he could not help looking around in nervous anticipation while riding away from the safety of the boat down this wooded road. Ambush was a favorite rebel tactic.

Except for rebs taking ineffective pot shots from the shore and a few pickets his troops had run off near the boat landing, so far the river expedition had been peaceful. Of course the pickets would have notified the main force, if it existed. Most of the Confederates in the area seemed to be massed around Jacksonville, making daily attacks against the Union occupiers.

Prescott and Owen split the troops and approached the McCoy plantation house quietly in a pincer movement. The house was a simple wooden affair like most of the country dwellings in Florida, with slave huts to the rear. Prescott sent Owen to secure the area while he rode up to the house with an escort of a dozen men. He dismounted, walked to the door, pistol drawn, and rapped with the handle of his weapon. "Open up," he shouted.

When no one answered, Prescott kicked it open and peered inside. He took pleasure in the panic-widened eyes of the woman cringing inside. With her was a young boy. "Come out, both of you," Prescott ordered. "You're under arrest." Prescott looked the woman over, a round, plain female, her clothes dowdy. She didn't move.

"Come outside," he repeated.

Slowly she obeyed.

"Where is your husband, McCoy?" Prescott asked.

"Outside with our people, putting in a crop."

"Our boys will find him." Prescott turned the woman and the boy over to his men to guard while he searched the house for anything of value.

*

Carrying his rifle, Isaac ran straight to the slave cabins. Right away he spotted his sons, apparently being supervised by a turbaned old woman who sat on a rocking chair outside one of the huts. The boys stared at him and the other soldiers in wonder. As his comrades ran past him, Isaac called his sons by name, and after a moment's hesitation, they ran to him, Micah toddling unsteadily but with determination. Isaac set down his rifle and knelt to put his arms around both of his giggling, delighted children.

The old woman walked over to him. "Bless my soul," she said. "You they daddy?"

Isaac nodded, unable to control the un-soldierly grin splitting his face. "Where's Lacey?"

"I been watching the children while she working." The old woman pointed with her chin. "Field's over that way."

"Thank you, Grandmother. Keep on watching my babies while I go find her," Isaac said.

She bent over and took each boy by the hand.

The people, attracted by the commotion, were coming in from their field tasks. Isaac scanned the half dozen wonder-struck, suspicious faces, looking for his Lacey. Then he spotted her and yelled her name. She ran to meet him, and they collapsed in each other's arms. Tears streamed down his cheeks.

"Look at you!" she cried, fingering his dark blue, wool jacket. "You a Yankee soldier now."

"I'm taking you with me."

"I knew you'd come for me," Lacey said. "I knew you'd find a way."

"You bet I would, sweetie. You bet. I be taking you to Jacksonville. You and the boys are free now."

*

Jack listened to Carlo's report with growing alarm. A few days ago the Confederate command had been surprised by hundreds of colored Union troops steaming into Jacksonville and retaking the town. Now the Yankees were set to dominate the river and bring whole regiments into the state's interior by boat. As far as he knew, only a small detachment of Dickison's troop had been left on the east side of the river, the main force having rushed to Jacksonville to oppose the invasion.

"Good work. Did you get the name of the boat?"

Carlo shook his head. "Couldn't make it out. Too far away."

"I'll get word to Lieutenant Brantley," Jack said. "Go back home and keep an eye on them for us. If it looks like they're landing on this side of the river, we need to know about it."

So far, while guarding the area close to home, Jack had felt his family was secure from Yankee molestation. Attacks on patrols had made the Yankees respectful enough to fear venturing far from their St. Augustine base.

How could they check an invasion by water? For the first time since he had joined Dickison's troop he feared Martina might be in real danger.

*

Prescott inspected the work his men had done so far. Under Owen's supervision they loaded bales of cotton, hams, and produce onto farm wagons. The men herded the livestock together to drive onto the boat. Two of the newly freed Negro men were helping while the others watched shyly, not knowing what to make of their new status. A couple of horses, of the small marsh tackey type common in these parts, were hitched to the wagons. The expedition was going splendidly.

Prescott was beginning to change his mind about the drawbacks of leading a company of colored soldiers. So far, under his command and Owen's training, the unit had showed a surprising level of industry. It remained to be seen how his troops would behave under fire.

McCoy, valuing his life, had given up without a struggle. He stood in sullen silence next to his wife and son while he watched the soldiers strip his property of anything the rebels might find useful. He was, no doubt, further stung by the indignity of being captured by colored troops and seeing his slaves carried off.

"Now that you are insuring our utter destitution, what are you going to do with us?" McCoy asked Prescott.

"We'll hold all three of you until all our men are safely on board. We don't want you informing the Confederates of our strength or what we're doing." Prescott looked the man up and down. "See here. I believe you must be in the rebel army. You look able-bodied enough to me. Truth be told, more robust than most rebels I've seen."

"No." McCoy shook his head emphatically. "I hired a substitute."

"We'll be taking you back to headquarters with us."

"You're going to keep me as a prisoner?"

"We'll take you and all your Negroes. We'll leave your wife and the boy at the wharf."

"I hope our men catch you and whip the daylights out of you."

Prescott guffawed. "Bring 'em on. We've been sending them off howling with their tails between their legs for days."

*

Lacey joined Isaac in the column as they marched back up Bellamy Road toward the boat, each of them carrying one of their children. Lieutenant Owen had given him permission to walk with the people from the plantation, though he carried his rifle in his free hand and was ready to fight back if the rebels attacked.

"Micah, Simon, we gonna take a boat ride," he told the boys. "We gonna go up and down the river, then we going to Jacksonville. You and your mammy are coming with me."

Lacey danced along, her joy overflowing. "When Master Miller sent us away, I didn't have no way to tell you," she said. "We wasn't sold. Master Miller just wanted us across the river on account of the Yankees. He leased us to Master McCoy. Master Miller wouldn't tell you where we were?"

"He wouldn't tell me nothing when Mr. Jack and I went to see him."

"I heared somebody killed Master Miller," Lacey said. "Then Master McCoy said he was keeping us because Master Miller didn't need us no more."

Maybe someday he would tell her what really happened to Old Man Miller. Not today. "I joined the Yankees so they would help me find you. It took 'em a long time, but we done it. You ought to thank Captain Prescott and Lieutenant Owen for bringing me here, sweetie. Colonel Montgomery, too, when we gets back to Jacksonville. He the head man."

He hadn't yet told her about his wad of cash, either. The cash he'd expected to buy her with. It was a surprise he'd save for later. Now she was his, earned by his willingness to carry a rifle for the Union Army.

Buoyed with pride and happiness, Isaac watched Lacey glance shyly at Lieutenant Owen, who rode not far from them. The officer grinned at her and touched his cap.

*

Martina had not considered the landing of the Yankee gunboat on the west bank an immediate danger because almost two miles of deep-channeled river separated her from the Yankees. Now the Union gunboat had left its moorings and continued south. Shading her eyes with her hand, she watched the boat until it steamed out of sight around the point of their cove.

"They aren't coming to this side of the river." The concern she had felt faded further. "They are going upriver instead."

"I'm going to ride back to the post and tell the soldiers," Carlo said.

"Yes, we need to keep them informed," Martina said. "When you come back, let's pack some things and load them in the wagon in case they stop at the Picolata landing on their way back." She did not want to abandon their comfortable home, but she would feel safer behind Confederate picket lines than amidst a horde of Yankees.

Knowing Jack and his friends kept vigil in the area, Martina had felt well protected. She had enjoyed the frequent visits from Jack, Ramon, and some of their comrades, even Captain Dickison. She and Carlo had taken picnic lunches to the picket post when Jack was stationed within a few miles. The Yankees had not made an appearance at their home in weeks, and she prayed they continued to stay away.

*

Prescott stood on the deck of the *Mary Benton*, the master of all he surveyed. His kingdom consisted of a boatload of Secesh prisoners and plunder, including cattle, a few sheep, trussed-up fowl of various kinds, and enough horses to mount half his company of soldiers. Adding to his crown of nobility was the batch of Negro slaves he had liberated during the trip upriver.

He had swelled the ranks of able-bodied Negro men who could be trained to be soldiers. His doubts over their fitness for soldiering had diminished after he and Owen had whipped the ex-slaves into shape at the Beaufort post. Although his darkie company had not yet been tested under fire, he had more confidence they would acquit themselves with skill and enthusiasm. They were going to make him look good.

Corporal Isaac Farrell and his wife were tearfully grateful for his making their reunion possible. That made the annoyance of the dark little children running about the deck more bearable.

Prescott was indeed a conquering hero, and he was prepared for further conquest. The last stop before they returned to Jacksonville would be at the Picolata landing, to investigate the location for a future garrison. They should arrive there some time after nightfall. He intended to add at least one more prisoner to his collection.

*

Carlo took a scouting trip toward the landing. He went on foot because if his suspicions were correct, he needed to be able to sneak in and out without detection.

During the night, suspicious noises had kept him awake. Metallic bangs, the hiss of steam escaping, and other sounds had floated through the night air. At first light he had gone out on the dock, but he saw no Union boats. That meant nothing, because the landing, a mere mile away by short-cut through the woods, was hidden from view by the bend of the cove.

The ominous sounds, a low hum of activity punctuated by sharper noises, continued. The effect was much like what he had noticed when the gunboat was loading and unloading across the river, only louder, and from another direction.

Leaving Nip tied at the house so he would not follow, Carlo picked his way south. In the early spring the woods were still fairly clear of summer undergrowth and progress was not difficult. Carlo had explored the area thoroughly since living here, and was familiar with every animal trail and had cut a few of his own. He figured he would see any Yankee soldiers before they saw him, if they had indeed landed.

The sounds grew louder as he approached the landing. The neigh of a horse, a shout, the thud of something hitting the ground. He slipped around the river bend, closer to the cleared area near the landing.

He peered through the bushes, noting the hotel, which had hosted no one since the Yankees had shut down the ferry. An abandoned house stood nearby, along with various outbuildings. Then he caught sight of the boat, moored at the dock, along with more Union soldiers than he had seen since leaving St. Augustine.

He made out the name of the boat, the *Mary Benton*. It appeared to be the same well-armed craft he had spotted across the river. A flurry of activity was taking place, unloading of horses and men.

He had seen enough. It was time to warn Martina, Jack and his other friends. He quietly withdrew and started back, staying low. Then he spotted a glimpse of blue among the foliage and froze.

"Who that? Halt!"

Carlo did not move, hoping the deep-voiced command was not directed at him. But who else?

"Stand up where I can see you. Keep you hands up." The soldier, a Negro, lowered the barrel of his rifle, pointing it in

Carlo's direction.

"I'm not doing anything." Carlo straightened, hoping the soldier would just let him go. "I live here."

"You sure 'nuff sneaking around. I got to take you to see the captain," the soldier said. "Less go. You try to run, I shoot."

Carlo had no choice but to go with the soldier out in the open and toward the landing. From the grim expression the soldier wore, and the way he held his rifle, Carlo did not dare try to escape. Carlo believed him when he said he would shoot. Surely the officer in charge would let him go home.

Right away he recognized Captain Prescott. Carlo looked for an escape route, but it was too late to try to run. He was surrounded.

"Well, well. What have we here? Still spying on us, Carlo?" The Yankee officer appeared to be delighted. "And where is your lovely sister hiding?"

Carlo would not answer.

"Cat got your tongue, boy?"

"I was just taking a walk, and this soldier stopped me," Carlo said.

"He has orders to take prisoner any civilians who come into our lines," Prescott said. "A job well done, I might add." He looked at the soldier. "My compliments, private. You did well to capture this boy. He is a known spy."

"That's just what you said." Carlo folded his arms across his chest.

"Martina must be staying around here." Prescott smoothed his moustache. "I've surveyed most of the places in the neighborhood but not for the past few months. You should make it easier on yourself and tell me which house. You know I'm going to search all of them."

Carlo shook his head.

"We'll start with the Farrell place. That's where you've been staying, isn't it?" Prescott loomed over him, his face glowering with menace.

Carlo didn't answer.

"I had a feeling about it last time I was there. I should have kicked Farrell out of the way and checked inside."

Carlo saw Prescott's fist coming but couldn't evade it fast enough. He reeled from the blow, tasting blood from his stinging lip. He glared at Prescott, hating him.

Prescott peppered him with more questions about Jack, Martina, and Confederates in the vicinity, pounding him every time he refused to answer.

Finally Prescott paused, rubbing his knuckles. "Private, keep him under guard and don't let him escape. If he tries to run, shoot him. We'll keep him with us while we check that house." The Yankee captain smiled at Carlo. "I have a hankering to see Miss Sanchez again. We'll have a touching reunion, I'm sure."

*

The boy's unwillingness to talk was of little concern to Prescott. The startled look in Carlo's eyes when Prescott mentioned Martina's connection to Farrell had given the truth away. Prescott recalled the conversation when she was oh, so worried about what he would do to that rebel, Jack Farrell.

Where Prescott found Farrell, he would also find Martina. The scoundrel probably had her hidden at his house during the last visit, before his patrol was attacked. He should have done something about it then, instead of letting Owen talk him into hurrying back to town.

Interesting that she would consort with that backwoods Florida Cracker, yet she would not let an upstanding Union Army officer touch her. If she was living with Farrell, didn't that make her a loose woman?

He would soon find out.

*

Where is Carlo? Martina paced between the house and the yard, loading the last of the provisions onto the wagon. She had hitched Ladybug to the traces, tied Nip to the wagon, and was ready to leave. She scanned the woods and the orange grove to the south looking for any sign of her missing brother. He had never returned from investigating the suspicious noises in the direction of the landing.

Heeding her fears about what the activity meant, she was ready to evacuate but could not leave without Carlo. It was not like him to fail to show up when she needed him. She heaved a

211

final bag of cornmeal onto the wagon-bed, and heard Nip bark. She looked up and spotted the Union soldiers.

They had caught her out in the open, and it was too late to hide. She reached into the wagon and gripped the shotgun, then hesitated. Showing the weapon would be an act of hostility, inviting retaliation. *Best see what they want.*

She looked up and realized Captain Richard Prescott rode toward her at the head of his troops. Worse, the soldiers had Carlo. He walked alongside Prescott, and his hands were tied together. His cheeks were bruised, and blood trickled from his split lip.

"Raise your hands, Miss Sanchez, or I'll shoot the spy," Prescott drew his pistol and pointed it at Carlo.

Martina did as she was told. She could only stand her ground, cornered, as the blue-coated soldiers surrounded the house and her wagon, all Negroes except Prescott.

"Miss Sanchez, we meet again. What a surprise." He swept off his cap and relaxed his gun hand. He smiled. It was not a good smile.

Carlo gave her a smile, too, but it was an apologetic one.

"Why do you have my brother tied up and under guard?" she asked. "He isn't a Confederate soldier. And what have you done to him? He's been beaten."

"He's a spy. We already established that," Prescott said. "I'm going to have to arrest you as well. Where is your consort, Jack Farrell?"

She pointed to the plain gold band on her finger. "He is my husband."

"Mrs. Farrell, then. Another surprise." Something unpleasant flickered in Prescott's eyes. "My, haven't things changed since we last spoke. I had no idea you were living here. And married? Oh, my."

"Since you had me banished, yes, things certainly have changed."

"It's hard to believe you would marry that worthless Jack Farrell." Prescott looked around. "Where is he hiding?"

"My husband isn't here right now."

"Is he with the partisans? Or skulking in the house? Or in the woods?"

She did not answer.

"I'm looking forward to having a chat with him," Prescott

said.

She tried another tack. "Haven't you talked recently with my father-in-law, Mr. Leon Farrell?"

"We are not garrisoned in St. Augustine any more. We're now in Colonel Montgomery's command. He is not acquainted with Mr. Farrell." Prescott dismounted, tossed the reins to one of his men, and looked into the wagon. "Were you planning to go somewhere?"

She did not answer. She locked eyes with Carlo, whose jaw was set and hands fisted within their restraint.

Prescott turned to one of the soldiers behind him. "Corporal Ross, take the wagon and see what contraband you can add. Assign two men to guard the prisoner and don't let him escape. I'll search the house."

"Sir, you wants any of us to stay and help you with that?" the corporal asked.

"No. I will deal with the house and the young lady myself."

She watched helplessly as one of the soldiers led Ladybug, pulling the wagon away, and a guard shoved Carlo into motion. "Don't hurt the dog," Carlo said to the soldiers.

The taller man guarding Carlo said, "That's Isaac's dog, boys. Best leave him be."

The soldiers moved around toward the back of the house, taking Carlo with them. Martina reached into her apron pocket and closed her hand around the knife handle. Prescott turned his weapon toward her. "Drop the knife."

"You're going to shoot me?"

"If you won't submit, what good are you?"

The look on his face told her all she needed to know. Martina tensed to run but feared he would shoot her if she did. She let out a choked cry, pulled out the knife and threw it down.

"That's better." Prescott stepped forward and grabbed Martina's wrist. "Let's go inside."

"No!" She tried to free herself, but he clamped her in a rough grip. If he took her inside, away from witnesses, what would he do to her?

"There's no use fighting me. I'm in charge here."

CHAPTER TWENTY-FOUR

From the underbrush across the road from the house, Jack watched in frustration and rage as the Yankee officer manhandled Martina. Holding his fire and his position took every bit of discipline he possessed.

Although he couldn't see them, he knew the rest of the troops should have dismounted by now and spread out in the woods between the house and the cove and on the left flank, closer to the landing.

River-based pickets had noted the arrival of the *Mary Benton* during the night and had sent word to the scattering of men Dickison had left in the vicinity. Because Jack's picket station was several miles toward St. Augustine, he had returned too late to warn his family. Instead, he had arrived just in time to see the Yankee detachment invade his homestead.

Jack raised the Enfield to his shoulder. "He's mine."

"You can't fire until we hear the lieutenant blow the cow horn," Cates whispered from just to his left.

"Damn the signal." Jack snarled. "That's my wife he's got." Prescott – he was sure he recognized the bastard even from this distance – was trying to drag Martina to the house. She thrashed about, fighting him every step. He couldn't shoot Prescott because Martina was in the way. If he rushed Prescott, the bastard would see him coming in time to harm both of them.

"Fall down, darlin'. Move away from him. Martina, get clear." Jack's hands were steady despite the struggle in front of him. He held his rifle carefully trained on Prescott, keeping his finger away from the trigger. Sweat popped out on his brow in terror of twitching at just the wrong moment and destroying the best part of his life.

*

Carlo trudged between the Yankee colored soldiers. He had

let Martina down by getting caught. What was Prescott planning to do to them? So far he had not found an opening to escape. Now, with his hands tied, getting away would be harder than ever. He tried to twist his wrists free, but the knots held them too tightly.

The soldiers spread out to find plunder, and his two guards did not seem to like having to stick with him. Stealing must be more fun than watching a prisoner. That gave him an idea. "You want whiskey? I know where you can find some."

The taller guard ignored him, but the fellow named Zeke took the bait. "Where?"

"In the woods. You'll never find it unless I take you."

The two guards looked at each other. The tall one said, "I don't drink no whiskey. I took a temperance oath."

"I didn't take no oath, and I'm thirsty," Zeke said.

"Captain won't like it."

"I'll give him some. That make him happy." Zeke nodded to Carlo. "Less go."

Carlo led the guards toward the woods. A shriek rent the air, and the three of them stopped and looked toward the house.

"What that?" the tall guard asked.

"That lady don't want the captain in her house, I reckon," Zeke said.

Carlo took advantage of their momentary distraction and ran toward the nearest cover, the orange grove. From there he could work his way around to the house and help Martina.

"Halt! Stop right there."

He kept running. The edge of the grove was close now. A fast runner, he could lose them among the leafy trees.

A rifle barked and his leg went out from under him. He tumbled and rolled. When he tried to get up, his left leg felt numb and paralyzed, then the pain shot through his thigh and he cried out. He ran his hands down to his leg, felt the warm blood soaking the fabric, and heard the footfalls of his guards running to reclaim him. "No!" He groaned in despair.

*

A gunshot from behind the house opened the fight before Lieutenant Brantley sounded the signal. Rifle fire from the concealed Confederates cracked all along the woods to Jack's right. Those to his left, their view blocked by the orange grove, held their fire. Braced against a tree trunk, Jack took a long, steadying breath, needing a clean shot at Prescott.

Prescott appeared to be startled by the gunfire. He let go of Martina with one hand to pull out his sidearm. She jerked away from him, the violence of her movement causing her to stumble and fall to the ground, clearing Jack's aim. Sighting on Prescott's chest, he gently squeezed the trigger. The solid recoil thumped his shoulder, and the smoke obstructed his view. Cates, with a clear upwind view, said, "You got 'im."

Jack broke cover and sprinted toward Martina, who had gained her feet and looked around in confusion. She started to run to him, but he yelled, "Go back! Inside! On the floor!" She obeyed instantly, whirled to the house, up the porch steps, and slammed the door behind her.

He drew his revolver and focused on Prescott, lying on his side, bleeding from his shoulder. The miserable bastard, still alive, raised his hand as though asking for mercy. He had dropped his revolver when he fell.

Breathing hard, Jack kicked Prescott's revolver out of his reach, thumbed back the hammer on his own Colt, and aimed at the bastard's black heart.

"Jack!" Cates shouted, "He's trying to surrender!"

Jack stood over Prescott, his hand steady. *Just one shot.* An instant kill to make sure he didn't waste another bullet. Prescott was blubbering now, sobbing and begging him not to shoot him again. At least Prescott was going to know who killed him.

Jack snarled, "Damn you. You should have left my wife alone. You won't hurt her again, you sorry –"

Cates knocked Jack's gun hand aside.

Jack gave him an angry shove. "Let me kill him."

Cates took a step back but didn't get out of the way. "He ain't worth it."

"How come you're so righteous?" Jack screamed. "Move!"

"Go see about your wife. I'll mind this trash."

Jack blinked through a red mist at the cringing Prescott. Reason returned to his fevered brain as he watched Cates reach down and pick up the Yankee's revolver.

"He's all yours." Jack let out his breath in a gasp, turned on his heel and ran to the house. "Martina! It's me." He threw the door open, and she flung herself into his arms. "Are you all right?" He moved his hand to her belly, which had been losing its flatness of late, reassuring himself that all was well with his wife and his little one. So much to protect.... "I came as soon as I heard."

She nodded, tears streaming from her eyes. "They've got Carlo. You have to get him back."

"I will. Where's the shotgun?"

"On the wagon. I never used it. My knife is on the ground in front of the house."

He rushed to the door. "Russell, find Martina's knife and give her Prescott's revolver."

"You know how to shoot it," he told her as he reloaded his Enfield. "Lie back down on the floor so you won't get hit by a stray bullet, and shoot if you have to. Shoot to kill."

"Jack, take care of yourself. I love you." She looked frightened and shaken. He wanted to hold her and keep her safe through the fight, but she would not be safe until the Yankees were gone. He pressed a quick kiss to her cheek. "I love you, too. And I'll get Carlo back."

He and Cates used the rope from Prescott's saddle to throw a quick loop around the bleeding, blubbering prisoner. They had more important things to do than guard him. A handful of steps took them through the dogtrot to the back yard. Jack slipped behind the tool shed for cover and scanned for Martina's brother.

The Yankees had run off. He spotted one who was left behind, apparently incapable of doing any more running. Looking out from behind the shed, Jack did not see any sign of Carlo.

Aware the enemy could shoot from the woods, the Confederates had emerged from their own hiding places in a wary skirmish line, jogging from one place of cover to another. It appeared the plunderers had fled, leaving the wagon still hitched to Ladybug, who was calmly cropping grass. He made out Nip hiding underneath.

Jack spotted Ramon and yelled, "Where's Carlo?"

Ramon shook his head. "Haven't seen him."

New gunfire broke out, in the direction of the road leading from the landing. "It's our boys on the left," Jack said. "More Yanks must be coming toward the noise."

"They'll need help. Let's go." Ramon jogged toward the fight.

Jack ran a different route, gaining the orange grove, where he could take cover and pot at the oncoming Yankees. Then he spotted Carlo.

*

Isaac ran with his comrades on the double-quick toward his old home.

He had heard the sounds of battle, and he knew right away where the shooting was coming from. Hurriedly, Lieutenant Owen had mustered up a squad to reinforce the captain's party of foragers, who must be under attack.

For some reason, after capturing Carlo, Captain Prescott did not include him in his foraging trip. Isaac was not disappointed, because he would have hated to watch the destruction of what he had helped build.

At the left turn that led to the Farrell place, the squad met Zeke and a half dozen other men from their company who said the Rebels had driven them back. The lieutenant brandished his revolver, ordering the retreating men to join the column, and they pressed on.

"What happened?" Isaac asked Zeke, who was blowing hard, rattled, out of breath.

"I was guarding that white boy. He run off. Mingo shot him."

"Why'd he go and do a thing like that? I know that boy."

"He was tryin' to escape, the fool. Then them rebs come out of nowhere. Shootin' and yellin'. Mingo got hit, too."

Isaac shook his head.

In sight of the orange grove, he spotted another straggler. He recognized Captain Prescott staggering toward them, the whole right side of him bloody, his face a sick grayish white.

"The devils ambushed us," Isaac overheard him telling the lieutenant. "They're crawling all over the Farrell place. They had me, but I got loose. Go kill them." The captain sank to the ground. The lieutenant told two of the soldiers to help Prescott to the boat, then ordered the column forward again.

More shooting broke the quiet. Isaac heard a plop, then the man to his left groaned and dropped like a fallen tree. Owen yelled for the men to spread out and form a skirmish line. Isaac took the left flank, toward the orange grove. He slipped through the leafy trees, inhaling the stink of burnt gunpowder. He figured if the Rebs could ambush, so could he.

*

Jack knelt beside Carlo, thankful the boy was alive. He had obviously taken a beating. Of more concern, blood soaked his pants leg.

"I am so glad to see you." Carlo clutched Jack's sleeve with his tied hands and managed a wan, blood-crusted smile. "I ran, and they shot me. Where's Martina?"

"Safe in the house. I'll take you to her." The leg wound was not bleeding much, so Jack hoped the wound would not be fatal. "Guess you'll be limping around for a while. Can't stay here any longer." The new wave of Yankees would find them excellent targets, and he dare not even take the time to free Carlo's hands.

Jack helped Carlo to his feet, then hooked the boy's bound arms around his neck. "Throw your weight on me." Gripping his brother-in-law's belt with one hand and his rifle with the other, Jack half carried Carlo back toward the house.

"Is your leg broke?" Jack asked.

"I'm using it some." The boy's harsh breath rasped in his ear.

"I'll get you there. If you can't stay on your feet, I'll carry you."

"Halt!"

The order had come from behind, from the orange grove. Jack hesitated and turned his head, feeling a prickle between his shoulder blades as though he could sense the exact place his captor aimed. He saw the rifle barrel amid the greenery of an orange tree, the dark face above the blue coat. He could not bring up his own rifle without inviting a killing shot.

*

Isaac felt the thrill of catching not just one rebel but two at once, even if Carlo didn't count as a real soldier.

He could have simply shot the grayback propping up Carlo, but he was feeling generous today after the reunion with his Lacey and the boys. He decided to give the Johnny a chance to live. He moved around for a better look at his captives.

"Drop that rifle," he snapped at the reb.

The reb didn't seem inclined to obey but didn't bring up his weapon, either. "Isaac," the Johnny said. "Don't you know me?"

Isaac stared at his prisoner, slowly recognizing the powder-smudged, unshaven face under the broad-brimmed hat. His former friend, the white boy he had grown up with, his ally against hostile

Seminoles, the man who had helped him find his sold-off wife and children, stood in front him. Yet Jack was an enemy and likely to shoot him, given the chance. Hands trussed up like a roasting hen, Carlo drooped against him, his battered lips white with pain.

"Did you find Lacey?" Jack asked.

"She's on the *Mary Benton* along with my boys."

"Good. I'm glad you set that straight."

"Mr. Leon wrote and said you married Miss Martina."

"Yeah." Jack flashed that smarty-pants grin of his, no matter the tight spot Isaac had him in. "She'd appreciate it if you didn't shoot us. Her brother is already shot anyhow, and he isn't even a soldier."

The rifle wavered in Isaac's hands. "I won't shoot if you throw down your guns and come in peaceful-like."

"You won't shoot me anyhow, Isaac. You owe me, and I'm calling in my chips. I never told a soul what I figured out happened to Miller, and I tracked down Lacey for you." Jack's smile had disappeared, and he was letting Isaac have it with his hard blue-eyed stare. "I will not die of scurvy in a hellhole of a Yankee prison. I'm leaving."

Isaac let out his breath but did not lower his rifle. He truly owed Jack, but if he let his old friend go, wouldn't they be shooting at each other sooner or later? He glanced around again, didn't see anybody watching, and decided he would deal with whatever happened whenever it happened.

That made up his mind. He could hardly believe what he was doing, but it felt right. "Git!"

"Thanks. We're even." Jack nodded and hurried away, supporting the wounded boy. Isaac looked around once again then brought up his rifle. He sought out another target, a distant rebel mostly hidden behind a pecan tree in the front yard, and pulled the trigger. Though he figured even if the fellow was hard to hit at this range, he might scare him to death. Jack did not turn around but kept on rushing toward the house.

Hunkered behind the skinny orange tree trunk, Isaac reloaded, regretting having worked so hard to keep the grove clear of underbrush. The zip of a bullet whizzed past, followed by the immediate snap of a rifle shot. Again Isaac looked around and did not see any of his comrades hiding in the orange grove with him. Seeing he was alone and overexposed, he worked his way back toward the road.

*

When Jack called out her name, Martina opened the door leading to the dogtrot. She gasped when he stumbled in carrying Carlo. Jack took her brother to the bedroom and set him down on the bed. "Take care of him. I have to keep them away." He turned around and ran outside.

"Oh, Carlo." She bent over and put her arms around him. "They shot you."

"Jack said I'll be all right. He said it isn't bleeding too bad." Stating his simple faith in whatever Jack had said, Carlo presented a brave smile through his broken lip. "Isaac wanted to capture us, but Jack wouldn't have any of it."

The shooting was still going on, but it sounded farther away. She set aside her rosary to free her hands so she could tend to Carlo.

At least one of her men was out of the way of the fighting. Directing her attention to Carlo's needs, she did not have time to worry so much about Jack and whether a bullet would find him, too. She attacked the knots binding Carlo's hands with her knife, untied the rope and slid it away. Then she ripped the leg of his trousers all the way up, exposing the wound. The bullet had stitched him through the muscle on the outside of his thigh.

"I'm thirsty," Carlo said. "Is there any water?"

Fortunately, this morning she had brought inside a bucket of drinking water. She dipped a cup into it and gave it to him. Then she cut off a length of sheet, soaked it in the water and gently washed some of the blood from his leg. The hole at the back of his leg was small, the opening in the front big and ragged. It was oozing but not bleeding freely. Noticing threads in the wound, she picked out a shred of his trouser material, despite his wincing protest. She cut more strips of the cotton sheet for a dressing and a length to tie around his leg.

"It hurts like fire." Carlo grimaced. "Does this mean I have to drink Jack's whiskey?"

*

Jack slipped out the door leading to the dogtrot, which gave him a narrow view front and rear. The Yankees must have been driven from behind the house, because he had not drawn fire while bringing Carlo from that direction. He stalked through the breezeway to the front, where he had a view of the drive, the road and the orange grove.

He didn't see Prescott. The son of a bitch had gotten away. Jack swore under his breath. He and Cates should have been less considerate of his pain and trussed him tighter.

Jack refocused his attention on the business at hand. From this vantage point he saw puffs of powder smoke coming from beyond the orange trees and from across the road to the south. The shooting had moved away from the house, down the road toward the boat landing.

He did not see any sign of fighting in the orange grove itself, though Isaac could still be hiding in there along with his fellow Yankees. Jack did not relish another confrontation with Isaac. The next meeting could not possibly turn out as well.

Jack ran off the porch and sprinted to catch up. The gunfire seemed to be slowing as he neared the landing where the Yankee boat was moored. He was only able to get off a few shots at the enemy before Lieutenant Brantley ordered the small force to fall back. When Jack started toward his house, Ramon fell into step with him.

"The Yanks ran to the protection of the gunboat," Ramon said. "The lieutenant thinks we've done all we can without getting ourselves killed. We're going back to the horses and pulling out before the boat starts a bombardment."

"I have to get Martina," Jack panted. "And Carlo's been shot in the leg."

"Holy Mary, Mother of God! Where are they?"

"In the house."

"I'm coming with you." Ramon looked around. "I'll let the lieutenant know."

Jack did not wait for permission. He ran toward the house.

*

"We drove them off," Jack said to Martina. "I brought the wagon around back. We're going to take you and Carlo with us. We have to hurry."

Ramon came in right behind him. Both men looked grim, their faces and hands smeared with burnt gunpowder.

"It's all right. I'm ready," she said.

She grabbed an armful of blankets and followed them outside, struck by how gently they treated her wounded brother. Just a few moments ago they had been trying to kill other men. She spotted the blue-clad body of one of their successes in the yard.

She decided not to worry about where she and Carlo would go next, just to trust her husband and her cousin to take them to safety. They lifted the boy into the wagon alongside another wounded man. Some of Martina's belongings and provisions had been dumped onto the ground to make room.

The injured trooper, a man she recognized from her visits to camp, sat propped up against the wall of the wagon. Blood covered his left side. He nodded to Martina, his expression strained.

Martina grasped Ladybug's halter to lead her. "Where are we going?" she asked Jack.

He pointed toward the north, away from the landing. "We have to go back to where we left the horses."

A distant boom, a howl made by no living creature Martina knew, then a nearby explosion of wind, heat and dirt made her cry out and duck. A dusting of earth rained down on them. She held onto Ladybug's lead as the blinkered mare fidgeted, tossed her head and began to rear.

Jack yelled, "Tina, get clear!" He ran up and grabbed the halter, pulling the mare's head down while Martina staggered out of the way. Her nostrils filled with the scents of burnt powder and earth.

"You all right?" He looked like a wild man, eyes wide, lips drawn away from his teeth, tension in every line of his body.

She nodded and moved away from the wagon, slapping dirt off her skirts. "I'm fine, Jack. Fine."

"Get in the wagon!"

She scrambled to do as he said and climbed in. Another boom. A shell shrieked by and exploded near the pasture.

Jack didn't join them as she expected but held onto Ladybug's halter and led her forward at a jog. She supposed he could better manage the frightened mare by controlling her head. Ramon, ranging alongside, said, "They're firing blind. If they hit us, it'll be by accident."

Martina found little comfort in his words. She glanced behind as another exploding shell fell short, tearing into the orange grove, sending bits of green leaves floating through the air. The shelling continued in slow rhythm as they gained the road. The two wounded passengers kept a stoic silence, ignoring the dirt that had settled on their clothes.

Carlo was pale and his face pinched, but when he met her gaze he managed a smile. She found the rosary in her apron pocket then crossed herself, giving thanks that her brave husband had saved them both, remained unharmed, and they were all together.

They hurried past three mounted troopers in the road covering the withdrawal. Charlie Colee rode forward, leading three horses, glanced into the wagon and shook his head. "I sure hope the Yanks look worse than y'all do."

"I'm taking them to the Miller place," Jack told him. "Leave us our horses."

"Charlie and I better go back and see if the other boys need help." Ramon took the reins of his horse. "Can you handle it by yourself, Jack?"

Jack nodded. "The mare's calmer now that we're away from the shelling."

Ramon helped Jack tie Choctaw and the wounded trooper's horse to the wagon, then mounted his own horse and rode off with Charlie. Jack climbed onto the driver's seat, shook the lines and clicked up the old mare to a gait quicker than her usual plod.

Martina caught her breath, though still tingling with apprehension. "Where is Captain Prescott?" she asked Jack. "What happened to him?"

"I shot him, but he wasn't dead. He was gone when I ran out on the porch."

She recalled the nearby gunshot, Prescott crying out, falling down, and Jack's sudden appearance. "He wanted me to go into the house with him." She shuddered. "I was afraid of what he would do to me."

"My aim was hasty." Jack's jaw tensed as he glanced over his shoulder at her. "I should have killed him. Cates stopped me."

His cold words chilled her further, but wasn't he merely putting her own thoughts into words? She studied his taut, war-hardened face. Jack was a dangerous man: dangerous to anyone who threatened his loved ones. "I knew what he intended to do." She placed her hand on her belly, dreading what harm would have come to her and the new life she and Jack had started, if Prescott had gotten his way. "At least he's gone. I don't have to be afraid of him anymore."

CHAPTER TWENTY-FIVE

Jack stopped the wagon under a shade tree in front of the Miller house and tethered Ladybug. Then he helped Martina down from the seat. Her pale face and drained expression worried him. She leaned into him, and he put his arms around her. "Are you feeling all right?" he asked.

She nodded and looked up at him. "What now?"

"Stay with Carlo and Henson. We'll leave them in the wagon for the time being, in case we have to move again."

"What about you?"

"I'll go back a ways and see what's going on. Shelling seems to have slowed down."

"Jack… don't be too brave. They aren't all like Prescott. If you have to give us up… just keep yourself safe."

"Take care of Carlo and let me worry about the Yanks." He kissed her on the forehead, gave her a final squeeze, and turned to mount Choctaw.

Jack dared to hope the Yankees were not planning a counterattack. If the enemy overran them, he would quickly surrender to keep Martina out of the line of fire. Surely they would not detain her or Carlo.

He turned in the saddle for a quick look at his beautiful wife. The thought of Prescott and what he had intended for Martina filled his mind. A bloody rage replaced the picture.

Surrender, hell. He could not allow such men near her, ever again. He heeled Choctaw into a gallop.

*

Isaac boarded the boat and stood on the deck beside Lacey and his boys. At every boom of the cannons, Simon covered his ears and made faces. Little Micah squalled in terror while Lacey cuddled him in her arms to try to calm him. Isaac watched the smoke and fire blast from the mouths of the big guns as the shells lofted over the trees to strike at his old home.

He did not regret letting Jack go free. He couldn't have shot him even if he was a Johnny. They were even now, and if they met again, he figured neither would feel obligated to show the other mercy.

The firing eventually stopped, and Micah's wails ceased. The little boy sucked his thumb, and his eyelids grew heavy. Isaac bent over and kissed him on the top of his head.

Isaac watched the crew bring in the lines and prepare to steam down river. Lieutenant Owen had told him they needed to get the severely wounded Captain Prescott to the hospital. A couple of privates needed a doctor, too. Another man was killed, his body left behind.

"When we get to Jacksonville, we'll find you a nice place to live," Isaac told Lacey. "Someplace white folks built for themselves. Someplace close, so I can come see you whenever I'm off duty."

"Where you get the money?" Lacey asked. "The army pay you that good?"

"I ain't got paid yet. Yanks don't believe in paying colored soldiers."

Lacy knitted her brows in concern.

"Don't you worry about a thing, sweetie." He stuck his thumbs under his armpits, threw out his chest and smiled at her. "Your man Isaac is a man of substance."

*

Jack walked to the end of the Miller dock in time to watch the stern of the *Mary Benton* disappear around a bend. Steaming north toward Jacksonville, it no longer posed an immediate threat.

After making sure the Yankees had all boarded the boat, he had returned to give Martina the only spot of good news on a disastrous day. Then he and Ramon had helped Carlo and Henson into the Miller house.

Prescott's attack, the exploding shells, and the threat of the panicked horse hurting his wife had shaken him to his core. Jack shoved his hands in his pockets, gloomily undecided about what Martina should do, where she should live, and how he could support his family without use of the farm. If anything happened to Martina....

He left the dock, found a bucket and filled it with river water, which he used to clean blood out of the wagon. When he returned to the house, Martina met him at the door. With the soft, responsive curves of Martina's warm body nestled in his arms, his spirits lifted. His woman was staunchly on his side. She carried his child, a fact that filled him with awe. Surely all would be well.

"The boat is gone, so we should be safe for a while," he said. "I'll take the wagon back to the homestead. Find out how bad the artillery hurt the place and salvage what I can."

"I'll come with you."

"How is Carlo?"

"He's resting, and so is Mr. Henson. Ramon is here if they need anything. Carlo doesn't want me mothering him."

Jack cracked a smile. "Yeah, he wouldn't."

"He's grown up a lot," Martina said.

"He'll be all right."

"Thanks to you."

"Tina, I'd have gone to hell itself to bring him back. He's more of a brother to me than my own brother."

She rested her head on his shoulder, and he held her, thanking God for her. She had married him knowing they could not escape hardships created by the war. She had thrown her fate in with his anyway.

He said, "Lieutenant Brantley is seeing about an ambulance to carry Carlo and Henson to Palatka where a doctor can see to them."

"When?" she asked.

"If he can't get hold of one by tomorrow morning, we'll take them ourselves in our wagon. We'll get it done one way or another."

"What do you think I should do?"

"You can go to Palatka, too. We'll find you a place." He held her away from him so he could see her face clearly. "I always want to keep you close by, as much as I can. Is that what you want, too?"

The warmth of her kiss told him the answer.

*

Martina sat down on the edge of the porch, where she and

Jack had shared so many companionable evenings. She looked out at the craters and the felled orange trees, then down to the pencil and a piece of paper she had found. While Jack inspected his still and the rest of the property, she wrote a letter to her father-in-law.

March 14, 1863
Dear Papa Farrell,

> *I hope when you find this that you and Margaret are well.*

> *It is my sad duty to tell you what happened, and I am leaving this letter for you because of our trouble getting it through the lines.*

> *The Yankee boat Mary Benton landed at Picolata last night, loaded with Negro Yankee soldiers. They took Carlo prisoner and Captain Prescott brought soldiers to our place. They shot Carlo in the leg and the captain made plain his vile intentions toward me. Jack and his friends attacked our enemies and ran them off. They wounded Captain Prescott but he got away. Your brave son and his friends saved Carlo from death and saved me from unspeakable insult. Jack said our men will bury the dead Yankee on the property.*

> *After the Yankees left, the boat shelled our place. You can see the damage for yourself. Some of the orange trees are ruined. They blew up Isaac's cabin. Thank the Good Lord they spared the house. One of our cows was killed and the men are butchering it so the meat won't go to waste.*

> *Isaac was with the Yankees. Our soldiers say the Union soldiers are stealing from people and making prisoners of them all up and down the river. I thought Isaac was better than that.*

> *Carlo and I are going to Palatka where we can see a doctor. Jack is sure Carlo will recover and I pray he is right. Jack won't let me stay here as long as the Yankees in Jacksonville are sending their boats upriver for plunder. He will try to sell the stock we can't take*

with us. I suppose he will be paid with Confederate
money, so it won't do you any good. We will repay you
when we are able.

> *Your son is a fine man and he is good to me.*
Carlo and I love him dearly. We are in for hard times
but as long as we have each other we can bear it.

> *I expect we will make you a grandfather in*
a few months. My prayer is that you and Jack will
forgive each other and forget your quarrels. I pray you
can accept our children as your own.

Martina had just finished the letter when Jack walked over. She handed it to him. "I didn't want to mention Isaac let you go. It might get him into trouble. Do you want to add anything?"

He sat down next to her and circled his arm around her. "You don't regret getting hitched to a beat-up rebel soldier with nothing to his name but a couple of horses?"

Despite her worry and sadness, she had to smile. "Read the letter, sweetheart."

She watched his jaw tense, and he took a deep swallow before he spoke. "Martina, I loved you the first time I ever saw you."

"I think I fell in love with you that night, too. If Francisco hadn't interfered...."

"If I hadn't acted like a jackass...."

She slapped him playfully on his thigh. "You sure did."

"Have I lived it down yet?"

"Heavens no. I'll hold it over your head forever." She laughed and kissed him, then said seriously, "I'll try never to hurt you like that, ever again."

Jack set the letter aside. "You're right about hard times ahead, darlin'. I don't know how to fix it."

She looked out over the field toward the shell-torn orange grove, craters and splintered trees. "I do hate leaving this place. It's been good to us. But we'll manage."

"I fear there's a lot of war left to fight," Jack said.

She regarded her husband, whose scars continuously reminded her that he was not immune to danger. Even Carlo had not escaped being shot, though he wore no uniform and belonged to no fighting unit. With her fingers she traced the faded marks on Jack's cheek down to where they disappeared into his short growth of beard. "First, keep yourself safe. That's the best way you can protect me and our little one."

"Me, a father." He grinned. "Fancy that." He stood and lifted her to her feet. "Are you ready to go?"

"Almost." She went inside, signed the letter and left it on the table. Then she gathered up a few household items she had overlooked in her previous haste. She took a lingering look around the house she must leave. She would not cry for the loss. Her time here with Jack, even after he had to join Dickison's troop, had been good. After losing Francisco and her St. Augustine home, she had gained a new start in life, thanks to Jack.

He took her hand in his and led her to the wagon. Heaven only knew what awaited them, but she was content to face it with the man she loved.

About the Author:

Lydia Filzen has written two award-winning Civil War novels, FIRETRAIL and PERFECT DISGUISE, under the name Lydia Hawke. She also wrote SILENT WITNESS, a suspense novel set in the world of dog agility trials. Her non-fiction work and photographs appear frequently in Clay Today and Civil War News with her byline Lydia Filzen. She is an avid history buff and lurks about Civil War reenactments trolling for stories and great pictures. Also, she shows champion Collies in conformation and agility. Lydia is a member of various writing organizations, Collie Club of America, Pals and Paws Agility Club, Greater Jacksonville Collie Club and Greater Orange Park Dog Club. She owns DesJardin Electrical Service with her husband, Larry. In her spare time she... Spare time???

Check her websites at www.lydiahawke.us and www.lydiafilzen. us, or email her at lydiafilzen@comcast.net

Civil War novels written as Lydia Hawke, available through your favorite bookstore:

Firetrail ISBN 0-9766449-7-5 published by Global Authors Publications
Now a feature-length movie by Forbesfilm!

Perfect Disguise ISBN 0-9766449-0-8 published by Global Authors Publications
Soon to be a feature-length movie by Forbesfilm!

Contemporary suspense novel written as Lydia C. Filzen:
Silent Witness ISBN 0-9766449-1-6 published by Global Authors Publications

Excerpt from Raiders on the St. Johns
Coming in 2010

Jack slid off Choctaw and handed the reins to Charlie. He left his Enfield in the boot, keeping the revolver as his only weapon. He and Ramon ran into the roadside thicket and crouched behind a convenient palmetto, the broad fronds concealing them from the road's view. Charlie trotted the horses away, the hooves drumming softly on the sandy earth. The hardware made no noise, as the scouts kept the sabers and other accoutrements muffled with rags.

Within minutes Jack heard the approach of horses from the opposite direction, from St. Augustine. He crouched lower and peered between the fronds at the two vedettes riding by. Close behind them, as though deliberately keeping within sight of the outriders, came the rest of the troop. No doubt fear of capture kept their formation tight, a tribute to the success of Captain Dickison's troop.

At their head of the main body of troops rode Jack's father astride his mule. Was he serving as a Union Army guide? Or had he joined the patrol to take advantage of an escort as the traveled to his farm on the river?

Riding with a Yankee patrol did not increase Pop's safety. If the Confederates decided to attack the patrol, his civilian status would not protect him. In the heat of a fight, such distinctions meant little.

Two blue-coated officers rode alongside Pop. Jack did not expect to recognize either of them. The only Yankee officer he knew was Prescott, whom he had put out of action, at least for a while.

But there was something about the captain....

Jack stared at the nearer officer, riding with his hand on his hip near his sidearm, his elbow cocked at a jaunty angle.

Couldn't be.

He felt the blood drain from his face.

What's he doing here?

He hadn't seen Dan in years, but the passage of time seemed to make no difference. He would have known his older brother anywhere.

Breinigsville, PA USA
22 December 2010
252007BV00003B/13/P